JOSEFINA

DAUGHTERS OF UMBRA

LEYA LAYNE

JOSEFINA
DAUGHTERS OF UMBRA

LEYA LAYNE

Trigger Warnings

While this book is meant to be a fun romance with spice, there are discussions of topics that could be triggering for readers. To be respectful to those who need warnings and those who see them as spoilers, I have placed the trigger warnings on my website. Scan this code to check the site.

For all women:
Some may try to bind your magic.
Others may call you mundane.
Never let anyone relegate you to the shadows.
Wield them instead to tie those fuckers in knots.

PLAYLIST

- Unwritten By Natasha Bedingfield
- Bonita By Juanes
- Tacones Rojos By Sebastían Yatra
- Imaginary By Evanesence
- Sisterhood By Mackenzie Johnson
- Dream By Fleetwood
- Take Me Back To Eden By Sleep Token
- Spin In The Dark By The Bela Vibe Design
- No Roots: Alice Merton
- Is This Real By Lisahall
- Echame La Culpa By Luis Fonsi & Demi Lovato
- Créeme By Karol G & Maluma
- Lose Control (Strings Version) Teddy Swims
- Ordinary By Alex Warren
- Ticking In The Dark By: Hellena Banner

MEET LA FAMILIA DE UMBRA

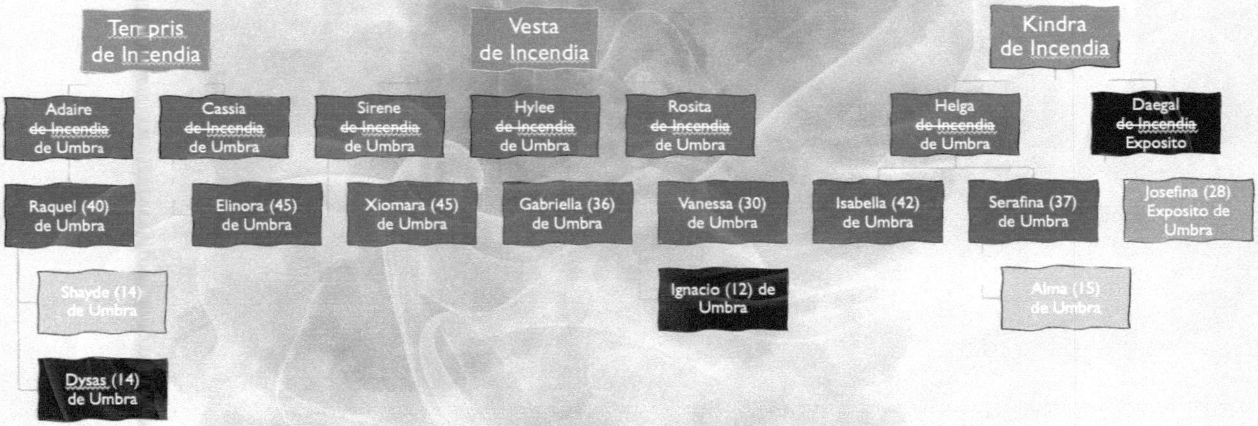

PROLOGUE

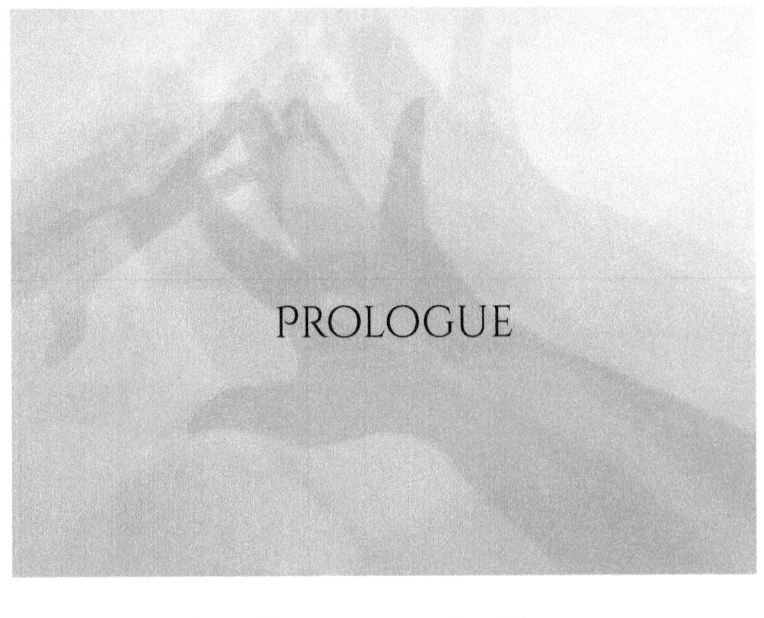

Five goddesses, powers combined in peace
Protecting people from deviant slight
Such as tragedy Umbra's shadows ceased
Or the vision from Incendia's light

New life sprang from divine intervention
Like Vienta's gifts: wisdom and healing
Suela's lessons to live with intention
Gave way to Yovizna's nurtured feeling

Until fire in one's virtuous maiden
Dried affection, a husband's lustful stare
Causing rifts dear sisters, fury laden
Redress the priestess' answered prayer

Incendia's daughters birthline exiled
Pitying Umbra embraced the reviled

CHAPTER 1
LAS MAÑANITAS
JOSEFINA

October 13, Three Years Ago

I scowl, looking around my empty vendor tent. The small two-layer cake sitting atop the makeshift counter is mocking me. I bought it this morning thinking it might help keep my spirits up or at least give me the sugar rush I'd need to make it through the night. Instead, it sits there with its tufted balloons and tiny writing taunting me with broken promises. I'd recently moved to Houston and started classes toward my master's at U of H. Anything to keep myself busy, to keep from thinking about everything, or rather everyone, I left behind. The move itself had been uneventful, and even changing school districts was a cakewalk. I roll my eyes at the poor choice of words. It appears even my brain wants to fuck with me today.

"Happy Birthday to me," I say aloud with a shrug.

Candlelight flickers around me as I begin separating the lid from the base, trying to keep anyone else from hearing the sad dirge of ratcheting that is opening one of these cake containers. Whatever company designed these things must've had one hell of a creative team meeting during the planning stage.

Hey, why don't we make it airtight.

Yeah. That'll make the cakes stay fresher longer.

If we make it hard to open, no one can steal a bite.

It'll be great for parents who want to keep their kids out of the cake.

Not only that, but it could be a deterrent for anyone trying to sneak food on their diet.

I don't think making something kid proof would help with that.

You know what would? Making it sound like a fucking machine gun when you pull the pieces apart. Now, that would deter me from sneaking a bite in the middle of the night.

Shaking my head at the ridiculous scene that just played through my mind, I pull the lid the rest of the way off like a band-aid from a wound. With a sigh, I stoop behind the counter to pull out the small packet of candles I'd bought at the same time as the cake. I really am my own worst enemy. Not only am I celebrating my 25th birthday alone, but I'd planned to light and blow out a small arsenal of candles. Maybe I'd wish for a magical brain transplant and get one that doesn't hate me. Until then, I'm stuck with this one and will follow right along with its bullshit plan. At least, that's the thought I have right before I find myself face to face with a god.

Okay, not a god, but damn if he doesn't look like a god made man. Dark hair, dark eyes, and a chiseled jaw that the flickering candlelight kissed in a way my lips are begging to try themselves. My eyes barely travel down his neck before he speaks, and my knees nearly give out.

"I heard someone say there was cake." His voice is like smooth silk, as if it alone could slide your panties to the side and catch every drop. Thankfully, my panties are safely ensconced in the shorts I have on under the bohemian skirt I wear to these events. When he smiles, though, I question their safety because spontaneous combustion is a real thing, a very real and possible thing. The smirk it slides into makes me choke on air.

Ridiculous. This whole moment is absolutely ridiculous. So

ridiculous, in fact, that I have to grab the counter to hold myself steady, spilling the box of candles. A couple of them land on top of the cake. Others clatter onto the counter, and half of those roll off onto the floor at his feet where my libido is now pooled. He chuckles, and it's a sound I want to bathe in. God dammit, how long has it been since I got laid?

"When I saw the candle shop sign, I didn't know candles would come flying at me from all angles."

All thoughts of climbing him like a tree halt as heat creeps up my cheeks. Shit. Not only had I been eye-fucking this stranger, I literally threw candles at him like they were dollar bills at Chippendales.

"I'm so sorry," I eke out and start collecting the offensive sticks by their wicks. Wicks, tricks, dicks. *No, no, NO!* I reprimand myself as my mind once again goes off on its own little tangent. I am a perfectly rational adult woman who can maintain an air of decorum around a delicious-looking man.

He laughs again before sobering. "I startled you. I should be apologizing. Since the tent flaps were pulled back, I assumed you were open. Then I heard the unmistakable sound of baked goods being opened and knew I had to come see what candles and cake had in common." I stare at him, mouth open, and he smiles again. He turns his head to the side and motions toward the entrance with his thumb. "I could go out and come back in. Maybe start this whole thing over?"

My eyes narrow. "Do I know you?"

I realize the question probably comes off rude, but I'm not taking it back. I've barely been able to say ten words since I found him staring at me from across the counter, so I wouldn't even attempt it. Besides, there's something in his profile that's vaguely familiar.

His head tilts to the side, and he gives me a quizzical look. "I'm not sure. I don't think so." He bends down, and it takes all my willpower not to lean over the counter to see... to see what he was doing. Yes, I definitely wasn't going to look over to check out his ass. I was simply curious about what he bent down to do. "This is my first time to the Renaissance Fair."

Shaking my head, it's my turn to chuckle. I live in Houston, but the fair is a good drive away, like almost everywhere in Texas, but he makes it sound like it's across the country. "Please tell me you don't believe we all live here in the fairgrounds. Anyway," I say, waving my hand toward him, "you look familiar, like maybe I've seen you on campus."

"Do you go to U of H?" He looks apprehensive when I nod. "Then maybe. I'm finishing up my doctorate there and am a TA for one of the professors."

I smile. "Now, I know. You came into one of our lectures and sat there until it was over."

Again, with the head tilt and smirk. "You remember me coming to your classroom one time?"

When he says it like that, I can understand the smirk. "Don't let your ego get away from you," I say before I can stop myself. "I remember thinking it was weird for someone to come in weeks after the course had started to just sit there and wait for the professor. I only ever saw you from the side, though."

Understanding sweep across his features, and his devastating smile returns. "I'll keep my ego in check if you tell me what we're celebrating." He holds up five candles, and it's all I can do to stifle a groan.

"How embarrassing," I mumble under my breath. The slight tic in his brow tells me he heard me but, thankfully, wasn't saying anything. Unfortunately, the way he patiently waits for my answer is just as unnerving. "My birthday."

"Really?"

The excitement in his voice has me lifting my gaze to his from where I had looked away to keep from seeing the pity in his eyes. I mean, how could he not pity me for being here alone in my tent with my tiny cake, about to blow out my tiny candles for a wish that likely wouldn't come true? Yet, there's nothing derisive in his expression. He looks genuinely excited...for me.

I sigh. "Yes. Today is my birthday, and here I am trying to quietly celebrate but failing miserably."

"Wish I could say I was sorry for crashing your party, but I'm a cake whore." My eyes go wide, and he must misinterpret the reason because he follows up with. "I'll sing for my dessert if you'll let me stay."

Looking around the tent, I check each corner making sure there are no hidden cameras. This has to be a joke. There's no way this gorgeous professor-to-be is standing here, excited to celebrate my birthday and calling himself a 'cake whore.' Who does that? I eye him skeptically.

"Is this a joke? Did someone send you here?"

His brows knit, confusion etching lines between them. "Is what a joke? My singing? Sometimes. But my rendition of Happy Birthday is top notch, or I can sing *Las Mañanitas* if you prefer."

Yes, please. My heart flutters, and I'm not sure if I've said the words aloud or not. Thankfully, his expression remains steady, and I'm able to take another breath.

"Both." He smirks, and I cut him off with a quick, "If you're going to make such a grand offer, I'm going to have to hear both, else you get no cake."

He nods before asking my name...in order to "finish the blessing of the birthday song." His words, not mine. Then, he lets loose a panty-soaking version of Happy Birthday, or maybe it's just his voice. Either way, my panties are no longer dry, and I will need some alone time tonight, preferably sooner than later.

"If I had a guitar, I'd do this more justice, but I was unprepared," he says, drawing my attention back to him before he slides into the second promised song. By the time he gets to the setting of the moon, tears sting my eyes.

Not for the first time today, I miss my parents. My mother died ten years ago, and that was the last year my father sang to me for my birthday. He's since remarried, but he's never regained the lighthearted joy that had been his constant companion throughout my childhood. I swallow back a sob as the man in front of me loses his smile.

"Are you alright? I'm sorry…"

I swallow and hold up a hand. "No, please, don't be. It was beautiful. Thank you. It's just been a long time since anyone has sung that song to me." I turn away from him for a moment, trying to get my emotions back in check. I wipe my eyes and take a deep breath to keep from blurting out more personal information this stranger didn't ask for before I turn back to face him. "Let me get a couple plates."

He puts the candles in the cake and lights them, creating a perfect circle of light. "Thank you for letting me celebrate this moment with you. I hope this circle, like these candles you sell," he says, gesturing around the tent, "sparks a light from within."

"That's quite the blessing," I say, expecting him to explain or to say something more, but he doesn't.

"Make a wish."

Closing my eyes, I try to picture a future far different from my current life, but the only thing I see is his smile. When I open my eyes and blow out the candles on top of the cake, the rest of the candles around the tent flicker, and shadows float around him like clouds. They swim through the tent, encircling his arms and caressing his jaw the way my hands yearn to. It has to be a trick of the light, a result of me cinching my eyes closed a little too tightly as I try to think of the wish I'd been formulating before he entered the tent. There's no way any of this is real.

"I forgot to ask if you liked carrot cake," I say to distract myself from the shadows that he doesn't seem to notice.

Without missing a beat, he responds, "If it's cake, I'm all about it," and I can't help but laugh. The shadows dissipate as a serve us each a slice.

When we finish, I thank him for the birthday wishes and for

saving me from eating the entire cake myself. He offers to help me douse the candles and close up the shop for the evening. I pretend not to notice how the tent fills with shadows right before we tie the flaps closed.

"You be safe getting home, and maybe I'll see you around campus."His tongue runs along the seam of his lips, and I wonder whether they taste like cake.

He's walking away toward his car when I realize I'm still staring at the spot where he'd been. I can't help but hope I see him again soon.

CHAPTER 2

JUST MY LUCK

JOSEFINA

April 20, Last Year

I sit up straight on the couch, a guttural 'fuck' falling from my lips. My eyes flutter as I try to steady my breathing, but it's really hard when my hand is still locked between my thighs, fingers pressed to my clit, and his face lingering in my mind. Normally, I wake in a panic as shadows descend out of nowhere. Those nightmares have been coming more frequently as of late, but occasionally, he invades my dreams, and I wake sweating for a different reason.

He's made himself scarce around campus since the day he'd walked into my tent and sang to me. He's probably busy with his own studies, I tell myself, or maybe he's graduated. Hell, we hadn't even exchanged names, and he doesn't owe me anything. Still, I can't help feeling disappointed that he hadn't looked me up in all this time. Obviously, my mind can't believe it either because it keeps conjuring him just like it conjures the freaky shadows that haunt my dreams. On a positive note, the shadows have only come while I've slept. I'd probably be on a grippy-sock vacation if they showed themselves again while I was awake.

The clock on the wall clicks. It's nearly 7pm. "Shit!" I jump off the couch and sprint to the bathroom. My friends will be at the bar by eight, and I've not even showered yet. Stupid afternoon naps always fuck me up. I either sleep too long and then can't sleep later that night, or I lose all track of time. There's only that tiny window for a perfect nap, and rather than creep through it, I crash into the wall like the damn Kool-Aid man. Throwing my hair in a bun on the top of my head, I jump into the shower and let the cold water punish me for my earlier transgression before the hot water kicks in, and I can make sure all the important parts are clean. It's a good thing I have no intention of hooking up with anyone. There simply isn't time for shaving anything.

Throwing my car in park, I power walk to the entrance, managing to make it through the door by 8:20. Two things spur me on, well, maybe three. One, my friends get real catty if anyone is late, especially for a birthday party, and it is Sofie's birthday. Two, the line starts wrapping around the corner somewhere between 8:30 and quarter to nine. And three, something about walking through the dark streets at night freaks me out lately. It never used to, but I've recently started to feel like someone, or something, has been stalking me from the shadows.

"Look what the cat dragged in," Christine says, her voice already slurring.

Sheer willpower is the only thing that keeps me from narrowing my eyes at her. "Where's Sofie?" I ask, refusing to let her chiding get to me. I'm never late. If anything, I always try to be early because I know how they are.

"It's her birthday. She can be fashionably late." Christine responds without looking at me.

"Well, she can be late. We all know she's not going to be fashionable." Taylor walks up beside me and puts her hand on my shoulder. She leans in conspiratorially and whispers, "Don't mind her. She and Kyle got into a fight today. What sounds like a pregame tipsy is really a heartbreak drunk." She shrugs and pulls me toward the bar. "Anyone else need anything?" she calls over her shoulder to the others, but everyone else already has a drink in their hands.

"Thanks. That sucks for her, but I just assumed she was being her wonderfully bitchy self."

"I'm sure there's some of that too, but she's been extra bitchy tonight." I nod and order my drink.

Thirty minutes go by before Sofie makes her way through the door and across the crowd that now fills the bar. Normally, we'd all be cutting up on the dance floor by now, but we've been patiently waiting for the birthday girl to arrive, and she looks just as pissy as Christine. Dammit, I should've kept my ass home.

"Who pissed in your cornflakes?" Taylor asks before Sofie even gets to the table.

"Fuck off and get me a drink."

"We had you one, but when you didn't show, or answer your phone, we drank it in your honor."

Taylor was joking, but the look on Sofie's face was murderous. Something was obviously wrong, but I wasn't close enough to the inner circle to feel comfortable asking aloud. It wasn't that I couldn't handle her answer one way or the other, but I didn't think it would do anyone, including me, any good. I call this group my friends because we come out to the bar every couple of weeks, but really, we're just a misfit bunch of full-time master's students who don't fit in with the undergrad crowd. Christine and Taylor are in the same program now while Sofie, Christine, and the others graduated undergrad together. I'm the only one without ties to the others besides the one class we took together earlier this semester. I'm the outsider with Taylor barely one foot in front of me, which is probably why I get along so much better with her.

"I'll get my own damn drink," Sofie says, stomping off toward the bar. When no one else moves, I follow behind her.

"Happy Birthday!" I say, trying to pump my voice full of more enthusiasm than I feel.

She snorts out a derisive laugh. "Thanks, but it's been absolute shit. If I didn't know how these bitches would shun me if I hadn't shown up, my ass would be at home with a bottle of tequila drinking myself into oblivion."

No sooner have the words left her lips than the bartender steps up, and she orders two shots of Patrón with a glass of wine. When he turns to me, I simply say, "I'll have what she's having," and pass him my credit card to pay for both. She looks at me sideways, and I wave her off. I've had some pretty shitty birthdays, and I hate to see anyone else suffering on the one day that should be just for them.

Sofie walks back toward the group, and a chill runs up my spine like all the body heat of the crowd has been sucked out of the room. My eyes catch sight of the mirrors behind the liquor bottles lined up against the wall, and tendrils of gray smoke begin to swirl around the glass, wrapping around the necks of each bottle like they would lift them off the shelves and begin pouring drinks. *Or smash them all to the ground*, my mind adds. The hair on my arms stands, and I cross them to warm my hands, which have turned to ice. The shadows move closer to the register, nearly touching the bartender before she turns back to me. I quickly put my card in my back pocket with my ID, add a tip, and sign the slip, my eyes trained on the shadowy substance that continues dancing around behind the bar.

Taylor's voice breaks my concentration. "Hello, Professor." She's directly behind me, but I can't see her because the mirror is now obscured in shadows. I don't have to see who it is to recognize the voice, though. It's the same one that has gotten me off in more daydreams than I can count over the past year or so. I down the first of my shots, pretending I have no idea there's a conversation happening not even five feet away. Then, Taylor leans in and whispers in my direction. "Turn around and meet the hottest professor on campus."

I turn my head slightly and hope he's looking elsewhere. With shit luck like mine, I should've known better. He might've been listening to whatever Christine was saying to him, but his eyes were trained on me, a sly smile playing at the corner of his lips. I pour the second shot down my throat like it was the antidote to whatever poison had my body overheating at the sound of his voice. I didn't even know this man, not really. We hadn't exactly exchanged names, nor did I see him again after that evening in my tent. Still, it's like he'd cast some kind of spell on me.

"Professor Seagal, this is our friend, Josefina," Taylor says, interrupting whatever Christine was saying. Christine's eyes narrow, but Taylor continues on unperturbed. "She's an Education major."

His smile widens, and I notice a dimple for the first time. How the hell had I missed that before? It's like every time I see him, he gets more attractive. Life just isn't fair.

"Professor?"

Something blazes in his eyes at the word, but it's quickly extinguished as he acknowledges Taylor standing by my side. "Yeah, Christine and I have a pharmacology basics course with him this semester," she answers, though I hadn't directed the question at her.

"Good to know professors are regular people who need to unwind with friends too," I say with a light chuckle I can't seem to contain. He tilts his head, and I shrug.

"You're welcome to join us," Taylor offers, her interest obvious. "We're here to celebrate Sofie's birthday."

"Maybe you could sing Happy Birthday." I take a sip of my wine before turning back toward the group, cutting my eyes toward the bar to find the shadows have receded to swirling within the mirrors. The warmth flows down my chest combining with the heat in my belly. Whether it's from the shots of tequila or the man stepping up behind me, I can't tell, at least not until he speaks so low and close to my ear that my core contracts.

"I only sing for those who need it."

I close my eyes and try to calm my fluttering heart. "Good to know."

"You ladies have a great night and be safe. I see my friend, so I'm going to leave you all to your celebration. Happy Birthday, Sofie."

And with that, he disappears into the crowd and takes all the warmth that had been flooding through my body with him.

"Why is he so fucking hot?" Taylor says once he's out of earshot. Murmurs of agreement buzz around our small group.

Great question. Why is he so hot, and why do I respond to him so strongly? A thought prickles at the back of my mind, and I turn around to find the mirrors over the bar have cleared, once again giving full view of the packed dance floor behind me. What the hell? My head swivels again, trying to find the elusive professor, but there are far too many people here. "Dammit!" I say aloud.

"What in the exorcist is wrong with you?" Christine asks, and I glare at her.

"You've been hopelessly bitchy since we got here, and you're asking me what's wrong? Take that shit elsewhere."

Christine's mouth drops open, and Taylor covers her mouth to stifle a grin. Sofie gives me a silent high five, but I couldn't care less about any of their responses. I'm clearly losing my mind, and it seems to be made infinitely worse whenever Professor Panty Drencher is near, which makes no sense. Movement near the door catches my eye, and a head of dark hair sneaks out amongst the throng waiting to get in.

"I have to go," I say unceremoniously. Taylor calls my name, but I've already crossed the dance floor.

The bouncer opens the door, and I squeeze my way past the knot of people waiting outside. *Shit, which way did he go?* My eyes scan the sidewalk in both directions before I catch sight of shadows toward the next side street. I must be out of my fucking mind. Not only am I chasing this man down dark streets, but I have no idea what I'm going to say once I find him. 'Excuse me, Professor, but are you controlling shadows? They seem to dance whenever you're around.' Somehow, I don't think that will make me seem very stable. Still, my feet keep moving forward. As I'm passing a dark alley, voices penetrate the self-deprecating conversation I'm having around this fool's errand, and I freeze.

"Looks like someone's lost," a male voice says from the darkness.

A shadow moves toward the mouth of the alley. "Maybe she's looking for a party."

"Well, she's come to the right place then," a third voice chimes in.

I turn my head slightly to look back toward the main street where the crowd is still gathered outside of the bar, and there's no way I'll make it past these men and back to my friends before they catch me. I don't run, especially not in heels. *Why the fuck did I wear heels?*

"You're not planning to leave so soon, are you?" the first man asks. Though his voice is calm, the words send a streak of fear up my spine.

"I've heard some women like to be chased. It gets them off," the man who had stepped to the edge of the shadows says, his words punctuated by an 'oof' as he doubles over.

"Don't talk about our guest like that."

"What do you want?" I ask, trying to buy some time while I cut my eyes to the other end of the street. It's just as dark and desolate as where we stand, as if the shadows have doused every light between the two corners. Maniacal laughter threatens to bubble up when I realize I'm in this predicament because of some imagined shadows. I'm in very real danger because my imagination perceived the light and dark dancing along the mirrors inside the bar. "Dumbass." Fuck, that came out of my mouth.

"Well, I was going to offer you a way out of here, but since you want to call names after crashing our party, I don't think I will." One of the men steps out of the alley, and my chest tightens. The man is huge, at least 6'5" and his face is hard. "What do you think fellas, should we keep her?"

Two more men step from the alley. They're both shorter than the first man but no less scary. The smiles on their faces turn my blood cold. *No, no, no.* When the fourth man comes into view, my feet finally start moving. I take one step backward away from the alley and out into the street.

"It's cute that you think you're going to just walk away from this," the man who is clearly the leader of the group says, his smile visible in the dim light coming from the streetlamps half a block away.

Another man steps into the street, and my mind goes hazy. At least, that's what has to be happening when that man snarls, and I see his teeth. Two jagged canines point down toward his bottom lip. *What the absolute fuck?*

"Stay away from me!" I yell. I want to take my shoes off to at least give myself a chance at running, but I'm afraid of letting any of them out of my sight. They all start laughing and panic sets in.

The two shorter men take two lumbering steps toward me, and my hands fly up as if I can ward them off simply by telling them to stop. When they step off the sidewalk and into the light, three things happen at once.

Tendrils of shadows pour into the street, and my sight goes dim.

Sounds of a scuffle, complete with snarling and screaming, play out around me.

A familiar voice calls my name.

CHAPTER 3
NOT AGAIN
JOSEFINA

Two days Ago

"Why are you being so weird?" Marcus says, disdain evident in his voice.

"What are you talking about? I'm here working. You knew what I'd be here doing. I do it every year."

"I knew you made and sold candles. I thought you'd have some little storefront, not be set up in some traveling circus of freaks."

My blood heats. This is the first time he's come to any of my vendor events, and his first thought is to criticize? How dare he? Things between us have been strained these past few months, but I've chalked it up to the stress of upcoming exams. His. I already graduated. If he thinks this is the way to repair the rift, he's woefully misinformed. Whatever this is goes way beyond uncertainty for the future, and it doesn't bode well for our relationship.

"What the hell is that supposed to mean?"

I'll admit, I take a lot of shit from people, especially if I have any kind of feelings for them, but I won't abide someone making fun of others. It's uncalled for, especially when you're a visitor someplace they're obviously comfortable. I won't allow his attitude to make someone else who might walk into my tent uncomfortable. I'm uncomfortable enough for all of us. I fucking hate confrontation, and I hate it even more when it calls for me to defend something I enjoy that shouldn't need defending.

"I just walked through a crowd of elves, orcs, and knights. Fucking knights in full chainmail. And here you are with pointy ears, dressed like a swamp witch."

"This is a Renaissance Fair, Marcus, not a pop-up in City Centre."

The laughter that bubbles out of me at his sneer is contemptuous. Marcus and I have been dating for a little over a year, but recently, I've seen a side of him that rubs me the wrong way. We both teach at the same school, and both of us are grad students, at least we were until I finished my requirements two months ago. The thing that caught my attention about him was how open and fun-loving he is with the kids. He's always smiling and even participates in the fun theme days, days where we all dress up as silly characters or in weird outfits that are sometimes inside out.

Early on, Marcus would go out of his way to make me laugh, and he'd sometimes join the girls and I on our bar-hopping nights. We have a lot of fun together. Well, we used to. Now, all he does is tell me what he doesn't like, and usually that's whatever I'm doing that doesn't directly involve him. It's like he hates the fact I've finished school and have more free time for other things I love, like my candle business and the book cons and fairs I participate in.

"No shit, Josie. No one in Houston would be caught dead dressed like this."

All I can do is shake my head. There's no point in telling him that half the cosplayers he walked past were likely from the city. That's the thing I love most about these events. People can come dressed how they want. They can be whoever they want. No one judges them for daring to be different. Well, except for uptight assholes like Marcus is being right now. Those of us who've worked the event for a while can spot the stick riders from a mile away, and I've always felt sorry for the group they come with. I never thought I'd find myself with someone so small-minded. I had hoped to find someone unafraid to be different. Immediately, my rogue mind travels to two years ago when Professor Panty Dropper waltzed into my tent and sang Las Mañanitas like he hadn't a care in the world, like he was having the time of his life here.

"Go home, Marcus," I say, my voice as level as I can make it.

His mouth drops, and genuine surprise streaks across his face. Surprise morphs into anger, and I take a step back before realizing my error. He moves in. "What did you just say after I took time out of my day to come support you and your little..." He waves his hand around my tent making the flames of the closest candles dance before turning his attention back to me. With a sweep of his hand, he gestures up and down, "costume party." He grabs my hand and pulls me forward before I realize what he's doing. His other arm wraps around my waist, pulling me close. "If I go home, you come too and make it up to me." His hand squeezes my ass and bile burns my throat.

I push against his chest, as well as I can with the way he has me pinned to him. "Let me go, Marcus. This is my business, my shop, my goods. I paid to be here. I'm not just leaving." My voice wavers at the end, and something terrifying flashes in his eyes.

"You'll stop this madness now and come home with me, or you'll wish you had."

Once again, I try pushing away from him, but it's a futile endeavor. For as much as Marcus might look the part of a nerd, he is pure muscle. I, on the other hand, have no strength in my upper body, and my legs are in no position to do much.

"Why are you doing this?" I breathe out.

His eyes catch mine, and for a moment, I think he might soften. The feeling doesn't last long as his gaze hardens. "Why don't you appreciate anything I do? It's like you think you're better than me." I shake my head. "You do. You used to laugh at my jokes. Now, you hardly laugh at all. You used to invite me out with your friends, but lately you've not made time for me." His grip tightens, and it gets harder to breathe. "You're supposed to be my girlfriend, but it's like I don't matter to you now that you've finished school. Was I just a study buddy all this time?"

"Let me go," I wheeze, trying not to let fear make my chest any tighter than Marcus' hold already has it feeling.

"Not until you answer me. Are you ashamed..."

I don't hear any more of his words as all my attention focuses on the wisps of smoky shadows traveling from the corners of the tent upward across the canvas roof. They swirl into each other, coalescing into puffy clouds that soon begin to fill the air above us. I turn my head to the left and see tendrils peeking out around the flickering candles, and the lights slowly extinguish one by one. My mind must be playing tricks on me. I'm quickly losing oxygen to my brain. Yes, that's obviously what's happening. There's no other...

One of the clouds thins out, a rope-like mass sliding around Marcus' neck. Suddenly, I'm gasping for breath and watching Marcus slowly dissolve into the smoke. Smoke? No. The only fires in here are the candles, though they're almost completely out. No, there's no fire. Shadows. Shadows just like when the professor sang to me. Just like when those men tried to attack me after I ran out of the bar. He was there then too. Was he here now? Gurgling sounds come from the writhing mass blocking the tent's entrance. Shit, Marcus is in the shadows. What do I do?

Feet shuffling through the dark, I step forward. I have to find him. I wanted him to let me go. I need him as far away from me as possible, but I don't want whatever is happening to him right now to continue. "Marcus," I call out quietly, not wanting to draw the attention of anyone outside of the tent. I have no idea what they'd see or what would happen if anyone tried to come in. Marcus doesn't answer. "Please, stop," I choke out on a sob. One of the candles flickers back to life on my right. "Stop. Please stop," I say again. Two more candles reignite. My breaths come faster and my head swims.

"Josefina!" A familiar voice calls my name. I can't tell if it's coming from the shadows, from outside the tent, or from my addled brain.

"Here. I'm here," I say, though I can't bring my voice to go louder than a whisper.

"Josefina, call them off."

Call them off? "I don't know how," I hear myself say.

"Are you alone?" The voice is louder now, closer.

"Marcus..." I can't get any other words to leave my lips. What else can I say? I don't know if he's even still here amongst the swirling shadows. Is he still breathing? I have no idea.

"Listen to me, *Muñeca*. I can't contain them. There's too many. You have to tell them to stop."

Tell them to stop? How do I tell them to stop? "I don't know how!" I screech. "I don't know what's happening." Panic grips my chest again as the shadows swirl around my feet. "They're around my feet. The shadows are everywhere. Please make it stop!"

"Breathe. They're responding to you, to your panic. Take deep breaths."

I inhale deeply and watch the shadows dance at my ankles. My exhale is shaky, and ripples run through the mass of shadows. Another inhale, and I close my eyes, trying to calm my beating heart. The shadowy thing around my feet settles, its wispy tendrils retreating.

"You're doing so good, Josefina."

More candles flicker as the shadows recede. I blink a few times to make sure I'm not imagining the steady dissipation. Then I look toward where the shadows are the thickest, and a knot forms in my throat. I start to take a step forward, afraid of what I might find there, when a figure steps into the light. A gasp leaves my lips, and my legs give out. Before I hit the ground, his arms wrap around me, holding me up, and pulling me close. Unlike with the fear that coursed through me the last time arms were wrapped around me, this time, I relax into him. Warmth and serenity flood my system, much as they had the first time he entered my tent.

"Professor?" I look up into his eyes, which are so dark, they remind me of the shadows. Oh shit, the shadows. Marcus. I stiffen in his arms and try to turn myself to look over his shoulder.

"Relax, *Muñeca*. All will be well."

I shake my head at him. "No, you don't understand. The shadows. There's someone."

"Shhhh," he intones, pushing a strand of my hair behind my ear. "Look at me." I turn my face back to his. "All will be as it should. But tell me, what did he do to anger the shadows?"

My hands push at his chest, his strong, very warm chest. No, don't think about that. "What do you mean by anger the shadows?" I step away from him. "You can see them? You know what they are?"

He smiles like he wants to laugh, but he controls himself. "Of course, I see them. Don't you?" He gestures toward the corner of the tent nearest the entry. The entry that is still very much obscured by the writhing mass.

"Wait, how did you get through there?" I can hardly see the open tent flaps, and I can't tell if it is still daylight outside or not.

"You watched me walk in here, Josefina. Do you not trust your own eyes? You called for help."

No, I hadn't. I was afraid of raising my voice and that people would come running to my aid only to be swallowed by the blob of shadows. There was no way I called for help. "And you just happened to be around? You happened to be the only one who heard me and came to check on me?" I took another step away from him. "Did you do this?"

Irritation crosses his face before his eyes soften, and he sighs. "I didn't do this. You did."

No. No, no, no. "I couldn't... I don't... This wasn't..." I know my eyes must be wide as saucers. I feel the wrinkles in my forehead, and I can't stop shaking my head back and forth. "Why is this happening?"

The dark mass starts gyrating in larger waves, and Professor Seagal takes a step toward me, but I put out a hand to ward him off.

"Don't," I say. "Tell me what is happening. Tell me why you're always around when it does."

"I..." He stands there staring at me before looking back at the growing waves. "You have to control it, Josefina."

"What the fuck does that even mean?"

"What did he do? The man the shadows took. The name you said earlier. Marcus. What did he do to you?"

"Oh my god, Marcus!" I turned my attention back to the front of the tent. "I can't even see him. Why can't I see him?"

"Did he hurt you?"

"He..."

"Tell me, *Muñeca*."

"Professor?" I look toward where he was standing only to find him a hair's breadth from me.

"Alistaire. My name is Alistaire. And I can't help him. No. I won't help him if you don't tell me."

I take a deep breath and swallow the embarrassment that rushes in when I think of Marcus' behavior and how I'd allowed it. I do not want this man, no matter how uncertain I am about his role in what is happening, to think less of me. I look over to where I think Marcus is laying and shake my head, but Alistaire puts his hands on my shoulder and turns me to face him.

"Your shadows are protecting you from him, and I need to know why. If he hurt you, I will let them keep him."

Your shadows. Not the shadows. No. He called them my shadows. They were protecting me. From Marcus. My mind traveled to the other times I'd seen the shadows. The first time right here in this tent. They'd licked around the man staring into my soul, trying to get me to confess Marcus', and by default my, sins. The shadowy wisps had caressed Alistaire's face, but they'd not been menacing. The same had happened when he arrived at the bar last year. They'd danced along the mirror and played around the bottles, hiding him from me until I turned around to stare into his face. On that dark street, though, the shadows hadn't been so playful. They'd filled my vision, hiding the men who threatened to attack me from my sight, or maybe they hid me. I'm not really sure because I still can't remember much that happened afterward other than Professor Sea—Alistaire—helping me to stand from the mouth of the alley and walking me to my car.

"What happened to those men?" I ask softly, my eyes pleading for explanations.

"Don't try to distract me or change the subject. What happened here tonight?" His hands still hold my shoulders, but his hold is soft and steady, not controlling.

My breath hitches, and he pulls me into his arms. I go willingly and wrap my arms around his waist. "He scared me," I say against Alistaire's chest. He stiffens slightly at my words, but his hands rub soothing circles on my back. After several seconds, I lay it all out for him. How Marcus and I met. The man I thought he was. The strange changes that have come over him, and the escalation and threats of tonight.

"He deserves far worse than a shadowy slumber," Alistaire says against my hair, his voice low and menacing. I try to lift my head to look at him, but he holds me in place for a few minutes longer.

"Do you have family?"

When I try to pull away this time, he lets me go. "My poppa's in San Antonio. Why?" I narrow my eyes at him.

"You should go there. Take some time to figure out what is happening. Family will know more than either you or I do."

"And Marcus?" I look toward where the tent opening sits covered in light shadows, showing that the sun has begun its descent. Now, the wiggling mass is little more than the size of

Marcus' frame. A shudder runs through my body. "Is he even alive?"

I don't realize the words have left my lips until Alistaire responds, "Likely. But the shadows won't let him go until they know you're safely away."

"I can't just go to San Antonio. The fair isn't over. I can't just leave my stuff. What about my job? My students?"

"Do you want something like this to happen at work? I can take care of everything else if you take care of you."

"But..."

He cuts me off by putting his hands on my face. "*Muñeca*, go to your father."

"Why do you call me that?" I ask at the same time he exhales, our breaths mixing.

"Because you are," he pauses, concentration written on his face, "precious. I knew the moment we met, before I even knew your name, that you were something, someone special."

His words catch me off guard. The earnest plea in his eyes like a bolt of lightning to my core. Tension coils between us, but just when I think it'll snap, and I'll do something crazy like lift onto my toes to kiss him, he turns me away from him to gather my personal belongings and head home. The weight of the past few hours falls heavily on my shoulders, and I have no arguments left in me. I grab my purse and keys. As I get to the entrance and give one last look toward Marcus covered in shadows, Alistaire's voice pierces my heart.

"I hope your birthday is everything you ever dreamed of."

CHAPTER 4

THE PAST 24 HOURS

Yesterday

Determination burns in my core when I wake up, and though I'm tired from replaying yesterday's events all night, I quickly pack a bag and get on the road. Alistaire's declaration that I caused the shadows has my stomach in knots, but if he's right, maybe there's also some truth to his promise of my father having answers. I can't imagine what those answers will be, though. The man hates my work with candles and that I dress like a fairy or a witch when I work the carnivals and fairs.

He always said that the supernatural was fake, but his insistence only fueled my interest over the years. As a little girl, I loved to read about witches and gnomes. Gnomes were my favorite. By the time I was a teenager, I was fascinated with vampires and the occult. Halloween was always my favorite holiday, but Poppa never allowed any of that in his house. He even refused to let me give out candy to trick or treaters. I couldn't wait until I moved away from home and could go to haunted houses and dress up with my friends. My first year away, I bought a shit ton of candy for the kids in my apartment complex and started my costume collection. Now, I somehow have to go to San Antonio and convince the old man that shadows are following me around and responding to my emotions. I need to get his advice on what to do, so they don't attack someone else like they did my boyfriend, ex-boyfriend, last night. I have to trust that he'll take me seriously.

"You've always had an overactive imagination."

"Poppa, listen."

"No. Josefina, what you're saying is impossible. Maybe all those candle smells made you woozy. Maybe the fight you had with that boyfriend of yours had you picturing something happening to him."

"Josie, it's not that he's not listening. It just all sounds so implausible. Fighting with your boyfriend can make everything feel off kilter."

I close my eyes and take a deep breath. Of course, my stepmother, Alice, would just go along with whatever he says. I've never known her to think for herself, never once had her take my side on anything, even when he was blatantly wrong.

"I knew you wouldn't listen," I say. "I should've just stayed home and taken care of it all myself. I survived the first times. I'll get through this."

"First times?" My father's tone has shifted from indignation to apprehension.

"Yes, it happened twice before. I told you that, but you didn't want to hear me." A scowl forms on his face. "You still don't want to hear me," I say with a sigh. "I tried to tell Alistaire--"

Poppa cuts me off. "Alistaire? Who is this Alistaire? Who else knows about this?"

My nose wrinkles at his ever-shifting tone. "Why does it matter?"

"Why does it matter?" he bellows in response. "Josefina Exposito, it matters because..." His voice trails off like he's not sure how to finish the sentence, or maybe because he doesn't want to finish the sentence. Finally, he closes his eyes and takes in a deep breath before speaking again. "What you are saying is not normal. People will look at you differently. They'll whisper behind your back. They'll make you feel like an outsider. They'll use the fact that you see the world differently against you."

I was ready to argue with him until that last sentence. The agony in his expression turning every retort to ash in my mouth. "Poppa, I have always been an outsider," I say, my voice softer than it had been. He shakes his head, but I continue undeterred. "Even with you. I have always been the dreamer, the hopeful one, and you've fought to keep my feet firmly on the ground. We are alike in many ways, but not in the way we see the world. Something is happening to me, around me, possibly coming from me. I don't know, but it scares me sometimes, and I was hoping you could help me."

When his face drops, I know there's nothing else to say, at least not tonight. Without another word, I leave him and Alice in the living room. After the lack of sleep last night, the three-hour drive here, and the past two hours trying to make him see reason, my reasons, I don't have it in me to keep fighting.

My childhood room looks nothing like it did when I lived here. It's like I packed up everything that mattered, and they made every remnant of me disappear. The accent wall of flowered vines has been painted over. The heavy wooden furniture that had once belonged to my mother and was covered in nicks and scratches from use has been refinished. Where I once had pieces of mom's artwork hanging over the bed, there's now mass-market frames and generic black and white photographs.

At the familiar burn of unwanted tears, I grit my teeth and make my way to the ensuite, the only positive renovation they've made. Steam from the shower, seeps into my stiff muscles, the heat of the water, helps me relax a bit. Unfortunately, the relief in my body releases the flood I've been holding back. Emotion overwhelms me, and I slide to floor, wishing for strong arms to hold me steady, and a soothing voice to tell me it will all work out. Consciously, I want those arms to belong to my father, but when I try to picture the man their attached to, the face I see is Alistaire's. Rather than fight it all, I let the emotions and longing run down the drain alongside the water.

Josefina

October 13

I cover my eyes from the light seeping through the blinds when loud crashing downstairs wakes me. It takes a moment to remember that I'm not home, and I'm damn sure not alone. My father's deep timbre penetrates through the house as he throws curses at whatever inanimate object pissed him off. It's no wonder I often apologize to my tables and try to soothe my plants. I learned from the best. When something else crashes, and I hear Alice's shriek, I groan and roll off the bed.

"Happy Birthday to me," I say to the empty room.

Downstairs, my father dances around the kitchen. I watch as he spins a grimacing Alice before turning back to the stove. The smell of pancakes warms my soul, and my stomach gives me away. I can't help but chuckle when they both turn in unison with mouths agape like they never expected me to be standing here.

"Good morning." My tone is light, and I keep my smile wide. Alice returns it easily enough, but Poppa looks at me skeptically.

"*Mi'ja,* I was going to bring your breakfast in bed like I always used to."

I catch a glimpse of disappointment in his eyes, but he quickly shifts his gaze and gestures toward the kitchen island. I lied. The huge bespeckled countertop is the second best renovation they made to the house, well, the entire kitchen renovation. It really brightened up the place and made it somewhere we could all hang out, work, cook, and play board games together. The dark cabinetry and tiny dining table of my childhood couldn't hold a candle to the space they've created here.

"Happy Birthday, Josie," Alice offers.

"Thank you." I ball my fists, pressing my nails into my palms to keep from cringing at the nickname. Normally, it wouldn't bother me much. Many people have called me Josie over the years, especially when I was a kid, but I much preferred my name, my given name, the name my mother gave me before she died. Josefina rolled off the tongue in a way Josie never could, at least not from those who didn't understand its meaning or me. Marcus had been one of those people. He'd refused to use my full name once he'd learned I sometimes let others call me Josie.

"Josefina," Poppa says, breaking me from my thoughts. His brows raise before he once again points at the island. *"Siéntate."*

I climb onto the nearest stool. These chairs were very cute, but they were not made for women with hips. I sent a silent apology to my ass for the impending discomfort before smiling at my father. Neither he nor Alice have ever had to worry about hip socket displacement in bucket seats, so I can't blame them for their poor furniture choices. Besides, I can't be mad at the man who immediately sets a short stack of pancakes in front of me and proceeds to light small candles sticking out of it in the form of the number 28. I can, however, bawl like a baby when he starts singing to me.

Once I have myself under control again, and the tiny wisps of smoke have cleared, I hurl myself into his arms. "What is that for?"

I open my mouth, trying to formulate the words to express how much I've missed these birthday morning celebrations, but nothing comes out. With a shake of my head, I climb back onto the torturous seat and ask what the plan is for the day.

"We thought we'd all head down to the river walk, do some

shopping and get lunch. That's if you want to," Alice responds when Poppa's mouth is too full to speak.

"I'd love that," I say and mean it. I've always loved exploring the shops along the river and riding the water taxis and listening to the tours. Not only would it be absolute nostalgia, but it would also be a welcome distraction from the turmoil of the past couple days.

CHAPTER 5
BIRTHDAY SURPRISE
JOSEFINA

Shopping has never been one of my favorite past times, especially not in the touristy area, including the river walk area. Finding clothes to fit my frame without going to a specialty store is near impossible. Thank goodness for online shopping and easy returns.

I do, however, love to walk along the shops and pop-ups the *artesanos* set up along the river to sell their wares. The vibrantly colored paintings and earthenware remind me of my mother's art and how I became fascinated with making candles in the first place. Mine are not your typical cylinders or tapers, though I have those too. They are layered jars with scents that intermingle as the wax melts. They are carved works of art in the shapes of dragons and fairies. Where other sculptors work with clay and stone, I work with wax.

Momma always encouraged my creativity, teaching me fire safety and how to layer my sculpting blocks. Poppa didn't mind my dabbling back then. He'd just walk by the art room, now turned family den, and chuckle at the mess Momma and I would make. In fact, he never even entered the room or bothered us about any of it until one of my teachers asked about the type of wax we used. It seemed that her bathroom had filled with smoke when she lit the candle I'd given her as a Christmas gift that year. To be honest, I didn't want to give her one. I'd made them for my favorite teachers. Poppa had insisted it would be rude to give a candle to each of my teachers except her. She was the only one I hated, and she didn't deserve one of my beautiful pieces. I complained the entire time. While the wax melted, I told Momma all the reasons I didn't like that woman. As I added the colors and poured the liquid wax into the cheap jar we'd bought, I ranted about how mean she was to so many of us. She was a total bitch who probably tried to burn her own house down just to spite me.

Needless to say, I couldn't have cared less about her little smoke debacle, but Poppa was mortified. I overheard him and Momma arguing that candles were a dangerous medium for my art. Momma would hear nothing about it and continued encouraging me while Poppa started spending more time sitting in the art room, his eyes locked on me during the melting and pouring phases. When he wasn't watching me like a hawk, he would read. At least, he'd pretend to read until I'd say something. The moment my mouth opened, he'd lean forward, tilting what he called his good ear in my direction. As long as I was silent, he was fine.

"How about a reading?" a lovely young woman dressed in black and silver offers, breaking me from my thoughts.

I shake my head while stepping past the woman, having learned long ago that the best way to avoid hawking and scams is to not make eye contact and to keep walking. "No thank you," I say as politely and coolly as I can, trying not to sound rude. The woman is just trying to do her job.

At my words, Poppa turns around from where he and Alice have walked ahead, and his eyes grow wide. "Don't..." he starts, but the words die on his lips as the woman grabs hold of my wrist.

Electricity zaps through my body, and I freeze in place. Not only have I frozen but so has everyone else along both sides of the river, everyone except the woman standing next to me. She screams and jerks her hand back as if she's touched a hot stove. I catch a glimpse of her hand, and her fingertips are stained black, her nails turning obsidian as I stare. *What the fuck is happening?* I look toward Poppa, and he stands there gawking, no words escaping his lips.

"What are you?" the woman asks, fear and reverence in her voice.

The tone catches me off guard, and I take a step toward her. "What do you mean? A person?"

Her hands fly up and she scuttles back away from me. "No. There is more, something more, something dark." Her brow wrinkles as if she can't quite put her finger on the words she wants to say. Finally, her eyes focus on her fingers that stand like beacons between us. "Look at my hands," she cries. "You're not human. You're not even a witch. The goddess..."

She doesn't get to finish the sentence when Poppa's voice rings out, "Enough. You don't know what you're saying." The look of anguish on his face cuts me in a way I didn't think was possible. Fear and anger shift across his features, but it's the devastation in his eyes that tightens the knot sitting right below my sternum.

"Poppa?"

The word might as well have been a flare, as chaos in the form of smoky tendrils swirl around us. They cover the river in a blanket of grays and black. The writhing mass spreads until it has encircled the woman who is still cowering on the ground. She tries to move away, but there's nowhere for her to go. I watch as her mouth opens in horror, and one of the tendrils slithers between her lips.

"No, Josefina," Poppa says, his tone calm and direct. I want to look at him, but my eyes are glued to the possession taking place not ten feet away. "*Mi'ja*, stop this now." He takes a step toward me, one hand outstretched. The random twitch of his fingers gives away the fear as he reaches out to touch my shoulder. "You have to stop them before they hurt her."

Hurt her. The words play through my mind. Why would they

hurt her? She hasn't done anything but try to get me to sit for a reading. She might be a scam artist, but that doesn't mean she deserves to be hurt. Not like Marcus. *Oh my god.* The image of Marcus' prone form encapsulated in shadows pierces my thoughts, and a sob leaves my throat.

"I don't know how." The words are a plea as Poppa wraps his arms around me.

"Breathe." He repeats the word several times before my brain acknowledges the message, and I take a deep breath in and let it out. On the second exhale, I wrap my arms around his waist. By the fourth, I relax against him. "Now, Josefina, tell them to stop."

I pull back slightly to look into his face. He doesn't shy away from my gaze, but I can read the discomfort in his tight smile. Please stop, I think, afraid to speak the words. For some reason, I'm afraid I'll be locked away if I say the words aloud. Who would take me away? I have no idea, especially since everyone else still seems frozen in time, including my stepmother. "Oh no, Alice," I say to Poppa, but he shakes his head.

"She'll be fine when this is over. We'll all be fine, but if you don't stop this, that poor woman will not."

"I can't."

"You must!" His voice raised slightly, and I flinch. Poppa almost never yelled at me. He rarely got upset at all.

"I'm scared," I admit softly, burying my face in his chest. "Poppa, I'm scared."

"Me too, but we can deal with it after this is over. Call them off, Josefina. You're the only one who can."

My thoughts drift to Alistaire who had said nearly the same thing. Bolstered by that thought, I take a deep breath. "I need you to stop, please. I'm fine and don't need you." The swirls slow as if understanding my words, and I repeat myself. "You don't have to do this. We're safe now." The smoke across the river recedes, and the wisps circling around our feet dissipate.

"You're not talking to children. Take control."

With a sigh, I release him and step back, so I can look toward the poor woman kneeling on the ground, mouth and eyes gaping wide. The smoke is coiled around her body like a snake, with that single thin tendril leading into the corner of her mouth. She looks like something from a horror movie rather than a living, breathing person.

"Release her," I say. "Stop this and release her."

It takes several moments that feel like hours before the woman pulls in a deep breath. Several more seconds pass before she stands on shaky legs. I take a step toward her, but Poppa grabs my arm and shakes his head. We watch her retreat into her tent, which she quickly closes.

"I'm sorry," I say under my breath.

Poppa and I stand, listening to the woman's sobs until Alice's voice breaks the relative silence. "You two look like you've seen a ghost. Is everything alright?"

Suddenly, my senses are overwhelmed by the rush of sounds and smells coming from every angle as if the dam that had been holding everyone frozen finally breaks. I swayed a bit, and Poppa let go of my arm to wrap his arm around my waist.

Turning toward his wife. "Yes, Josefina was feeling a little dizzy. It's probably time we go home."

"Oh, you poor thing," she says, completely oblivious to everything that has happened for the past several minutes. Thankfully, her lack of awareness makes it easy for Poppa to direct her toward where we had parked the car.

CHAPTER 6
HISTORY REVEALED
JOSEFINA

"*No te hagas*, Helga! You know better than to think I would just make something like this up."

Poppa's booming voice breaks through the quiet of my room, jolting me awake. How long have I been asleep? Wait, what day is it?

"The high priestess was wrong!"

"What in the world?" I say to the empty room before moving to get up from the bed. At least, I try to get up, but my head has other plans as dizziness forces me to sit much longer while I wait for the world to stop spinning. It's only the murmurs of Poppa's voice still trickling up the stairs that keeps me from getting back under the covers. Even when he raised his voice at the river... Oh fuck, the river. The shadows. That poor woman.

Visions of the woman's body with coils of smoke leading to the tendril that fed into her mouth flash through my mind, and I double over dry heaving with my head between my knees. I swallow back the bile burning my throat. *What have I done?* Without Alistaire's presence, there was no one else to blame for what happened with the smoky shadows.

"I need your help. My daughter needs your help."

Poppa's pleading voice brings me back to the present. With a few deep breaths, I stand and make my way downstairs. The living room is empty and so is the kitchen. There's no way Alice is sleeping through his barks of anger, so she must be gone somewhere. I find Poppa pacing the den, phone pressed to his ear, and a gloomy look on his face as he listens to whoever is on the other line. I take a tentative step into the room. "Poppa?"

He startles but catches himself, quickly giving me a small smile. "*Me tengo que ir,*" he says into the phone while gesturing for me to give him a moment. His face is a mask, but his eyes can't hide relief that washes over him at whatever the person on the other end of the line tells him. "Tomorrow" is the only other word he says before ending the call and sliding his phone into his pocket.

"*Mi'ja,* how're you feeling?" He walks over to put his hands on my shoulders. I stare into his eyes for several seconds, holding his gaze until he sighs and looks away.

"Who was on the phone?"

"*No te preocupes.*"

"Poppa..." He gives me a look that says leave it alone, but I can't. "Don't tell me not to worry, and don't act like that call wasn't about me. I heard you say I needed whoever it was you were talking to. So, who was it?"

He looks up toward the ceiling like he's praying for patience, but then he lets out a long sigh. "Your *tía.*"

My eyes go wide at that unexpected response. As far as I know, he hasn't spoken to my *Tía* Helga, or any other member of his family for that matter, since I was a child. I can barely remember what she looks like, and that memory is only because of the photos I've looked through hundreds of times over the years. Confusion must be written on my face because Poppa turns away and walks toward the built-in bookshelves. He runs a finger over a photo of me and Momma on my 15th birthday. I had wanted a *Quinceañera* full of family and friends, but Momma's illness put a damper on the celebration. Still, Poppa took me shopping, and he bought me the gown Momma had dreamt about. I got my hair done professionally and had pictures taken before twirling around Momma's hospital room with Poppa. After our impromptu father-daughter dance, I climbed into the bed with her, hoop skirt and all. He took that picture in the final moments before I drifted off to sleep and she fell into oblivion.

"Why?" The question comes out as a whisper, yet it fills the room with all the heaviness of those memories.

I'm not sure how much time passes before he finally turns back toward me, but there are tears in his eyes, and it looks like he's aged 30 years since he first touched the picture. "Sit down, Josefina." A knot forms in my throat, but I do as he says. Rather than join me on the couch, he sits on the coffee table directly in front of me and takes both my hands in his. "I owe you an apology, *mi'jita*." I open my mouth to tell him he doesn't have to, more out of habit than meaning because I have no idea what he might need to apologize for, but he silences me with a shake of his head. "I do. Everything that's happening to you, everything that happened this morning, is my fault."

"Your fault?" My voice pitches high with incredulity.

"Indirectly, but yes, my fault. You should have known, should have been prepared. The possibility was there, I guess, but we thought for sure..." His voice trails off, almost as if he's forgotten I'm sitting here. He is obviously trying to work through something in his mind, but my patience is impossibly thin.

"What do you mean? What should I have known? Prepared for what? Poppa, please tell me what is happening."

Again, his eyes lift heavenward. For a man who claims to not believe in anything, he definitely looks the part of a devout father exasperated with his heathen daughter. I've seen that look often over the years since mom passed. What I've never seen until this weekend is the hint of fear that's clouded his warm, caramel-colored eyes since I arrived in a flurry of chaos yesterday.

"I'm sorry, Poppa. I know you're scared." He flinches, but I press on, my voice softer. "I see it in your eyes that you know something. Whatever it is can't be as bad as the unknown."

He snorts out a derisive sound, and my jaw clenches. How can he not understand that having all of this happen without explanation is infinitely worse than being able to address it head on? We can't hide from everything. We can't escape every conflict. We can't just run from every difficult conversation. I'm so far inside my own head, I hardly recognize when he starts speaking.

"From the day we found out your mother was pregnant with a girl, I've done everything possible to protect you from the shadows." He shakes his head and rolls his eyes with a weary smile. "I know that sounds ominous, but I'm not afraid of the shadows harming you."

"I hope that statement wasn't supposed to make this less scary," I say under my breath, and he nods in agreement.

"You're probably right, but that's the best way I can describe it. I spent most of my life surrounded by shadows, running around, and trying to hide from the smoke and mirrors. My life was like a funhouse, or at least my house was, except it wasn't very fun...for me."

Have I stepped into some alternative universe? What in the hell is he talking about? My brows furrow, and my eyes narrow. If he doesn't get to the point soon, I'm going to lose it.

"Imagine being in a family where everyone can wield those smoky tendrils, everyone except you."

I sit back, shock settling in. "Are you saying you've seen this before?" No, that can't be right. Poppa told me, insisted that, magic, including religious miracles, were all a hoax. He said there was no such thing as the paranormal.

"I couldn't keep up, couldn't hold a candle to them. I found myself hating them all, hating my mother and the goddess. Just because she only allowed the matriarchal line to be priestesses didn't mean she had to leave us out of her favor altogether. We still carried their blood, even if we couldn't carry the line."

"I'm not following."

"I was the only one without magic. The only one, and they never let me forget it. As soon as I could, I left. I came out here and never looked back, at least not until you were conceived. Your mom was so excited to be pregnant and ecstatic that she'd get to have a little girl, a mini her, and you were her twin in every way. As soon as my aunt, the High Priestess of Umbra heard you were born, though, she sent for you."

"Sent for me? What? Why?"

He stands from where he's been sitting in front of me and starts pacing again. I don't move to follow. This is his story to sift through, and it doesn't seem like it's going to come out in an easily decipherable way. None of what he's saying makes any sense. His family members have magical powers? The shadows are controllable? I have so many questions, but the first one I need him to answer is the last one I asked. What did he mean by sent for me?

"I'm probably not the best person to explain this all to you, Josefina. I'm just an old man who's been running from the family truths for decades. My perception is skewed, and I hate that my anger may have left you vulnerable." He comes back to the couch and wraps his arms around me. "I was wrong. We were all so wrong, and I'm so sorry."

"Wrong about what? You can't just apologize and not explain what you're apologizing for."

He pulls back and stares at me for a long time. I get the feeling he's trying to work out how he hasn't explained it. Such is my father's way. I ask a question, and he talks in circles until he thinks he's told me all I need to know, and I'm left having to look that shit up myself. Unfortunately, I don't know that any of what he's told me will be found on the internet.

"Ok, let's start with this," I offer, breaking his trance. "Who is Umbra and who or what did you mean by the High Priestess?"

He blinks a couple times and then smiles, the first genuine smile I've seen on his face since I arrived yesterday. "Oh, yes, Umbra is the Goddess of Shadows. She is the patron goddess of our family. Your grandmother and mine before her served the goddess as her priestesses here on Earth."

If that doesn't sound like something from a children's story, or ancient mythology, I don't know what does. Though I don't want to interrupt him, I can't help it. "What happened to religion being a huge scam?"

Poppa sighs, and his lips turn down. "*Mira*. Listen. If you spent your entire childhood knowing that your family was the servants of a goddess, but you weren't privy to any of the benefits of everyone else, you'd think it was a scam too."

My eyes narrow. "So, you're telling me that you do believe in myths and magic, but you told me not to? You made me feel like an outcast because I made candles and loved all things supernatural. You pushed me away out of spite for something your family couldn't control?"

The gasp that comes from my father sucks the air from the room. I hadn't meant to be so harsh, but none of what he's saying is believable to me. In fact, it's so incredible that I almost ask if he'd tried to keep me from having magic intentionally. There isn't any need for me to ask.

"I felt like I had been punished for being born without a womb. I was the outcast. I was ignored and overlooked and different. By the time I was in my late teens, I knew I had to move away and just live a mundane life. As soon as I could, I left. I left and pretended the family had abandoned me. In a way, they had. They'd let me go. Other than Helga, no one even reached out to check on me. Not until you were born."

All the anger and frustration that had been brewing at his cryptic and vague explanations disappears as my heart breaks for him. He may have left his family out of anger, but he was obviously brokenhearted too. I reach out and lay my hand on his. I'm still not fully sold on the idea of shadow magic and family service to a goddess, but I know that he's never hurt me intentionally. When he lifts his eyes to mine, there's gratitude in them.

"Why didn't you tell me any of this before?"

"It should've never been something you needed to know." I draw back as if he'd slapped me, but he grabs my hand in his. "You weren't supposed to have magic. The shadows should've never found their way to you. According to our history, the goddess's favor passes down through the matriarchal line, and a male child breaks that line. That's why I kept you here far away from the family. I didn't want you to feel the same way I did for being different, for having your birthright withheld for something out of your control. I didn't..."

He trails off, but I'm able to easily finish his sentence. "You didn't want me to blame you." He gives me a sad, watery smile, and I scoot forward to wrap my arms around his neck. "Poppa, I don't blame you for any of this. I'm still not sure exactly what this is, but I don't blame you." I don't. Not really. I'm upset that he's kept such secrets all these years. I'm sad that I've been without the benefit of an extended family. And, if I'm being honest, I'm hurt that he couldn't support me in the things I love because they remind him of what he couldn't have, but I don't blame him.

"Well, you might be angry with me again when you hear what I have to say now. You're going to want to fight me on it." He lets out a deep breath. "You're going to argue that you can't be forced, but I need you to listen to me when I say you can, and you will."

My head tilts to the side. If I had been looking in on this conversation, I'd probably see myself looking like one of those cartoon dogs when they hear something that shouldn't be happening. I don't get a chance to say anything before he pushes on.

"*Las Tias*, the Daughters of Umbra, are sending someone to get you tomorrow. They will pick you up here, take you home to pack, and you'll be in Onyx Junction before the week is out."

"Poppa, I can't go anywhere. I have to work tomorrow

afternoon. I have a job, a life. I need to check on my stuff from the fair."

"Do you trust that your shadows won't release on the middle of campus? Do you have enough control to keep them from wrapping around a student? What about that asshole ex of yours? If he got free, how will you handle seeing him at work?" I open my mouth to speak, but I don't know what to say. Poppa doesn't give me a chance anyway. "No, you will go to Onyx Junction. You will learn our family history, and you will figure out how the magic you weren't supposed to have found you. You would hate yourself if something happened to one of your students or a colleague, and I won't let you take that chance."

"I don't have the luxury of taking time off."

"You don't have a choice. The High Priestess is sending someone for you."

CHAPTER 7

RECKONING ON THE HORIZON

ALISTAIRE

"Alistaire. Wait."

I close my eyes for a moment, willing my jaw to unclench, before I turn around. Doctor Edwards is not the reason for my foul mood, and though he is terribly droll, he doesn't deserve the anger and frustration roiling inside of me. As his footsteps shuffle closer, I take a deep breath, plaster a smile on my face, and turn to face him.

"Professor Edwards."

"Doctor Edwards," he corrects, and I give him a curt nod. "You know the protocol, Alistaire."

Yet you never call me Professor, you hypocritical bastard. Of course, I don't say the words aloud. I'm not worried about anything he might do, but I may still need this job sometime in the near future, and burnt bridges within the same century never bode well. They make things messy.

"How may I help you, Doctor Edwards?" Acid burns my tongue as I'm force to play nice when all I want to do is head back to my office and sulk, perhaps head home and down a bottle of bourbon.

"I'm needing someone to cover my classes next week. I had

meant to reach out to you about it a couple weeks ago, but time got away from me. I'm sure you understand."

My fists clench and unclench. *You want me to play substitute for your boring ass lectures, but you don't even respect me enough to give me the courtesy of time to prepare. Typical.* Again, I school my features and give him a remorseful smile. "My apologies, professor. I will be on leave for the foreseeable future. There has been an emergency, and I must take some time off. Had I known ahead of time, I might have been able to adjust my leave, but that's just not possible at the last minute."

Edwards sputters with indignation. He can't believe he's being told no, especially not by an adjunct professor and doctoral candidate. The joy it brings to have burst his entitled bubble is delicious, and though I'd love to stay here and fuck with him some more, I really have to get things in order. After all, I was only half lying.

"I'm sorry, professor. I really must go." Turning on my heel, I walk away without a backwards glance. Odds are, the old ass will be dead before I come back here anyway, unless the news I got was wrong.

The moment my office door closes, I drop everything--my bag, my keys, and the mask I'd been wearing since this morning's phone call. *Fuck!*

A listaire
        Three hours pass before I'm back in my apartment, clothes thrown haphazardly in a suitcase and the bourbon I'd been craving settling warmly in my stomach. It takes far more than the average amount to affect my senses, but I do love the feel of it going down. At least, the burn is better than the knot I had to

lecture around this afternoon. Prattling on about the history of modern-day pharmaceuticals, as if they haven't always been a scam, is much harder to do when my balls are in danger of being ground to powder with a *pilón* while still attached to my body.

I'd had one job. Well, I've had multiple jobs, but only one important task--keep the girl safe from herself. It's not like I haven't tried. I'd checked in on her 25th birthday, and she seemed unaffected. I'd watched her from a distance while she was on campus. I'd even ground my teeth during her early courtship with that fucking idiot I'd had to save from her shadows. Lucky for all of them, I'd chosen this weekend to attend the Renaissance Fair. Unlucky for her boyfriend, that moron decided to show his ass on her birthday, the day her magic decided to take over. Still, I shouldn't be held responsible for any of that. I couldn't just interfere in her life on a daily basis and make my constant presence seem a coincidence. What the fuck did they expect me to do? Stalk her?

The thought has some merit. Standing from the leather chair I'd plunked down in after pouring my drink, I start pacing my home office. Not that any new plans matter now. Now, the high priestess knows Josefina ascended and I hadn't been there to keep her from doing any damage to the life she'd created for herself or the coven's secrecy. Not that the idiot boyfriend knew anything about the coven or even understood what had happened to him. *I should've let the shadows consume him.* At least, that's the thought I've had plaguing me all fucking day. Whatever he had done to her, the shadows were hungry enough to devour him. Still, I followed protocol and released him and ensured he received medical care all while making her tent and every scrap of evidence against her disappear. I did everything right.

Except sending her home to her father, my inner demon chastises.

Okay, maybe that was a poor decision. Maybe I should've kept her with me. I could've explained what was happening to her. I could've helped calm everything down, ensured she was protected, and then contacted the high priestess myself.

We could've brought her back here with us.

Thoughts like that are exactly why I couldn't bring her home with me. Those thoughts are exactly why I've kept my distance since that first evening in her vendor tent. Her beautiful face. Her plush curves. Her sass.

Her vulnerability.

"Shut up," I yell aloud, throwing the glass in my hand. It shatters against the wall, tiny splashes of amber liquid splattering the paint.

Stop pretending you don't want her. Stop lying to yourself.

"I can't want her. I'm not worthy of her."

The disembodied voice snarls out, *and that's why we're being called in front of the high priestess,* before going silent.

We've had this argument many times over the past few years. Hell, we've had similar arguments many times over the past half century. Still, he torments me with thoughts of what can never be.

CHAPTER 8

WHERE DO YOU KEEP THE BROOM?

JOSEFINA

I have never been a morning person, but the mixture of uncertainty and excitement for today's visitor has me awake at the ass crack of dawn. An hour. I spend an entire hour staring at the ceiling, willing myself to go back to sleep. Poppa isn't even up yet, and he is the literal early bird. If I were home in my apartment in Houston, my blackout shades would make the endeavor a little easier. Here, however, I'm lucky that the blinds haven't all turned to dust.

Before I even hear stirring through the house, the smell of brewing coffee lofts up the stairs and into my room. I smile at the predictability. I don't know whether Alice is aware, but my father was never a big coffee drinker. Sure, he would have a cup after dinner with his dessert, but it was never something he needed or wanted first thing in the morning. My mother, on the other hand, would not start her day without it. She was the one who insisted we have a coffee pot with an automatic start, so a cup would be ready when she got out of bed. Something about the continuation of that tradition made me feel a little better. My life was falling apart, and yet this one little piece of normalcy is what finally brings tears to my eyes.

The shower does little to brighten my mood. I spend most of it letting the tears fall and hoping the pounding water covers my sobs. Maybe I'm a little more nervous than excited at the prospect of being uprooted and thrown to *las tías*, as my father calls them. All my life, the only person he ever talked about was my *Tía* Helga. I had assumed she was the only family member who hadn't disowned him and, by extension, me. I have no idea how big his family is nor do I know what to expect once I arrive halfway across the county.

"Elinora," my father's voice booms from the front door.

"*Tío! Tanto tiempo,*" a woman's voice follows suit.

I had just finished getting dressed and packing my few belongings into the overnight bag I had brought with me. If I'm being honest, I've taken far longer than necessary up here. I don't want to see the look of concern on my father's face or the fear in his eyes. I also don't want to see Alice acting as if everything is normal when nothing is normal anymore. It's as if I've forgotten how to play my role in the family when the stage is about the be overrun by additional actors reading lines of script I hadn't received.

"Josefina, come down here," Poppa yells from the bottom of the stairs.

"*Voy,*" I say. I'm coming. With a final look around the room, and a sense of finality that says I likely won't make it back here again, I open the door and head into the past and the future simultaneously.

Elinora isn't at all what I had imagined when Poppa said one of my cousins was coming to get me. Poppa and I both have dark hair, sun-kissed skin, and stand on the shorter side. My cousin, however, could easily pass for a plus-size swimsuit model. Her hair is long, thick, and blonde. There are red and brown streaks in it that I'm almost certain aren't natural. She doesn't seem to favor Poppa or the one photo I have of my *Tía* Helga. Her eyes, though, unlike my own, do have the same caramel hue, one that seems to glow from within.

I have always gotten compliments on my eyes, especially from people who struggle to find something positive to say about my body instead of just keeping their mouths shut. Still, I would've gladly given up the muted blue for eyes like my Poppa. It's as if his have light illuminating them from behind rather than reflecting from some other source. Elinora's eyes have that same internal fire.

I've never really felt insecure or inadequate, but for some reason, this beautiful Amazon bending down to wrap me in a hug has me shrinking inside. Is this what the entire family looks like? Is everyone in the family this intimidating? I don't realize I asked the last question aloud until Elinora bursts out laughing.

"I'm not sure it will make you feel any better if I say yes, but it would be a disservice to tell you no. *Las Tías* are scary as fuck!"

Despite my discomfort, I laugh, and some of the tension I've been holding seems to evaporate. "How many are there?" I ask with more than a little trepidation.

"*Tías*? Six in total if you count my mom. There are more of us than them, especially with you joining us because it's hard to count Raquel."

Poppa's eyes jump to Elinora's face from where he's been staring into his coffee. "What's wrong with Raquel? Is she unwell?"

"No, *Tío*. She's healthy as the goddess herself. She just, how do I put this, already thinks herself a *tía* because she's in line to be head priestess."

Poppa nods solemnly. All I can do is look between the two of them. Though they're speaking aloud, it's like they're having this unspoken conversation with me sitting right here. Not that I'm upset about not being the center of attention. I'd rather not relive everything that's happened this past weekend, especially not with this complete stranger.

A noise from the kitchen grabs all of our attention, as Alice let's out an expletive. Poppa takes off running toward the open doorway with me hot on his heels. Considering I've never heard the woman say anything stronger than "damn" in all the years they've been married, something must be wrong. I nearly run into his back when he stops just inside the doorframe, but I manage to catch myself before bowling him over. Peeking around his shoulder, the first thing that catches my eye is Alice on the floor surrounded by at least a dozen cookies, some of them broken into pieces.

"Are you alright?" Poppa's voice carries a hint of worry, though we can easily see she's unharmed. When she looks up at him, though, there are tears in her eyes. There's something else as well, but I can't quite place it.

"What happened?" I ask, squeezing around my father to help pick up the metal tray haphazardly flipped against the table leg.

My eyes drift to Alice where she still sits looking between my father and the corner of the kitchen near the pantry door. Poppa helps her up from the floor and wraps her in his arms. I take the opportunity to let my gaze drift to the spot she'd been eyeing. There was something along the edge of the door that seemed to disappear before I could focus on it fully, but maybe it was my imagination. I turned back to the task of cleaning up the wasted cookies when I noticed Elinora standing just inside the kitchen. She, too, was looking toward the pantry.

"Tío, take your wife out into the living room. We'll get this mess cleaned up," she says without looking away from the closed door. A shiver runs up my spine.

At first, Poppa doesn't move. It's obvious from the look on his face that he's guessed something is up, but he gathers Alice against him and follows Elinora's directions. She shuts the door behind them, without so much as turning her head, even when she speaks.

"Does your stepmother normally drop trays of food all over the floor, *prima*?"

I shake my head, but when she doesn't respond, I realize she's waiting for a verbal answer. "No. She's never wasted food as far as I know, but I haven't been home in a few months."

"Where do you keep the broom?"

"In the pantry." I stand and place the tray on the counter. Her head nudges toward the door, and I get the odd feeling that we're about to play out one of the worst scenes in every horror movie where everyone knows the killer is in the closet, but the actor has to go investigate the weird sound anyway. "You want me to get it?" Though I try to mask the terror rising in my chest, my voice cracks a bit.

"Just open the door, and I'll get it."

Jesus Christ, this can't really be happening right now. What the fuck does she think is in there? It was just a play of the light, nothing more. At least that's what I'm telling myself. With a deep breath, I take the few steps across the room and reach my hand out toward the knob. Elinora walks up behind me and steps over until she's directly in front of the door. Before my fingers can touch the metal, her hands are outstretched. By the time, I twist the knob and look back at her for the signal to pull the door open, her entire countenance has changed. Her face is taught. Her caramel eyes are black as coal, and her fingertips have turned the dark gray of the night sky.

"Now," she says at the same time a gasp leaves my lips, but I manage to follow her order and yank the door open.

A gust of air blows out from the pantry as the shadows that had filled the room dissipate. Elinora steps in closer, but light from the open kitchen window fills the small room. It's completely empty. My heart races, and I struggle to get my ragged breathing under control when Elinora sniffs in deeply, her head tilting to the side. Without warning, her eyes flash from the black orbs that had nearly scared me to death back to the backlit caramel of earlier. Likewise, the gray of her fingers recedes to their normal flesh tone, at least I'm guess the lightly tanned hue is the normal one. *Gods, I hope that's the normal one.*

"What was that?"

"I'm not entirely sure," she responds simply.

"I meant with you. What the fuck happened to your eyes and your fingers? Is that going to happen to me?"

She shrugs, and my temper flares.

"That's it? Poppa says I have to go with you to learn what the hell is happening to me, and all I get is a shrug?"

"*Mira, prima*, I was told late last night that I had to make this trek out here. I'm working on nearly no sleep. I got no explanation of why or what I should expect to find, just that I was coming to Tío's house to get a cousin, a cousin I didn't even know existed."

I bristle at the last part of her statement. "I didn't ask for you to come. I didn't ask for any of this. You're bothered that you were sent to find one person when I didn't know we had an entire family out there. I was the one caught unawares. I'm the one all this shit is happening to. I'm the one having to uproot my life, and for what?" My hands have balled into fists, as anger rolls off of me in waves I know she has to feel.

Suddenly, her demeanor changes again. "What do you mean you were caught unaware? *¿Qué te pasó?* What happened?"

I deflate against the rollercoaster of her emotions. "It doesn't matter," I say, turning to leave the kitchen.

"Hey." She grabs my arm, pulling me to a stop. I try to pull out of her grasp, but the bitch is strong.

"I'll work it out. If this is how the rest of the family is, I'll just figure it out on my own."

She releases me, but before I can make it to the door, her words stop my progress as quickly as her hand had a moment ago. "No, you won't."

I roll my eyes and push through the door into the living room where my father sits with Alice cradled against him on the couch. One look at my face, and he stands abruptly, startling Alice from where she must've dozed off after the adrenaline of her scare wore off.

"*Mi'ja, ¿Qué pasó?*"

I shake my head and start up the stairs toward my room. "I'm going home, Poppa. I have work in the morning."

Elinora must've followed me out the room because he asks again, "What happened in there?"

"Nothing," Elinora lies.

"¿Cómo que va a trabajar mañana? She can't. It's not safe."

Without waiting to hear her response, I close the door to my room and lean against it, trying to get my emotions in check. There is absolutely no reason I should be this angry, but something about her nonchalance, like I should be fully aware of what's happening, rubbed me the wrong way. If everyone else in the family is going to treat me the same way, I'd rather not know any of them. I might as well keep my ass home and let whatever happens happen.

CHAPTER 9

GO AWAY...NO WAIT
JOSEFINA

Three hours later, I'm back in my apartment, looking around at everything that makes up my life here in Houston. Books litter the kitchen table. The trash is filled with to-go containers from where I grab something quick on the way home from work each day. And the walls are bare except for one tiny shelf that holds three candles in front of an oval mirror. They're the only ones I have left from the last batch Momma and I made together before she got sick. I never lit them because I didn't want them to become another distant memory like everything from my childhood. Now? I swallow the lump in my throat and grab the lighter from the counter. Now, I hope they'll make her feel a little closer.

As soon as the first candle flickers to life, warmth settles over me, and I smile for the first time today. The second and third candles dance against the wall, and I sit on the couch to watch the show. The weight of the weekend and the past 24 hours seems to melt off my shoulders as I lean my head back against the cushions. My eyes flicker shut, and I'm whisked away to some quiet place in the oblivion. No more worries weigh me down, and my heart is light.

I have no idea how long I stay like that, lost in the sweet feel of nothingness surrounded by fluffy tufts of gray and white clouds that cushion my body and cocoon me in tranquility, but when I wake, the candles have burned down halfway. The first thing I notice when my eyes flutter open is that the sun has moved to the other side of my building. Shadows obscure the hall that leads to my bedroom and office. A few stay tucked around the corner into the kitchen where I can't see from my place on the couch. The flickering light from the candles catches my eye, drawing my attention to the mirror where tendrils of smoky shadows dance alongside the light as if made to be partners. I nearly smile at the thought, but the escape of a single tendril from the mirror has my lips open in a silent gasp instead.

The vine-like wisp slithers down the wall, growing thicker as it moves. It crawls across the floor toward the couch, covering the beige carpet in smoky gray. I pull my feet up, nearly doubled into the fetal position as fear skitters under my skin. I blink multiple times, afraid to take my eyes off the thing reaching for me while wanting to wish it away at the same time. Still, it creeps closer.

A voice enters my mind just as terrors beings to constrict my chest. "You can control it, *Muñeca*." No, I can't. I can't control it. I don't even know what it is.

"Please stop," I finally say once the tip of the tendril reaches the couch cushion. It's progress halts, the tip moving back and forth in a sweeping motion like a snake. It stays there for mere seconds before it begins to lengthen again, the tip spreading out into what appear to be fingers. "I said stop." My voice is a little more forceful than the first time as I remember Alistaire telling me that I had to mean what I was saying when I talked to the shadows.

They come from you, Josefina. They are yours to control.

This scary ass vine didn't feel like mine. It sure as fuck didn't come from me. It came from the mirror as far as I can tell, but who the hell am I to question it. It's not like I have any idea what in the hell is going on in my life anymore. Where are you, Alistaire? You'd been there when I needed you before, when the shadows were too much. Where are you now?

Just then, a knock sounds on the door. I let my eyes flicker toward the entry and then back to the shadow tendril that, much like the candlelight, dances back and forth. The person knocks again, but neither I nor the tendril move to leave our position.

"Josefina, are you home?"

My hand clutches at my chest. There's no way. I look toward the door again.

"Josefina, I have your tent and wares from the event this past weekend. I have to leave town and didn't want to not return it."

Holy shit, he's here! I start to unfurl my legs and then remember the shadowy vine that I nearly kick with my feet. "Shoo, go back in the mirror," I whisper, afraid Alistaire might somehow hear me through the door and think I've completely lost my mind. The tendril doesn't move except to swing its tip back and forth as if following my gaze to the door and back.

"Josefina, are you alright? I know your car's here."

"Go away," I say more forcefully, swatting my hand at the shadows, my fingers cutting through it. The tendril rears back like it's been hurt, and I watch in astonishment as it recedes the way it came with tiny wisps floating off in waves as if it were bleeding along the way. My heart sinks, and I'm ready to apologize to the incorporeal form when something thumps on the landing, and Alistaire's voice seeps through the door more quietly than before.

"I'm sorry. I'll just leave everything out here for you."

I jump up from the couch, nearly tripping over my own feet. "No, wait!" I yell. Scrambling for the door, I yank it open to find him with one step on the landing, as if he had already begun his descent. He turns, and though there are dark circles under his eyes, I'm still floored by how absolutely gorgeous he is. "Hey," I say, unsure any other words would come out coherently. It's still hard to believe he's standing here after I just called for him to come save me.

"Hey yourself." He points to the boxed-up tent, tables, and boxes of items sitting in a pile next to the door. "I came to bring you your things and didn't want to just leave them out here without you knowing."

A smile tugs at the corner of my lips. "Thank you."

We stare at each other for a few moments. He looks me up and down like he's trying to make sure I'm whole. When he seems satisfied with his initial assessment, he returns my half smile. "Is there somewhere you'd rather these be than right here?" he finally asks.

I blink away the stupor that has me staring at his lips while he talks and look back into his eyes. "The tent usually stays in my car during the season, but I guess that's over for me now, so it can all go into my office." I make a show of leaning over to pick up a box, unsure what else to do. It's like something is pulling me toward him, but I'm not sure it's safe to take that step. He really does seem to always be around when the shadows take on a life of their own.

"Do you need my help?"

His question gives me pause. I don't need his help. I've been moving this stuff around on my own the past couple years. It's not like I can't, but I'm not one to turn down the opportunity to watch a beautiful man work. "Thank you. That would be..." I pause and narrow my eyes. He tilts his head, confusion written on his face.

"That would be..." he repeats, waiting for me to finish the sentence.

"How'd you know where I live? And how is it you always show up when..."

"When what?" he asks, immediately on alert and looking around us. His eyes take in the entry over my shoulder. I follow his gaze, but the only thing visible is the flicker of light reflecting from the mirror onto the walls. "Is everything alright in there?"

I let out a breath. "Yes. All good." His shoulders relax, and I raise a brow, crossing my arms over my chest. "I'm still waiting for an answer, Professor Seagal."

I don't know what makes me use his title, but something flickers in his eyes. A spark perhaps. I'm not sure, but his eyes narrow in on mine as if he's staring into my soul, and heat, rather than fear, curls in my belly.

"So, it's professor now, is it?"

My shoulders shrug, and while I'm aware this might be a dangerous game, I just can't seem to help myself. "Whatever it takes to get your attention back on the conversation at hand."

He leans against the railing, crosses his legs, and slides his hands into his pockets. "You wanted to know how I got your address, right?" When I don't say anything, he smirks. "Would you believe it if I said that your friend Taylor gave it to me during class today?" I raise a brow. "That's a no, huh?"

"I'll accept that as plausible if you answer the other question I didn't get to finish. You know, the one that sent you into protector mode."

His lips purse, and his Adam's apple bobs. He's not nervous, but I can tell he's weighing his options.

"Look, Professor, I have been through the absolute ringer this weekend, and I've already dealt with one person who refused to answer my questions. I don't need that shit from anyone else. So, if you're not willing to be straight with me, then please leave." I try to hold onto my serious stance, but I feel myself deflating the longer he stays silent.

"Can I come in? This is probably not a conversation for outside and random ears. I'm already in enough trouble."

I eye him suspiciously. "Trouble?"

He just shakes his head. "That's nothing for you to worry your pretty little head about. But I can answer your other questions or at least give you some answers that might make all this shit make sense. At least, I hope I can do that for you."

A few moments pass as I calculate the risks of letting him

inside my house. He, obviously, has some kind of strange abilities. There's some reason he keeps showing up when weird shit is happening. And I really don't feel like carrying all this crap into the apartment myself. What's the worst that can happen? He kills me, or I jump his bones. The way my emotions have been going, I'm not sure which would be preferable.

"Help me carry this stuff in, and I'll give you a chance to explain yourself, Professor."

He sighs. "Can you please call me Alistaire?"

"Not when you seem to like my calling you by your title so much," I mutter under my breath. Heat floods my cheeks when he chuckles behind me, but I refuse to turn around.

CHAPTER 10

MAKE IT ALL GO AWAY

ALISTAIRE

I should already be on my way to Onyx Junction. The High Priestess only gave me until tomorrow afternoon to show my face before the council. I'd literally rather cut out my own tongue than do that, so here I am doing the one thing that might bring me a few moments of joy before hell takes me. Watching Josefina bend down to pick up a box in front of me is pure joy. She disappears through the door, and I adjust myself before picking up the unwieldy tent and follow behind her.

"It smells divine in here," I say as we pass through the living space and down the hall. I get a tiny glance into her bedroom and recognize the corner of a wooden sleigh bed before she turns into another small room off to the side. It must be her office. Considering the bedding choice, I'm surprised to walk into a sparsely decorated room. There's a small self-assembled desk in the corner and a shelving unit where she's stacked boxes along the back wall.

"It's the candles. The ones burning in the living room are old, so they're quite potent. I needed something to help me relax."

She speaks of the candles as if there's nothing more to them but wax and oils, but I can feel the magic swirling throughout the apartment. I didn't get that feeling in her tent on either occasion I visited the Renaissance Fair, but it's here now. "How old?" I try to keep my voice light and unassuming. I don't want her clamming up on me. No matter what I saw happen with her, there's no way she faked the terror coursing through her the other day. She has no idea what her magic is capable of. I wouldn't be surprised if she didn't know she had magic at all.

"They were the last candles I made with my mother before she passed away. I was ten."

Josefina leaves the room, but my feet are glued to the carpet. Ten years old? In all my years of service, Umbra has never bestowed magic on anyone younger than fifteen. All her priestesses have ascended at fifteen. In fact, one of the young ones is ready to go any day now. Ten?

"Professor?" Josefina's voice breaks through my stupor. "Don't worry about the boxes in there. I'll get them lay..."

Her words cut off as we nearly collide, and I grab her waist to keep her from falling backwards when she stumbles. "Sorry, I didn't mean to scare you," I say, trying to straighten her, so she's able to stand. Her hand cups my cheek, and I make the mistake of looking down into her eyes. Those amazingly pale blue eyes that make me want to bathe in them, bathe in her. "Muñeca" is all I manage to say before her other hand slides around my neck, and our lips meet.

I have no idea what comes over me, but the moment his hands touch my skin, an inferno courses through me. Doubt has kept me wondering if he's as aware of me as I am of him until he stares into my eyes. His take on that glow I've seen every night in my dreams, and when he calls me his doll, I can't hold it back anymore.

My hand locks into his hair, and I pull his lips to mine. If I have to be on fire, he's going to burn with me.

The kiss is something otherworldly. I feel like that smoke tendril slowly losing wisps of myself in each caress of our tongues and each nip of our teeth. I want to wrap myself in the sensations like a warm blanket. The air swirls around us, warm and comforting. That's what his touch is. It's comfort, like coming home. He pulls his lips from mine just when I'm moments from losing my breath, and I whimper at the loss.

"*No te preocupes*," he says, brushing my hair back from my face, "I'm not going anywhere."

Without warning, he pushes me against the wall outside of my bedroom and runs his nose along my jaw before kissing his way down my neck. Every touch is a spark, a tiny little flame along my skin. Soon, I'll be the candle melting all over the carpet.

"Alistaire." My voice is breathy, but it gets his attention. His eyes are molten when they meet mine, and there's no way my panties, or my sanity, are going to survive this man.

"Tell me what you want, Josefina. What do you need from me?" His voice is gravely, and my knees shake at the desire emanating from him.

I've been with other men. Hell, Marcus and I had been dating for over a year, and fucking since before then, but I've never felt as wanted as I do when he looks at me like this. It's like he's pleading to serve me and yet wanting to devour me at the same time, and hell if I don't want him to do both. I hadn't been lying when I said he always showed up right when I needed him, and tonight is no different.

"Make it all go away, please."

Our bodies spin as if we've been pulled into a tornado, and when I catch my bearings, we're in my bed. Alistaire leans over me and rubs his nose against mine. The gesture is so intimate that my throat tightens. His hand slides up my arms, goosebumps following in the wake of his fingers.

"You're so beautiful, Daughter of Umbra. Fuck, I've dreamt of touching you for so long, it's..."

I interrupt him with a primal "What?" that takes both of us by surprise. "What the hell is that?"

His wide eyes tell me he doesn't even realize what he's said. We lay there staring at each other for what feels like forever before I finally catch my breath and manage to push him off of me. He sits back on his heels, but he says nothing. I don't know whether to slap the surprise from his face or scream again.

"What did you just call me?"

He swallows and closes his eyes for less than a second. When they open, it's obvious by the remorse I see there that he has replayed his last words. "I'm..." He inhales deeply and backs off the bed. After a few more moments of silence that nearly send me off the rails, he looks up and says, "I think it's time for me to give you those answers you asked for earlier."

I climb off the bed, sniffle back the frustration and anger threatening to boil me from the inside. Without looking back to see if he follows, I make my way to the kitchen and put on a kettle for tea. The wait gives me a chance to simmer and to recuperate from the thrumming in my veins. I'd love to say it's all righteous indignation, but I'm still not sure what I'm angry about. What I do know is that there's a healthy dose of feminine pride and disappointed libido warring inside of me too.

Neither one of us speak until I set the tray with two steaming cups of water and different flavor teabags on the plushy ottoman I keep in front of the couch in place of a coffee table. He watches me while I steep the chamomile tea that I hope will help calm the raging inside. I can feel his gaze, but I'm not ready to look into his eyes and see... I don't even know what I think will be there. Pity? Caged desire? Or maybe it'll be worse, and there will be nothing in his eyes. I'm not sure my heart could take all that after these past few days.

He opens his mouth to speak, but then says nothing. I can

hear his jaw ticking, though I still haven't turned in his direction. After the same thing happens twice more, I can't take it anymore.

"Just spit it out, Alistaire."

"I'm sorry."

When he says nothing else, I finally turn my body, so I can take him in. He's sitting up straight, almost too stiffly for the man I've seen relaxed in every situation until now. Though his torso is rigid, his shoulders are slumped.

"For what?" If he thought I was going to let him off easily, he is sorely mistaken.

"For all of it," he says, and an almost inaudible sob leaves my throat before I can stop it. Unfortunately, he catches the slip, and his hand reaches toward me before he pulls it back. "Let me rephrase. I'm not sorry for everything. I'm sorry for what came before, what I didn't protect you from, and I'm sorry for ruining the moment and failing you again."

As if I haven't been swallowing back tears for days now, they threaten to show their faces again. I'd rather be angry if this is the only alternative. "I don't understand any of that cryptic shit. C'mon, you're a fucking professor. You can do better than that. Explain it to me like I'm five."

"I can't explain it all." When I glare at him, he holds up his hands. "I wish I could. *Te lo juro*. I swear, I do, but I can't."

"Then start from the beginning and tell me what you can or get the fuck out of my apartment."

CHAPTER 11
MAKE IT MAKE SENSE
JOSEFINA

It's a calculated risk to give him an ultimatum, but something in his eyes tells me he isn't ready to leave, and thankfully, I'm right. Rather than standing up and storming out with a devastating 'fine' like so many other men I've known, including my ex, Alistaire smirks and leans forward, grabbing the cup of hot water and a teabag. Something in my chest loosens at the realization that he plans to stay for a while longer.

"What do you mean by protect me?" I'm not sure why that is the first question I ask. Once it's out of my mouth, though, I know it's the one that feels the most important."

"As I said, I can't explain everything because I don't have all the answers." He leans back into the couch and takes a sip of the scalding hot tea without so much as a flinch.

My eyes narrow slightly, but I force them back open. It's obvious there is more to Professor Alistaire Seagal than it seems, so I can't be surprised the man can drink liquid fire. Tapping my nails on the cup in my own hands, I feign impatience rather than disquiet.

"I saw you that day in your classroom. The day I came to

observe your professor. No, saw probably isn't the right word. I felt your presence behind me. The entire hour in the lecture hall was an exercise in control each time the urge to turn around came on. I had no idea who you were, but I knew you were there."

The swallow of tea I hurriedly down to keep him from seeing my surprise burns my throat. Not enough to cause lasting damage, but damn if it doesn't nearly take my breath away. Once I'm able to open my mouth without breathing fire, I say, "What do you mean?"

"Are you saying you don't feel anything when I'm near?"

He leans forward until his face in directly in my periphery, almost daring me to look at him, but I hold steady. "No, not until I hear your voice."

A light snort is all that follows my lie before he settles back into his seat. "Anyway, after that I would watch for you, but I rarely caught a glimpse until you were too far away for me to catch your eye." I turn back toward him again, and he smiles. "Until that day at the Renaissance Fair. Imagine my surprise when that mysterious feeling prickled my skin as I was walking past this random tent advertising candles for all occasions outside. You were hiding behind the counter, but I knew you were there. That spark of recognition told me you were there."

"I thought you said you came in because you heard the cake container opening," I blurt out, and his smile widens. Fuck, he really is a beautiful man. *No, pendeja, no falling for his beauty. You need answers.*

"Oh, I did hear the cake container, and that just gave me the perfect excuse to approach you without making it weird." My head tilts, and he shrugs. "I mean, how would you have taken it if I'd walked into your tent, snuffed out all the candles, and said, 'I've been chasing the feeling of you for centuries?'" His brow raises, and I roll my eyes.

"I'd have said you were full of shit and sent you on your way."

"Exactly, so my love of cake was my saving grace that day."

I purse my lips and give him another eye roll, which makes him chuckle, and dammit, that sound sends quivers down to my core. *Stop that right now, Josefina. Answers. You're here for answers.* "So, you're saying it was completely happenstance that you showed up at my tent at the fair, not that you were stalking me. Right. Ok, and the second time?"

"The, um, second time?" His voice had pitched up slightly. "Well, that time I did go looking for you."

"And the bar?"

"You're not going to make this easy for me, are you?" I just stare at him. "I'm gonna need something stronger than tea."

Now, it's my turn to smirk. "You know, Professor. I might almost feel sorry for you if you would have answered at least one of my questions already." I raise a brow in challenge. I know that he's trying to skirt around the things he doesn't want to say, but I'm not having it. It is my life being turned upside down, and it all seems to have started from the moment this man walked into my tent.

"I thought I was explaining how I know where you live."

My mouth opens and closes as my brain works to put the pieces together. I was absolutely lying when I said I can't feel when he's nearby. I knew it was him outside my door earlier before he said anything. I knew he was outside my tent before he walked through the smoke obscuring Marcus and the door. And I knew he was behind me at the bar even though I couldn't see him in the mirror. Would that feeling lead me to him if I had known what it was? My face softens a bit at that question because I don't have a response, and he must see that reaction as a cue to continue.

"So, what started as happenstance turned into an awareness I embraced. That's what led me to you tonight."

"And I suppose it's also a coincidence that you seem to find me," I say while making air quotes around find, "when something weird is happening and I'm a little emotionally out of control."

His mouth quirks to the side. "Well, there might be something to that." He shrugs. "We could call it my spidey sense?" I shake my head at him. "Bat signal?" I put down my tea and cross my arms.

CHAPTER 12

YOU WEREN'T THERE

She's really not going to make this easy for me. Among the other things I could feel from her, I already know that she's smarter than any of her friends, and probably more so than any of them give her credit for. Brains and beauty. A deadly combination, and the way her lips purse keeps drawing my attention back to her mouth. My demon wants her back in our arms, every glorious inch. She might never let me touch her again. Hell, I shouldn't have touched her in the first place. But now that I have, now that I've tasted her lips and run my hands over her soft skin, I'll never be the same. Another thousand lifetimes won't purge that feeling from my mind.

Her throat clears, and I realize I've been lost in my own thoughts. My demon chuckles, and it's all I can do to keep from rolling my eyes. The last thing I want or need is for her to think I'm not taking her seriously regardless of my little jokes about this connection between us. I don't know how else to explain it. At first, I thought it was something the high priestess had done to help me identify Josefina the first time on campus. Not that I didn't have a photo, but the high priestess was just untrusting enough to conjure another way to ensure I don't miss her, as if blazing her image into my psyche wasn't painful enough. A shudder runs up my spine as that thought reminds me I have to stand before the council tomorrow and explain what's happened here when I don't even know.

"Are you the reason for the shadows?" she asks, and my heart stops. How the fuck do I answer this question truthfully? If she doesn't already know about the coven, then I can't be the one to tell her.

I let out a heavy sigh, and her brows furrow. "No, I'm not responsible for the shadows. Those are yours." The way she deflates at my words does something to my soul, at least what's left of what's inside me. I don't want to hurt her. This shouldn't hurt her. She shouldn't have been caught so unaware. "Has no one told you anything about the shadows? What about when you went home to your family?" I pause for a moment. "You did go home when I told you to, right?"

She nods, but there's little life behind it. Without thinking, I reach over and grab her hand. Her eyes meet mine, and I give her a smile that I hope will help calm her nerves. Though she might not believe it, I'm here for her.

"I went home and told my father. He basically said I was imagining things. Then I mentioned your name, and..." She stopped to look at me. "Why would my father freak out at the mention of your name?"

My heart nearly beats from my chest. Fuck, I didn't think the old man would remember me. It's been ages since we've crossed paths, far before he even met Josefina's mother. Hell, before he left the coven. Trying to portray as much confusion as possible, I shrug.

She stares into my eyes like she's trying to discern the truth, but then she returns the shrug. "Maybe he was thinking of someone else. It's not like you all are even around the same age." I simply blink at her. If she only knew how wrong she is about both of our ages. Instead of saying anything, mostly because I'm afraid my voice will betray me, I gesture for her to continue. "Anyway, he acted like it was all my imagination. At least until we went to the River Walk the next day."

"What happened at the River Walk?" I ask, though I'm afraid of the answer. Whatever happened is likely the reason I've been summoned to the council.

She stands up and wraps her arms around her midsection before turning away from me and looking into the mirror behind the candles still flickering on the wall. "I, um... I think I nearly hurt someone," she says, anguish in her voice.

"If you're talking about that ex of yours, the one rolled up like a burrito that day in your tent, he's fine."

Her head shakes emphatically. "No, not Marcus. He deserved whatever happened to him for being an ass to me that day." She starts pacing. "You know, I thought, no, I hoped it was you controlling them. I almost let myself believe it was you because they only ever showed up when you were around." Her feet stop, and her eyes catch mine. "Except, you weren't there in San Antonio, were you?"

The look she gives me is less pleading than resigned, yet the urge to wrap my arms around her and reassure her is intense. Unlike the hope she just expressed, we both know I'd be lying if I said I had been there. "No, and I'm sorry I wasn't there for you."

A sad smile passes over her lips, and she starts pacing again. Eight steps. That's how far she goes from left to right, but I can tell her mind is traveling much further, taking her back to the moment that seems to have changed everything.

"There was a medium set up along the river. There's always at least one, but I've never actually talked to one before. Poppa said they're all charlatans trying to steal your money and everything they say is a generic lie."

I bristle as my mind conjures the likely events of that day, but I don't interrupt.

Josefina turned pleading eyes on me. "I tried to be kind and tell her I wasn't interested. She was just trying to make a buck, right? But Poppa screamed, and the woman grabbed my wrist, and the smoke. My god, the whole river filled up with smoke, and tendrils crawled into the woman's mouth, and I couldn't make them stop. The woman's eyes. Her fingers turned black from where she touched me, and her eyes. I was hurting her, but they wouldn't stop."

From the corners of my eyes, I catch sight of shadows creeping up the walls. Josefina's panic is going to reenact the very thing that has her spiraling now. Within seconds, I have her in my arms, holding her tightly like a weighted blanket. "I know, *Muñeca*. I know you would never hurt anyone intentionally." My hands run over her hair and her back as I try to soothe her in the only way I know how. She trembles in my arms, and her tears soak through my shirt. I don't care. A thousand ruined shirts would be worth it if she didn't have to suffer.

"Her mouth was stuck open in a scream by the smoky tendril. It was the most terrifying thing I've ever seen, and you're saying it really was my fault?" she asks with her face pressed against my chest.

Putting my hands on either side of her face, I lean her back slightly, so she can see the sincerity in my eyes. "If I could make this transition easy for you, I would. You have no reason to believe anything I say, but please believe that I would spare you all of this." I hold her back against my chest. "I should've been there," I say with a growl that's a little more forceful than it should've been. A shudder runs through her, and I curse myself.

In an effort to once again soothe her fears, I let my fingers run through her hair. This time when she trembles, a small whimper reaches my ears. It might have been imperceptible to anyone else on the planet, but my demon roars to life at the sound. *We could make her forget all of this.* I close my eyes and pull her in tighter, as if that will somehow protect her from the thing inside of me. *You heard it too.* My head shakes of its own accord as I fight the urge to scream at the lecherous voice. She's scared and vulnerable. I'm not going to let him, us, take advantage of her, no matter how soft and pliable she feels in my arms. That thought is enough to wake my dick up, and I nearly throw her away from me to keep her from feeling it.

Startled, she looks up at me wide-eyed. "Sorry, I had a thought," I say, taking the opportunity to step back from her. I grab her hands and lead her to sit back on the couch, so I can sit until this wayward erection goes down. "There's been no news stories of anything strange in San Antonio." Her head tilt has got to the be the cutest thing I've ever seen, and I can't help but chuckle. When she frowns, I shake away the laughter. "Sorry, I was simply saying that the town and the medium must be fine, else there would've been something on the news."

Something like hope lights up in her eyes. "Do you really think so?" I nod with as much enthusiasm as I can muster since I have no earthly idea whether everything is fine there or not. "Well, I mean, I guess you have to be right." She clutches her hands together in her lap. "The people did all seem to go back to normal once the smoke lifted, and the shadows released the woman." Again, she looks to me for reassurance. This time, though, I can't hide my surprise.

"What did you mean by all the people went back to normal?" My chest starts tightening as I play through all the possibilities.

"It was like everyone froze in place, everyone except Poppa, me, and the medium. All sound stopped, and, you know, I'm not even sure if the water was flowing. It was really weird."

She says it all with a nonchalance that's staggering considering how upset she had been just minutes before. I, on the other hand, am fighting my own version of a panic attack. No fucking wonder the council has called me back. There hasn't been a chronomancer born in my lifetime. *What the absolute fuck?* I clear my throat, trying to dislodge the terror. If she's able to control time... No, I can't even think about that.

"What did your father do?" I ask, my voice tight.

"He called my *tía*, and she called the rest of the family." She shakes her head, and I start to ask another question, but she continues, clearly agitated. "They sent this bitchy *prima* who tried to act like all of this shit was completely normal, and I wasn't supposed to ask any questions. That's why I came back home. I wasn't going to sit there and listen to some stranger and Poppa continue to pretend like this..." she waves her hand around but says nothing else.

Fuck, no wonder she was freaking out and begging me for answers. The damn family still didn't explain anything. "So, no one told you anything?"

"No!" She throws her hands up. "You've told me more than anyone else, and you've barely told me anything."

I can't do very much but give her a sheepish smile because she's not wrong. Knowing they did nothing to help her work through this pisses me off though. Why even bother sending one of the priestesses if they weren't going to tell her what's happening?

"They should've explained what was happening to you, Josefina." She gives me a look of 'no shit,' and again a chuckle bubbles up. This time, however, she laughs with me, and I want to bottle that sound. "Like I said earlier, I can't explain much of anything, but I can say that powers like yours..."

She cuts me off. "Powers?"

"Shadow magic, Muñeca, is some strong magic. So, yes, power like yours. They're usually passed down through the bloodline. It's not like there's a spell book you can buy on the Internet for that." She stares up at me expectantly, and it's all I can do not to tell her everything. Something about her has me wanting to break my vows of service and condemn myself. My demon stirs with impatience, and I take a deep breath, trying my best to settle the evil bastard. "That's why I told you to go home to your family. My hope was that they would give you the information you need to ascend without panicking."

"Ascend?"

Shit! Dammit, Alistaire, why can you not learn to keep your fucking mouth shut!

"I'm sorry," she says, and I open my eyes to see the apology in her expression. My brows furrow, and I nearly flinch when she reaches a hand out to smooth them down. "You told me that you couldn't explain everything. I believe you."

I grab her wrist and place a kiss on her open palm. "I don't deserve your trust, Muñeca, but I do appreciate it."

"Oh," she says with a smirk, "I didn't say I trust you." My mouth gapes, and she winks.

Standing from the couch, I walk toward the door. "On that note, I think I've done enough damage here. I have a trying day tomorrow and really should get going. I hope you get the answers you need in the least painful way possible," I say when she comes to stand beside me at the door. I lean down and kiss her forehead. My only hope as I walk out the door is that I'll one day get to see her again.

CHAPTER 13

NOT YOU AGAIN
JOSEFINA

The smell of dying candles hits my nostrils moments before someone tries to knock down my door. I've barely had time to realize that the sun's not yet up when the banging starts again. "Jesus Fucking Christ!" If we weren't along the beltway where there is always noise happening, the neighbors would be calling the cops. *Oh shit! What if it's the cops? What if that woman wasn't ok?*

"Dammit, Josefina, if you don't open the door..." a vaguely familiar female voice penetrates through the apartment.

Though the words are clearly agitated, I'm not entirely sure she's yelled them. They seem oddly calm, and a shiver runs down my spine. *La prima.* That's who's at the door. Thanks to Alistaire, I now understand that sensation as her power meeting mine.

"Keep your panties on," I say with the same calm she'd expressed, though I'm anything but calm.

"What do you want, Elinora?" I say before I've fully opened the door.

"Good morning to you too, sunshine," she says with a smirk. Before I can hurl all the insults my sleepy brain is slow to produce, she holds up a bag from Shipley's.

"Are they fresh?" I ask, still blocking her entrance.

She rolls her eyes. "They'll be soggy if they stay in this bag any longer. Will you just let me in? Please."

The earnestness of her plea, more than the word, and far more than the donuts, is what makes me step out of the way. After what I learned last night, and what I still need to know, I'm willing to overlook her bitchiness and hear her out.

Rather than head for the couch, which was going to be my suggestion, she walks to the small, square table that serves as a dining room placeholder. I don't think I've ever eaten at the table in the two years I've lived here. I shrug and close the door. She pulls a chocolate glazed donut from the bag and takes a bite, her eyes rolling back in what I know to be ecstasy. I can smell the warm chocolate and gooey glaze that hasn't yet solidified.

"How'd you know?" I ask, gesturing toward the bag with my lips.

She smiles slightly around the mouthful. "*Tu papá*. He said they're your favorite, and I needed a peace offering." I eye her suspiciously. She swallows the bite. "No, I mean, I had mentioned needing a peace offering, and he suggested I stop at Shipley's on my way here." I chuckle and am about to tell her it wasn't necessary when her eyes light up. "A tea kettle!"

That really does make me laugh. I don't know many people who prefer tea to coffee in the morning, but by her enthusiasm, and the fact that she didn't carry in a cup, I'd say Elinora is one of the few. Without asking, she hurries over and turns on the kettle and then starts opening cabinets looking for mugs. I'm a single woman living in a tiny apartment. I literally have two, and they're both in the sink, but I don't bother to tell her that. Then she'll start asking questions I don't want to answer. I'm still trying my best not to think about all that happened last night.

"You seriously only have two?" she says, though she doesn't look toward me like she's needing an answer. Instead, she just washes them out and grabs the tin of teabags, carrying them to the table.

"Make yourself at home," I tell her, popping a piece of the delicious pastry into my mouth.

She sits down on one of the stools and sighs. "Look, we definitely did not get off on the right foot yesterday. There was a lot of shit I didn't know, and I made far too many assumptions." I raise a brow but say nothing. "I'm trying to apologize here, *prima*. I don't do that well. We, um, our family. We're not very apologetic."

"So y'all are just a bunch of assholes then?" I scoff. "If that's what you came to tell me, you could've just gone back to wherever you came from and left me to what I already figured out."

"No, that's not what the fuck I mean. Dammit, Josefina, will you just let me get this out?"

I release my shoulders with a deep breath and try to soften my expression. Hopefully, my gesture for her to continue is more generous than I'm feeling.

"I've never met anyone else with magic who didn't know they had magic. So, let's start there. When I was sent here the other night, I was told that a cousin had ascended far later than expected, and I was to bring her home."

"Later than expected? What does that mean?" Her eyes narrow at my interruption, and though she really is intimidating, I hold her gaze and pop another piece of donut into my mouth for good measure.

"The women in our family usually ascend when they turn fifteen, so, you're about..."

"Thirteen years late."

"Yeah, something like that. Anyway, I had no idea how little you knew about what was happening," She eyes me nervously this time and reaches for the bag, pulling a regular glazed out. "How badly did I freak you out when I had you open the closet?"

I nearly snort tea out of my nose at the question. "Oh, you

mean when you went from blonde-haired, caramel-eyed bombshell to something from a damn horror movie with black eyes and grayish-black fingers?" My lips twist, and I shrug. "Seemed pretty normal to me."

"That's what I thought."

We sit there, no other words passing between us as we drink our tea and finish off the half-dozen donuts she'd brought. A couple of times, I catch her watching me, like she's trying to get a read on me, but she doesn't say anything. Another time, I look up to find her staring at the shelf where the burnt-out candles sit, wax melted down the shelf. She gets up and walks over to look into the mirror.

"You know, it's weird," she says without looking at me, "I feel your magic. It's new and a bit chaotic, but not as chaotic as Alma's. Hers is roiling in preparation for her Ascension in the coming days. The point is that while I feel your new magic, I also feel old magic here." Her eyes never leave the shelf. "Where did you get these candles?"

I join her in front of the mirror. "I never thought I'd burn these. They've been sitting in a box for years. But when I came home yesterday, I needed something soothing."

My mind plays back over the way I stormed through the apartment as soon as I got home. I might have been my own little tornado. Anger, frustration, disappointment. They were all waging war inside me, and I couldn't think straight. In fact, the only thought I had was how much I wished my mother were still alive. Normally, I'd pick one of the broken or messed up candles in my collection. Sometimes I'll finish burning the ones left over from the vendor events. Last night, however, something pulled me deep into the walk-in closet. Digging through the boxes of items I brought from my parents' house but never unpacked, I found the candles. They were buried beneath teddy bears and my baby blanket, but the scent of sandalwood was just as strong as it had been when we first cured them.

"My mother helped me make them."

Though Elinora wears a curious expression, she smiles. "I saw the photo of the two of you at the house. You're a perfect combination of your parents. Even the color of your eyes is distinctly your own. You'll find that most of us have the dark hair and caramel eyes, but not you."

I shake my head and look away from her gaze in the mirror. She doesn't need to know how much I always wished for eyes like hers. I'm not ready to be that vulnerable with her, family or not. I don't know her like that. In my periphery, I see her reach out a hand but then pull it back. She opens her mouth to say something, but it's several seconds before any words are exchanged.

"Wait, didn't your mother die when you were ten?" I bristle at the brusqueness of her question. Who says things like that without an ounce of empathy?

"Have you ever lost someone you were close to, *prima*?" Turning back to face her directly, I shoot her a scathing look. "I'm guessing not based on how callously you asked that question." With that, I turn and walk down the hall toward my room. I need to get away from her for a few minutes. Of course, she doesn't take the hint.

"Do you always think the worst of people?" She yells at my back before her footsteps start following me. "Also, are you twelve? Who the fuck just walks out on a conversation the way you do?"

I turn to close the bedroom door, but I'm not quick enough to stop her from getting in. It's unnerving how much taller than me she is, especially when she's pissed, though I can't see what she has to be angry about. She'll turn around and go home, and her life will be just as it was. Mine, on the other hand, will never be the same.

"Stop acting like a child, Josefina, and talk to me."

Her face is in mine, and I have to lean back to keep our noses from touching. I try to take a step back and run into my dresser. My heart rate picks up, and I can't seem to catch my breath.

Movement in the corner of the room catches my attention, and my eyes go wide. She must sense the change because she stands up straight, and her eyes start changing.

"Are those yours?" she asks, turning those black eyes on me, but I can't answer. She looks down at my hands and back at my face. "I need to know they're yours and not someone else attacking us." The shadows creep closer, swirling and writhing like a snake. Elinora lifts her hands protectively and steps between me and the shadows. "Are they yours or not, prima?" Black and grey seep into the tips of her fingers, and wisps begin to dance around her nails. Still the mass moves toward us. "Am I protecting both of us or just myself, Josefina?"

I blink at the question. "You," I say, somehow secure in that answer. Without a doubt, the shadows looming closer are not here to harm me. They're coming to protect me.

"And why are you sending them after me?"

"Have you seen yourself?" Though her eyes are completely black, I somehow know that she's rolling them.

"Call them off, Josefina."

The small bit of laughter instantly dies. "I don't know how."

She shakes her head. "By the goddess, what in the world have I walked into?" She reaches out, smoky tendrils escaping her fingertips. They spread out over the shadows along the wall and engulf them. Within seconds, the tendrils return to her and disappear. By the time she turns back to me, her hands are their natural color, and her eyes are once again melted caramel.

"Pack a bag, *prima*. We need to get you somewhere more contained until you learn how to control yourself."

I stand my ground. "You know that was your fault, right?" She tilts her head. "It is. You stood your scary ass over me."

"You have goddess-fucking-given shadow magic. What the hell do you need to be afraid for?"

Wringing my hands, I answer, but my voice starts much softer than it had been. "I'm afraid of the shadows. No, not the shadows.

I'm afraid of what they might do. I can't control them, Elinora. I don't even know where they come from or when they're going to show up. I can't stop them because I'm not the one who calls them."

She nods in understanding, and it's the first time since I met her that I feel like she finally sees me.

"Get some things together. Whatever else you need, we can take care of in Onyx Junction." She must see my reluctance because her voice softens. "Let us help you through this. You should not have had to ascend completely alone without warning."

The empathy in her voice combined with the way she was able to corral the shadows breaks my resolve. I pull two suitcases out from under the bed and begin throwing clothes into them. Elinora returns to the kitchen and makes herself another cup of tea while I run through the apartment like a tornado, grabbing toiletries, random items I might need, and some of my candles. I can't go without taking some of my candles. They bring me comfort like nothing else. The place is a mess by the time I'm done, but, for once, I'm not worried about how things look.

CHAPTER 14
JUDGMENT
ALISTAIRE

Stop pacing, Alistaire. Just stop. If only I could take my own advice. It's not that I'm nervous. I'm not. Well, maybe a little. It's not like they can hurt me...much. My mind conjures Josefina's face, and I know that's a lie. They could definitely hurt me.

We should have made her ours.

I shake my head at my demon. No. She's not ours to claim. She's one of Umbra's daughters.

She felt so good. Her arousal smelled delicious. We should have tasted her.

My eyes close at the thought. She was so fucking soft and so sweet.

And she wanted us.

"She wanted me," I say aloud to the empty room, and the demon scoffs. "She doesn't even know you exist. If she did," a shudder runs up my spine. If she knew what was inside me, she'd have likely attacked me with her shadows rather than with her lips. Those lips. I still feel the way they moved against mine. *No, stop this too.* Thinking about that kiss, about the way she felt beneath me...fuck...none of that is going to help me with the council.

Go back to her and try again.

"Now, that's the smartest thing you've said in a century."

No sooner do those words leave my lips than the door opens, and a pair of caramel eyes backlit by their own preternatural light narrow on me. "Who were you talking to just now?"

I swallow. Do I tell her the truth? There's no softness to her, nothing saying she's remotely amenable to my plight. I look her in the eyes and say, "Myself."

If I never have to travel to Onyx Junction again in all my lifetimes, it'll be too soon. I won't say that Houston is the best place I've ever lived, but I'll be damned if it isn't better than being directly under the thumb of the coven.

You're already damned.

"Shut up, demon!"

A wicked laugh penetrates my mind, and I once again wonder at the efficacy of lobotomies. If I could exorcize that fucker, I would. Instead, I'll just drink myself to sleep until I no longer hear his obnoxious ass. Besides, it'll feel good to sit on my comfortable furniture in front of my cozy fireplace and not those hard chairs in the frigid room the priestesses had me waiting every day for the past week. I understand they don't see me as human, but would it be too much to ask for some minor comfort.

I still don't understand why it took them the entire week to finish their investigation. Their questions were arguably mundane compared to what I expected when I was called. *Who else saw the shadows? How quickly was cleanup handled? Why was Josefina sent home to her father? Where was I when all hell broke loose in San Antonio, and how'd they manage not to end up on the news?* Though I had been beating myself up about not being there for her, I was infinitely grateful to be able to claim ignorance of those events. I had no inclination to explain to the priestesses that Josefina might be able to control time. Nope. I'll just keep that little bit of information to myself until I know for sure.

Looking up at the stone building just inside the gate, my heart stirs. I had intended to go directly home and unwind. My plan was to check on Josefina in the morning. It wouldn't be right to expect her to welcome me in this late at night. My feet, however, had other plans because here I stand outside her complex willing her to look out her window, so I know she's awake. The apartment is still, strangely still, eerily empty. I can't feel her magic. I've always been able to feel her magic from this close.

My eyes look toward the parking lot, and her car is there in the same spot it was last week. The car is here, but she's...

Where is she? My demon roars, sensing my increasing unease.

Before I realize what I'm doing, my hand is connecting with her door. The knock seems to echo against the silence. It shouldn't be so quiet. I knock again, but there's still no movement, no sound at all from inside the apartment.

Break down the door!

She'd never forgive me if I destroyed her home. "Josefina, are you home?" I knock again, though I know it's futile. She's not here.

Let me go!

"No," I say aloud, though quietly enough to not draw the attention of any nosy neighbors.

I can find her.

My head is shaking before I can even think the word. He is not trustworthy. He barely behaves on the inside. Letting him out is a recipe for disaster.

Either let me out or break down the door. She could be hurt, he hurls at me, knowing I don't have many options.

"The last time I set you free, you destroyed the family we were meant to protect. Two decades. We spent two fucking decades in a cage because of you."

That was only one time.

"And the time you burned down the temple? I was barely able to hide the fact we had been there."

You're wasting time, and she could be dying. Besides, I'd never hurt her. She's mine.

"No!" I say much louder, and a dog barks inside one of the neighboring apartments. I step into the shadow of her porch. Anyone who looks outside will think I'm a trick of the light, and in a way, they'd be right. "You can't have her," I snap back at my demon. If I can't have her, he certainly can't.

He growls in response and then says the one thing that I can't argue. *If she's hurt, and you've done nothing to help her, the priestesses will tear your soul apart.*

"Fuck," I mutter under my breath, and he chuckles, knowing he's won. "If you harm her or destroy her home, I will destroy us both before the coven has a chance." Then, I throw open the chains tethering him to my body. As I feel him stretch and wriggle free, I can't help but wish it were that simple to rid him from my psyche. Unfortunately, the head priestess made that bit of relief impossible.

His disembodied voice plays through my mind. *The apartment is empty. She's not here. Everything is a mess.*

"What do you mean a mess?" Her apartment wasn't a mess that night when... I shake my head free from that train of thought. If anything, her apartment felt lonely, like she didn't want anything around. The only decoration on the wall had been that mirror and candles. Even her bedroom was sparse, though I was far more focused on her than the decor.

Come look. At those words, I hear the click of the lock before his presence once again fights for space inside me. Oddly, though, he doesn't try to take over. Instead, he returns to the area along my spine and sulks. Something inside the apartment must've bothered him.

Pushing open the door, I sniff along the edge. Something is off. A few steps inside tell me someone else has been here, though it's not clear who or when. The candles she had lit the night I was here still sit on the shelf, though they've worn down the entirety of their wicks. Still, the essence of the magic within them lingers. My fingers tingle with the urge to touch them, to read the memories infused within, but something else pulls me toward the hall. An unexpected sight catches my attention on the way. Two mugs sit on her small dining table. She definitely had company.

Her office is a mess like the demon said. He grumbles something about me not believing him, but my attention is on the disarray. Boxes lay in various piles rather than on the neatly stacked shelves where we'd placed them. Some are open, and others are just on the floor, as if someone had gone through looking for something specific. The bedroom has a similar feel with things thrown haphazardly on the bed and the floor. The smell from earlier is stronger in here, and a different emotion vies for position against the worry that has been constantly nagging since I saw her car in the parking lot. I tamp it down and refocus on the scents. Magic. Hers and something more potent, something older. *Where the fuck are you, Muñeca?*

On my way to the door, my eye catches on the mug I had used that night. Josefina washed it before I left, which means whoever was here last must've been the one using it. I reach out a hand, and my demon whimpers. My hand freezes in midair. In all our years together, he's never done that before. "What do you know?" I ask aloud. Though I know he can likely hear my thoughts as well as I hear his, he's never answered me when I don't actually speak. He doesn't answer now. I look back at the cup with trepidation, but I have to know.

I barely hear the demon howl when memories flood my mind. "Shit!" Not her. Why couldn't it be any of them but her?

CHAPTER 15

YOU'RE NOT ALONE

JOSEFINA

The closer we get to Onyx Junction, the supposed home of my father's extended family, the more unsettled my thoughts become. There's been a steady pulse of impatience wafting off Elinora since we left Houston, almost as if the thought of the nearly fifteen-hour drive was irritating her. It made no sense to me when she'd just driven eighteen hours to get to San Antonio two days prior. She shouldn't be surprised at the distance. I can, however, understand her being tired of driving, but this feels different, like she knows a shortcut but is pissed because she can't take it. I shrug to myself. I'm far too tired to try and decipher Elinora's moods.

Still, my own mood wanes as the hours pass. Unlike my cousin, I'm not wanting the time to pass any more quickly. The feeling that I'm walking into something bigger than myself is one I can't shake.

"I feel you thinking," Elinora muses from behind the wheel. "Why not take a nap or something? Your anxiety is wearing on my patience."

I scoff. So much for the empathy she showed me earlier.

"Funny, you've been in a mood since we left the city. Maybe it's your impatience that's triggering my anxiety."

She laughs. "I hate driving this damn car, but *Tía* Helga insisted. She claimed my bike wasn't appropriate. I'd have been home in my bed already if we were riding. Instead, we're stuck following the fucking traffic."

I turn in my seat to face her, eyes wide. "Wait, you ride a motorcycle?"

"We all do," she says with a smirk, "though, they're not quite what you think." Before I can ask what she means, she continues. "Hang out with us long enough, you'll ride too." My head automatically starts shaking of its own accord, and she laughs again. "Don't be so quick to say no. It's a verifiable man magnet. Every *pendejo* who ever thought himself bad ass offers himself up on a silver platter for a chance to ride. Women, too, if that's your preference."

An unladylike snort leaves my nose, and my mind travels back to a certain professor. I can't imagine him being wooed by a woman on a motorcycle. Though he wasn't scared of my shadows like most normal people might have been, he seems more the luxury sedan type of guy. "I think I'm good."

"Suit yourself, *prima*, but it is the most efficient and exhilarating way to travel. Ask any of the *primas...tías* too."

"Tell me about them," I say, trying not to sound nervous about meeting everyone.

Thankfully, Elinora seems glad to have something else to pass the time than silent driving. She spends the next two hours telling me about the rest of our cousins, each of their parents, and the few teenagers in the family. Apparently, our family isn't big on just pumping out babies, and for some reason that makes me feel better. I've never really had any desire to be the traditional housewife and mom. I think I'd be happier as the crazy cat lady down the street who has candles burning in all her windows. Maybe I'll decorate my house for Halloween and never take the decorations down. Even before this whole magic thing, I've had the witchy vibe down. Now, I can at least own it as a way to keep the neighbors from visiting more than once a year. I chuckle to myself, and Elinora looks at me sideways with one of her perfectly trimmed brows arched high.

"What's so funny?"

I almost laugh again at how defensive she sounds, but I won't do that to her. *La Familia de Umbra* might be brand new to me, but she is obviously a proud member.

"It's not what you think. Sometimes my brain makes ridiculous associations, and I was thinking how I could totally play up my new-found witchiness by being permanently decorated for Halloween and owning a herd of black cats."

Elinora lets out a hearty chuckle. "Oh, you and Serafina are going to get along so well."

"She's the one who's daughter's magic is coming on too, right?"

"Yes, we're preparing for her Ascension, though it's not been easy."

"What do you mean? Didn't she know what to expect?"

Her shoulders droop slightly. "Ascension isn't easy for anyone, even when we know it's coming. That's why I was sent for you. No one should have to go through that shit alone."

I nod in agreement and turn back to watch out the window. If the teenager who's spent her whole life knowing what she was and what would happen is struggling with her magic, what the fuck am I doing?

"Why is this happening now?" She squirms a bit, but she doesn't answer. I watch her from the corner of my eye trying to decipher what she's not saying. "I mean, why didn't it happen earlier. If, um, I forgot her name..." I wait for a second, but when Elinora still doesn't speak, I press on. "If she's going through her, what did you call it? Ascension, now at fifteen, *¿Por qué no me lo pasó a los quince?* Shouldn't my magic have come in when I turned fifteen?"

She sat silently for several minutes, and I'd just about given up on getting an answer when she spoke. "Alma. Alma is preparing for her Ascension now. And it should have happened when you were fifteen. I'm sorry," she says with a shake of her head.

"Sorry for what?"

"I'm sorry I can't tell you why it didn't. Just know that fifteen was never when yours would have happened."

I purse my lips. "What do you mean mine would've never happened then? Obviously, it didn't happen then. I'm fucking 28 years old. It shouldn't have happened at all."

"*Tienes razón.*"

"Jesus Christ!" I mutter under my breath with a groan of frustration. What the hell am I right about? The fact that I shouldn't have magic? If I get all the way to Onyx Junction and don't get straight answers from anyone, I'm really going to lose my mind.

CHAPTER 16

I'M NOT A DAMN CHILD!

JOSEFINA

We pull up in front of a gray house with a black door, but Elinora doesn't shut off the car. I look at her, but she doesn't pay me any attention. Instead, she pulls out her phone and dials. "*¿Dónde estás?* I'm sitting outside your house." A few seconds pass by, and though I can't hear the person on the other end of the phone, I can tell that Elinora is not getting good news. "*Voy pa'lla,*" she says before disconnecting the call.

"Is everything alright?"

"What? Oh, yeah. That's Serafina's house, but she's not home."

Again with the cryptic messages. For someone who complained about my anxiety, Elinora sure sucks at not inducing it. Does Serafina even know I'm coming? Had she agreed to let me stay with her? The woman has a daughter going through the same shit I am. Why the hell would she want to take on two of us?

"I could stay in a hotel if it's easier on everyone."

Elinora shakes her head. "Absolutely not! No, we're going to *Tía* Helga's house. Serafina and Alma are over there."

I clasp my hands together on my lap trying to hold in all the questions. There's no use getting into an argument here when I have no easy way of getting back home. Still, she and I are going to have it out the moment I get my bearings because she's really shit at this whole make me want to join the family thing. It's not like I have a choice anyway. Blood doesn't lie, and apparently, I'm part of this weird ass shit whether I want to be or not.

In less than ten minutes, we park in the driveway of another two-story house. This one is a little brighter than the gray and black, but no less imposing. I guess maybe it's the uncertainty of what I'm walking into than the house itself that makes it feel so uninviting. Without warning, Elinora grabs my hand and squeezes it.

"You'll be fine. No one inside is going to hurt you. Well, I wouldn't go attacking them with shadows like you tried with me." My eyes snap to hers, and she winks. "Stop worrying. You're family, and we take care of our own."

Swallowing back the bile threatening to come up my throat, I open the door and step out. When I start to walk around the car to grab my bags, Elinora waves me on.

"Don't worry. We'll make sure they get inside," she says and ushers me to the front door.

We're not even onto the porch when the door flies open, and a tornado of a woman at least four inches taller than me twirls around me in a flurry of movement I can barely catch. "Josefina," she says, her hands pressed firmly to my cheeks. "*Por* Umbra, you have grown so beautiful." Her smile is infectious, and I recognize her immediately from the photo Poppa has on the mantle. Her hair has far more salt in it than it had back then, but she's still very much as vibrant with her backlit eyes that see more than I want to show. The door opens and closes behind her, and another woman steps out onto the porch. Her arms are crossed, and I get the feeling she's not as elated at my arrival as *Tía* Helga. Still, I welcome the distraction her presence provides.

Helga seems unperturbed by the other woman's distrust and continues clucking around me. Out of the corner of my eye, I catch Elinora climbing the stairs and overhear her call the woman Sera before wrapping her in an embrace. Serafina's response is terse, and her eyes never leave me. She says something else, and Elinora turns to look down at me standing here like a mannequin while our *tía* flutters around, grasping my face and pulling at my hair. Once, I imagine the pinch of a strand being plucked, but that couldn't be right. I shift my attention between my aunt and the two women on the porch until finally Serafina calls out.

"*Ya, mamá,* let her come in the house at least. Accosting her in the yard is a little much."

"*Cómo qué* accosting? Can't I be excited to see my *sobrina* for the first time in ages?"

"Seriously, *tía*, it's barely been decades," Elinora says, giving me a wink before holding the door open for me to escape through.

"Qué decades y decades. She's already grown."

Both of the younger women roll their eyes, but there's loving amusement in them. Apparently, they're both used to entertaining her eccentricities, or maybe they're tired of trying to corral her. Either way, I'm glad to not be dealing with her alone. Before I can sit on the sofa, Helga is coming from the kitchen with a tea kettle and four mugs. She moves unbelievably fast for an old woman.

"*Mamá*, must you? Let our guest sit down at least before you ply her with food and drink." Serafina turns in my direction. Her eyes are still wary, but there's not the same level of animosity that had initially colored her expression. "Please forgive my mother. She's a pistol most days, and she's even worse when new people come around."

"She's not new. I met her when she was a child. This is your cousin Josefina."

Serafina's eyes widen. "Cousin?" She looks between Elinora and her mother before turning her gaze back on me. "What do you mean cousin?"

I shrug. She's not going to get the answers she's looking for from me. "Your guess is as good as mine, *prima*." I say the word sarcastically. "I just found out all of you existed about 72 hours ago, I think, maybe less."

"How?" she asks, staring at her mother. When Helga ignores her and pours the tea, she turns her questioning stare on Elinora who stiffens. Not for the first time, I get the feeling she knows more than she's saying.

"Stop harassing your cousins, Serafina. *Lo único que necesitas saber es que Josefina es tu prima.* She's my brother's daughter."

"Your brother?" Serafina shouts. "You said that *Tío* Daegal died more than thirty years ago! *¡Treinta años, mamá!*" She gestures in my direction. *"Esa cría no puede ser su hija."*

My blood boils. I've already put up with enough bullshit from Elinora that there's no way I'm letting anyone else in the family talk to me any kind of way. "I'm sitting right here," I say, "and last I checked, I'm fully grown, not a damn child." A muscle tics in Serafina's jaw, and Elinora sits up straighter. Even *Tía* Helga turns her full attention on me. There's so much I want to say. So many questions I want to demand answers for, but I'd literally rather be anywhere but here right now. I stand and start toward the door. I don't make it five steps before my aunt has grabbed my shoulders.

"Stay. Please."

The earnestness in her voice surprises me. She's been all energy and sass until now, and the shift captivates me. "How do you do that?" I ask before I can think better of it.

Her brows furrow. "Do what?"

"Fly around the house, *tía*," Elinora answers for me. "Josefina is new to this whole magic thing, so your constant movement from one place to another must have her feeling a bit unsettled."

She's not wrong. It's definitely unnerving how quickly the woman moves, but her speed is not the only thing bothering me. My eyes flit to Elinora. "I thought you said the family has shadow magic. I've not seen a single shadow, but..." I trail off, letting my gestures mimic Helga's movements.

Serafina, who has remained silent since my outburst, glares at Elinora. I can only imagine what she might be thinking.

"You're telling strangers our secrets now, *prima*?"

If Elinora had been an animal, her fur would've stood on end with the way she just bristled at the accusation. She doesn't get to answer when footsteps invade the pregnant silence.

Serafina stands, her gaze landing on the stairs where a younger version of her stands watching. "Alma, go upstairs and stay there until I say you can come down." The teenager's gaze lands on me, and her head tilts, but she follows her mother's instructions. No sooner does a door close above us than Serafina turns wrathful eyes on Elinora. "What were you thinking? We made a vow."

Elinora's shoulders square, and her voice remains steady. "She needed to know. She deserved to know."

"Why? Because you believed she was our long-lost uncle's spawn. Under what authority did you make this decision?"

"¡Ya basta! That's enough, Serafina," Helga reprimands. "I sent her. Daegal called me a few days ago terrified for Josefina and asking for my help again. I told Elinora to bring her here to me, to us."

"*Mamá*, my daughter...Alma is upstairs going through..." She doesn't finish the sentence. "Why would you invite..." Serafina seems to deflate before our eyes, and Helga is at her side in an instant.

Their arms wrap around each other, and a sob lodges in my throat as I wish my mother were here to wrap me in her arms. I turn away from the scene and feign interest in the photos hung along the walls. My eyes land on one that has tears streaming down my face. My parents smile out at me from their place alongside a two-tier wedding cake. The joy on their faces breaks me in ways I didn't know I could be broken. I miss her so much, and right now, I'd give anything to have her here.

"Sera," Elinora's voice breaks through my silent sorrow, "you know I'd never do anything to compromise the coven, and I'd definitely not put Alma in danger. I could not leave her there to ascend alone."

Time seems to freeze as all eyes bore into my back. The urge to run courses through me. Serafina is going to decline to help and will probably kick me out of the house. I imagine Elinora is already regretting the decision to bring me here, and *Tía* Helga, well, I'm still not sure about her. Honestly, I can't blame any of them for their decisions. I'm a stranger coming into their world. There's not reason for them to trust me. Hell, I can't even trust myself, especially not with this gods' forsaken magic I've been straddled with. Peeking over my shoulder, I catch Serafina's stare. There's wariness still, but not the utter disdain I was expecting. Instead, something else, something pained plays along her features. She looks like she wants to say something, but the words freeze as another voice interrupts.

"You're ascending too?" comes a soft voice from the stairs.

CHAPTER 17

THROW ME A LIFELINE

Energy swirls through the living room as we pace back and forth, me wearing a hole in the carpet, and my demon beating a steady drumming in my mind. How the hell did this all go so wrong? Eighteen years. I've been in this fucking state just waiting for her to show herself for eighteen years, and now, she's gone. They just took her. "What the fuck!" I yell and throw the glass in my hand against the wall. The demon howls in frustration, probably wishing he could throw something as well.

They called us away, he snarls. *They took her while we were gone. She's ours.*

I can't argue with him. We were barely gone a few days, and they took her in that short period of time. Why send us back if she's no longer here? I flop on the sofa staring into the fireplace as the flames dance with tiny crackles from the alcohol dripping all around. Where the heck is she?

Those bitches have her.

That's obvious from what we found in her apartment, but why? Why would they take her? If the whole point was to simply keep an eye on her, there was no reason to take her across the country. And what would that fucking bitch Elinora want with her? Just the thought of that witch has me seething. She's the whole reason I'm in this mess and cursed to spend eternity losing my goddess-damned mind. If she does anything to Josefina, I'll forget my vow of service to the coven. Damnation and the goddess's wrath would be worth the chance to tear her apart.

Yes, the demon whispers. *They will pay for any harm that comes to her.*

As my mind starts to play over the torture I'd rain down on her, my phone rings. I know who it is without even looking. Why the high priestess doesn't just speak to me directly like she used to a century ago, I don't know. It's not like we need this modern contraption for her to control me. My demon whimpers and I freeze. Is it possible she heard my thoughts? Could she have felt the threat through our bond? I pick up the phone and stare at the screen for several seconds before tapping the accept button.

"Head Priestess," I say in greeting.

Where the fuck is she? comes the angry voice through the phone.

"What do you mean? Who?"

Are you going to lie to me and say Josefina is there in Houston under your careful watch? She says the word 'careful' with much more sarcasm than anyone her age should be able to muster.

I swallow, trying to make sense of her anger and her questions. The demon bristles under my skin, confusion pulsing through him as well.

"Is she not there in Onyx Junction?" I ask, trying to force a calm that I don't feel into my voice. This feels like a test, and I have no idea how to answer.

Let me rephrase the question, Alistaire, Son of Brevard, Servant of Umbra, and Protector of the Priestesshood. Why is she in Onyx Junction? And why, por Umbra, are you not here watching her?

"Head Priestess?" Wait, was she not the one who sent for her? Did Elinora act on her own? No, that can't be. No one acts on their own in the coven. They all defer to the head priestess.

Except for other high priestesses, the demon adds, and I mull over that thought, a question forming.

Adaire de Umbra, High Priestess of the goddess Umbra, and head of the coven, roars through the phone. *What?*

"Did you not know she was there? Did you not send for her?"

I can picture her pinching the bridge of her nose as she's done at me many times since I took over my father's position. "Why would I be calling you if I knew she was here? Why, *por* Umbra, would I be asking why you're not here if I had sent for her?"

The demon whimpers again, and I feel the same fear wash over me. "I... There was an aura from a priestess left behind. I assumed..."

"You assumed? I sent you back to Houston with express direction to watch her with your life. If I had known she was being brought here, I would have kept you here."

The phone falls from my hands as tendrils of smoke seep from the screen, her anger permeating the line. "I'm on my way there, Head Priestess."

J osefina

I bolt upright in bed. The room I'm in is dark and the bed is small. *Where the fuck am I?* My breath hitches as I listen for sounds that might give me some inclination...

"Did you have a nightmare?" a quiet voice asks from within the room, and I jump. A small click and then a light flickers to life as the teenager whose face looks vaguely familiar turns on a lamp, "Sorry if I scared you. I kinda got startled myself when you sat up like that. I'm not used to anyone being up here with me except my mom, and she sleeps like the dead most of the time."

"Alma, right?" She smiles and nods. Memories start flowing

back into my mind as I stare at the beautiful girl in front of me. I remember her being a little taller than me, though that's hard to see with her sitting cross-legged in the bed. "Sorry to have invaded your space up here."

Alma shrugs. "No worries. I've not really liked sleeping alone recently." Her eyes flick to the corner of the room and back to me like she's afraid something's there. The move reminds me of that day in Poppa's kitchen. I knew I had seen something but still questioned myself as if trying to make it not be true. My eyes follow to where her gaze lands, and there's a mirror sitting against the wall with a blanket thrown over it.

"Not a fan of mirrors?" I ask with a half-smile. Most teenagers can stare at themselves for hours.

She shrugs again. "Not anymore."

There's a sadness to her tone that pulls at my heart. The girl is beautiful, so body dysmorphia shouldn't be an issue, though I know well enough that's not always a given. "What happened?" I ask, keeping my voice soft.

She looks back toward the mirror and then at the floor. We sit in silence for a few minutes, long enough for me to consider telling her she doesn't have to answer, when she finally starts talking. "There have been some incidents, some scary shit," she says before quickly clapping her hand over her mouth. "Sorry."

I chuckle. "I won't tell if you don't. I've had some scary shit happen recently too."

Alma perks up, readjusting herself on the bed. "So, it is true that you're ascending too? I know I asked last night, and you said yes, but I thought Umbra always calls us at fifteen." She looks toward the stairs and then leans in toward me conspiratorially. "*Mamá* says that no one's Ascension is easy."

"Funny, Elinora told me the same thing when she showed up at my house the other day to bring me here."

Her head tilts to the side, and I watch her expression shift as she ponders some thought going through her mind. "Is it true that you didn't know you had magic?" Her hands grip the blanket on either side of her hips, and she nearly bounces up and down with energy.

"You were listening the whole time, huh?" A sheepish grin grows on her face, but it doesn't dampen her excitement. If I'm being truthful, I'm grateful for her glee. It helps to know that I'm not alone and that it doesn't have to be all doom and gloom. This young girl has known she'll grow into her magic all her life, and yet it's been a difficult transition for her too. It also helps to find someone in this family who isn't condescending as fuck about what I don't know. "My poppa was adamant that magic didn't exist. He hated my obsession with all things spooky." Actually, now that I think about it, maybe he was a little too forceful in trying to steer me away from all things spiritual or mystical.

She gives me a pensive look, tapping her finger on her chin. "I bet he was trying to protect you," she says without judgment. "*Mamá* does everything she can to protect me. I even overheard her threaten to not take me before the council to complete the rite."

"The rite?" I ask, my voice cracking and stomach knotting with the question.

Her shrug is equal parts a response and a tic. I can tell she doesn't really know what the rite is and that the unknown makes her nervous. It probably doesn't help to know her protective mother is willing to keep her from having to go through it. Though I'm not willing to admit it, knowing Serafina's worried about Alma's Ascension doesn't make me feel any better about the process either.

"I thought *mamá* was relaxing some, but then she and Mr. Santos got into an argument, and she's been even more on edge."

That piqued my interest. I didn't get to learn much about her mother last night, other than she can be a raging bitch, so learning what makes her tick from her daughter might be helpful. "Mr. Santos?"

"He's my English teacher. The first time something weird happened at school, he helped me. He's really cool and kinda hot. He kissed *mamá* in the car..." She looks at the stairs again before finishing her sentence. "I thought she liked him, but then she had Vané pick us up from his house. They all threatened him." She punctuates the story with another shrug. "She's been acting weird ever since. She's not usually as mean as she was to you last night." Her tight-lipped smile makes me feel a little better.

I return the smile and then yawn. It's still the middle of the night, and sleep is calling to me again. Without another word, Alma turns off the light, and I lay back against the pillow. So, Serafina has a thing going with Alma's English teacher. Her cool and hot English teacher, I think and have to hold back a laugh. My smile falls as my mind conjures another hot teacher, or rather professor.

Did Alistaire make it back from whatever unexpected trip he had to take? He had seemed apprehensive, but I was so worried about what was happening to me that I didn't even ask him whether it was something dire. If he has made it back to Houston, has he looked for me? Is he worried that I'm not home? He did always show up when I needed someone, when I needed him. We should've exchanged phone numbers.

Alma's soft breaths signal that she has fallen asleep, and I envy her. Then I remember seeing my purse on the floor next to the bed. Trying not to make any noise, I roll to the edge and feel around until my hand finds the leather bucket bag. Slowly rummaging around inside, my hand clamps around my phone and pulls it out. Thankfully, it still has a charge since I had kept it plugged in for the entire drive. Going through my contacts, I click on the first person who came to mind.

> ME: Hey, you don't happen to have Professor Seagal's cell number, do you?

> TAYLOR: Josefina? It's nearly midnight.

ME: It's not like you were asleep.

> TAYLOR: Well, no, but he might be.

ME: Yes, well, he has something I need.

Taylor sends back a gif of someone with raised brows, and I nearly groan aloud at the unintentional double meaning of my text. Images of his mouth on mine and his hands on my body flood my mind, and I have to fight the urge to moan. I turn my head to the side. I may not be able to see Alma in the dark, but focusing on the fact she's there helps cool my overactive libido.

ME: Not like that. He helped me pack up my stuff from Ren Fair when I had to rush to my dad's place in San Antonio, and there's something I can't find.

It's at least partially true. He did pack up my stuff. I did go to San Antonio, and there are some things I can't find. It takes a couple minutes, but she finally texts me back with his number.

> TAYLOR: Please don't tell him I gave this out.

ME: I won't. Thanks, chica!

Without giving myself a chance to overthink, I open another text thread.

ME: Hello, Professor.

Ok, maybe I'm overthinking a little as I stare at the text without pressing send. I should probably tell him who I am, right?

Yes, of course I should. I don't get the chance, though because the phone slips from my hand and when I pick it back up, the blue bubble gives me a menacing glare. Quickly, I start typing in a follow-up, but a response comes through before I can get one word finished.

> UNKNOWN NUMBER: Are you alright? Where are you, muñeca?

I feel the panic in his questions, but warmth spreads through my body at the same time a smile breaks across my face. That one little word has calmed my heart more than anything else could.

CHAPTER 18

CALM BEFORE THE STORM

JOSEFINA

My nostrils are assaulted by the battling aromas of coffee, bacon, and is that myrrh? Why in the world would anyone be burning that, or better yet, cooking with it? I climb out of bed and throw on a pair of leggings, crop top and a loose sweater with some flipflops. The looks of wonder at my ensemble tell me most people here are not used to wearing flipflops in October. I laugh and wiggle my perfectly manicured toes. I might not have the height and natural beauty of Serafina or the model look of Elinora, but dammit, I have pretty feet.

My smugness dies when two new faces come into the room from the kitchen. They also take me in from head to toe. Thankfully, one of them is closer to my height, maybe even shorter than me. That one gives me a warm smile that I return gratefully because the other's stare is burning holes through me right now, and it's all I can do not to glare at her. So much for the contented feeling I'd had upon waking.

Finally, I had gotten enough sleep, and my text conversation with Alistaire gave me a sense of calm no one else has been able to bring. He tried calling me after our initial texts, but I couldn't answer. As much as I wanted to hear his voice, I hadn't wanted to wake Alma after she'd sat up talking me off a ledge. She needed her sleep too.

"You must be Josefina," the shorter woman says, and her voice is just as warm and inviting as her smile. "I'm Gabriela, Gaby. Welcome to the family." Without warning, she wraps her arms around me in a hug, and I can't help but reciprocate the embrace. She's incredible warm, and our equally soft bodies just kind of meld together. Of everyone I've met thus far, I see the resemblance between the two of us most. "That's Raquel. She always looks grumpy, so don't take the scowl to heart."

I cough to cover the giggle that bubbles up from nowhere. "I'll take that under advisement," I say.

"Don't let our little cousin make you believe anything you haven't seen for yourself. Sometimes, her glasses obscure her vision," Raquel says in response before giving me a nod of acknowledgment.

It isn't exactly the warm welcome Gaby provided, but it's a far cry kinder than Serafina's. Though, I had thought Elinora warm and friendly when we first me too until after the pantry incident. My eyes flit back to Gaby who is chattering away with Alma, the young girl laughing at her antics. New voices come through the kitchen door right before it swings open, almost hitting Alma in the back. Without looking up, Serafina flicks her wrist, and a cushion of smoky shadows deflects the impact. My eyes must fly wide because Raquel shakes her head at me.

"You really are as naive to our magic as they say, huh?"

My back stiffens, and I take in a deep breath, but the chance to retort is stolen away when another small group of women exit the kitchen with *Tía* Helga. She catches sight of me and smiles brightly before setting down the tray filled with cups. One of the other women carries in a platter of scones, and the other, the one with the odd-looking eyes, brings in a large incense-burner wafting white smoke.

"Did someone say something about visions?" she asks, eliciting chuckles from everyone else around the room.

Raquel clears her throat. "*Tía*, this is all nice and cozy, but have you told my mother about your little visitor."

"She is family, Raquel, and you will do well to remember that I, too, am a high priestess. I do not need your mother's permission for everything I do," Helga says before I can manage to roll my eyes at once again being called a child by these women who are barely a decade older than me.

With a nod of her head, Raquel sits down, though I can tell she's uncomfortable with the response she received. Whether it's for being reprimanded in front of everyone else or genuine concern that they might all be in trouble for my being here, I don't know. Suddenly, a soft voice echoes in my ear, and I quickly rub at the offending appendage.

"Don't mind her. She's in line to lead the coven, and she's a rule follower. *Tía* Adaire is intimidating, but she's also understanding."

I look around the room, trying to find the source of the voice and see Gaby staring at me, her mouth moving slightly as if she's mumbling to herself. I tilt my head to the side and raise a brow in question.

"Of course, it's me. It would be far more intrusive and obvious for me to walk over there right now with *Tía* Helga and Raquel glowering at each other than for me to explain it like this."

Finally, someone puts a cup of tea in front of my face, and I accept it eagerly, glad they hadn't offered me the coffee I'd been smelling. "Thank you," I say to the woman who could literally pass for Serafina's twin.

"That's Isabella, Sera's sister," Gaby's voice buzzes in my ear. "That bad ass bombshell with the red hair and funky eyes is Xiomara. She's our in-house medium."

My eyes dart nervously to the woman who appears to be looking at me, but it's hard to tell when one of her eyes has the milky blindness and the other could be looking at any of our other cousins. My hands start sweating, and I have the urge to run. After my last encounter with a medium, I have no desire to be in the same space as one.

"Don't worry. She's harmless," Gaby says. "You look like you're about to bolt, and you definitely don't want to do that."

I clamp both hands around the mug and take a sip while letting my eyes drift around the room to the other women. Eight women that I'm supposedly related to. Eight women who share the same bloodline. Eight witches. My heart rate picks up. I'm in a room with eight witches who have far more control of their magic than I do. What if they brought me here to make sure their coven stays as is? What if they're planning to get rid of me?

"Josie," Alma's voice cuts through my spiraling thoughts. She looks into my eyes and silently mouths the words 'are you okay?' before asking aloud if I'd like a scone. I nod and thank her as much for the lifeline as the flaky pastry. It takes a few minutes before I realize she'd called me Josie, and I didn't hate it.

"Now that we're all settled, let's talk about the Ascension rite."

Just then, the door flies open with a bang, and an older woman, much older than *Tía* Helga, walks through the door followed closely by the last person I expected to see here. What in the hell is happening?

CHAPTER 19
NOT HELPFUL
ALISTAIRE

I'd have given anything to not enter this house at this moment with the head priestess. My hopes of being able to fully explain things to Josefina before she found out who I am was shot to hell when she wouldn't answer my actual phone call. There's no way to explain that I'm a life-long servant to the coven and the errand boy of Adaire, the head priestess and coven leader. Not via text message.

My eyes find her immediately, and the shock followed by confusion, hurt, and then anger guts me as if she were brandishing a knife. I want to say something to her, to soothe her however I can, but I have a role to play.

"Did someone call a family meeting without me?" Head Priestess Adaire asks, and I know she's not expecting a response. She is the queen of rhetorical questions, a painful lesson that took me ages to learn. "Come in, Alistaire. No need to linger at the door. Everyone here knows who you are, well, except maybe for Alma."

Squaring my shoulders, I push the door closed behind me. I catch Josefina's gaze and have to clench my teeth, especially when all eyes turn in her direction after the great reveal. Yes, Alma is the only one in the house I'd never met.

"Alma, go upstairs," Serafina says, shooting daggers in my direction.

"No, let her stay," the head priestess commands, and there is no doubt to anyone in the room that her words are indeed as a command.

"But *Tía*."

"As your head priestess and coven leader, I insist. She is ascending, is she not?" Serafina's eyes drop, as do her shoulders, but she nods her head. "And when were you planning to bring her before the council?"

"That's what we were about to discuss," Helga says, stepping protectively between the head priestess and all the other women in the room.

The temperature rises uncomfortably, and there's a shift in pressure as the two elders face each other. Still, my eyes stay locked on Josefina. I see the moment she feels the change, and fear clouds her anger.

"So, let's discuss, cousin. Let's also discuss how you have skirted around the council, around me, to bring someone untested into our midst."

"And you don't possibly think that this display might be the reason why? Seriously?" To her credit, Helga doesn't back down. If anything, she looks even more determined to protect the two young women. "My granddaughter and my niece need some additional support for their Ascension before they'll be ready for the rite. You would have been called in far before that."

"I should have been called as soon as it started. I should have been called as soon as your brother's child showed signs of having magic."

"We didn't know until recently!"

"Bullshit!" Adaire bellows. "You knew years ago. You knew and found a way to hide it."

I take a step back. I knew this wasn't going to go well, but it is going so incredibly wrong. *Protect her,* the demon yells in my head. I look up at her again, but her eyes are fixated on the head priestess. There's curiosity mixing with her fear. So much has been kept from her that the eagerness to know the truth is going to put her in danger. *She is ours to protect,* he protests. He's right, but how do I protect her from...herself? Now that she's here, how do I pull her away from this world? *You should have told her the truth when she was in our arms.* "Not helpful," I say under my breath. Thankfully, no one seems to have noticed, at least I think that's the case until Josefina turns her gaze to me. My lips murmur an apology, and she stiffens, turning her attention back to the elders.

"Who told you that?" Helga asks, taking a step forward.

Instinct tells me to get between them, but my loyalties are torn. *Umbra, please don't make me choose. You called my family to protect your priestesses, to serve the coven, but nothing in the covenant explains what is to happen when the battle is within.* My silent prayers are followed by the demon's push to protect Josefina. He has nothing to lose in this choice. I, on the other hand, have the family legacy to uphold. Though, if I'm being honest, I'd watch it all burn to the ground to know that she is alright. I simply hope the goddess doesn't let it come to that.

"You may be quick, little cousin, but you have never been stealthy. You choose to do things that have obvious repercussions. No one with our blood is going to wait an additional decade to ascend without intervention, and we both know your worthless brother couldn't accomplish it."

"Don't talk about my father like that," Josefina says, jumping to her feet. Conflicting emotions swirl across her face, and I feel her magic struggling to break free. A quick glance around the room says that none of the other women recognize the conflict roiling inside her, though I doubt it will take the head priestess long to sense it. It's as clear to me as my own. "He told me how you all disowned him and basically chased him out of town. I didn't want to believe him, but if this is how you've always acted, then it's no wonder he kept me away from everyone."

"Josefina," Helga hisses, "you don't know what you're talking about. *¡Cállate por favor!* Let me handle this."

"Handle what, *Tía*? Handle how you also kept your distance from your only brother. How you failed to show me what he couldn't."

No, no, no, Josefina, I scream internally.

"She protected you. Tried to keep you from having to deal with any of this until you were older, more mature," Elinora defends.

Every set of eyes turns in her direction. My jaw clenches and unclenches as it does every time I'm in the same room with her. There's no time to focus on my own issue with the witch when the head priestess rears back.

"What do you know about it?" She takes a step toward Elinora, but Helga steps in the way.

The other women all jump to their feet, and I inch my way closer to Josefina who still hasn't reclaimed control of her emotions. Magic permeates the air as everyone prepares for the inevitable clash.

"I expect this type of shit from Helga. She's always thought herself too good to follow protocol," Adaire grounds out through clenched teeth, "but you, *sobrina*. I never expected you to betray the family."

"Josefina is family, *Tía*. She is one of us, and Tío was so scared for her." Elinora's pleas give me pause. I've always thought her hard and unfeeling, willing to do whatever dirty work the coven required. There's no telling what she did, but she seems genuine in her reasons.

"He should've been scared for her. He chose to leave the safety of the coven."

"You chased him away," Helga roared. "*Tú le decías inútil* and constantly made fun of his lack of magic. He'd have brought her back here had he thought she'd be safe. *Habría regresado si no fuera por ti.*"

The entire room goes silent, except for Gabriela's quiet sniffles. She's always been the most empathetic of this generation's witches, maybe the previous generation too. Still, she isn't the one who should be upset about these revelations. If anyone, Josefina should be livid, and yet she stands against the wall completely still. The calm before the storm.

CHAPTER 20

FURY UNLEASHED

JOSEFINA

My eyes go back and forth between the old women and then from them to Elinora. So many fucking secrets. The hair on the back of my neck stands on end as *las tías'* fingertips darken and their eyes shift. They're both wrong on so many levels, and now they want to throw their power around like that's somehow going to make things easier for me and Alma? I see Alma wrapped in her mother's arms from the corner of my eye, her face buried in Serafina's chest, and my anger spikes.

Shadows swirl along the wall, rising from the floor and covering each of the family photos, photos that barely acknowledge my father's existence and ignore me completely. A family that would rather forget we exist. Around the room, the women stand wide-eyed, their attention focused entirely on the two women who've caused my father so much pain and contributed to my childhood isolation. None of them notice the whirling smoke settling around everyone's feet.

"That's enough!" I cry out. The energy in the room shifts as my shadows cover the windows like blackout curtains. "How fucking narcissistic are the two of you that you've made this entire situation about you? This is my life. My fucking life. This is Alma's

Ascension. Her fucking life." My heart rate has doubled, and my breathing is ragged. Elinora moves, her mouth opening like she wants to say something again, but I beat her to it. "What did you do to me? You seem know so much about my magic, why not just say it?" She doesn't respond right away, and my fists clench. Her nostrils flare like she wants to attack me, and I'm ready for her this time. "*¡Dale pues!*" Her mouth snaps shut, and she looks at the floor only to snap her eyes back up to mine.

"Josefina," she says softer than her expression portrays.

"Not this time, *prima*." My shadows wrap around her legs, and she gasps.

It's then that everyone else notices the wisps of smoke swirling throughout the room. Confusion fills the air as the women begin to climb up on the furniture. The two elders aren't near any of the furniture. They spin in different directions, hands outstretched, trying to find the origin of the smoke. I nearly laugh at the way they try to contain it, but I'm not ready to let it go. They have done far too much damage and need to answer for it. I start to tell them so, but another voice echoes through the silence.

"*Mamá*, what's happening?"

A twinge of guilt constricts my throat. I don't want to hurt Alma. I really don't want to hurt any of them. I just want answers and need these *viejas* to stop their bickering. I just want...

"That's enough, *muñeca*," a soft, deliciously familiar voice comes from my left. "You got them to stop. Now, let it go."

Alistaire touches my shoulder, and my eyes land on him. He shouldn't be here. Why is he here? Why did he come in with her? All the questions I haven't had time to ask flood my brain, recharging my anger and concentrating it on him. "Don't touch me!" I grind out between my teeth. "You lied to me!"

He shakes his head, and sadness coupled with regret shows in his face, but he stands resolute. His resolve pisses me off even more, and smoky tendrils make their way toward him, wrapping around his legs and tying themselves in place like shibari. This time, I stand transfixed, my eyes tracing up and down his body from where the smoky knots sit to his face. There's no fear in his eyes. If anything, there's a spark of something darker. As the tendrils reach his upper thighs, he leans in closer to me until his lips are a hair's breadth from my ear.

"If you want to tie me up, *muñeca*, all you have to do is ask."

A surprised gasp leaves my lips, and it's enough to break the spell over the room. Suddenly, voices crowd in from all sides, the unknown *tía's* the loudest of the bunch.

"You? You're doing this?" She eyes me warily, looking between my face and my hands. *"Por Umbra, cómo es posible?"*

Tía Helga twirls her hand around like she's trying to gather up my smoke and shadows, but they simply wrap around her hand. She looks up at me with her head tilted slightly. She takes in a deep breath and lets out a sigh. *"Tienes razón*, Josefina. You deserve answers, and yours and Alma's safe Ascension is what matters most." She releases her magic, and her eyes return to their natural color.

I start to relax. I don't know how to call the shadows back, but they've stopped spreading. Turning toward Alistaire, I give him an imploring look. I'm still angry with him, but he's always been able to disperse the shadows somehow. The corner of his lip starts to quirk up, and the knots around his legs fall away. His arms open, as they've done the previous times, and my body leans toward his. Something shifts, and his eyes turn red. Before I can react, an angry scream pierces the silence.

"Adaire, no!"

"¡Herencia Maldita!"

I have no idea what she's talking about. Cursed heritage? What? Alistaire jumps forward, his body blocking my vision. Air whooshes from his lips and he slumps back slightly. I can't process what's happening, but my arms instinctively wrap around him as sounds of toppling furniture and surprised voices fill the room.

Get out of here, Gaby's voice says in my ear.

My focus returns to the man in my arms. He's breathing but he's also still leaning heavily on me. "Are you alright?" He doesn't answer, doesn't even turn his head in my direction. "Alistaire, are you hurt?" Still nothing. Again, Gaby's warning comes through. "*Por favor*, Alistaire, *contéstame*," I say at the same time the priestess yells from further into the room where I can't see her for his body blocking me.

"She shouldn't exist. *¡Nos va a destruir!* Don't you see? She's not one of us!" she repeats like a mantra.

Suddenly, Alistaire stands up fully, nearly levitating from the floor, tendrils of smoke around him. "I cannot let you hurt her. *Es Hija de Umbra* and mine to protect." The priestess yells again, calling him a liar, telling him that he's failing the coven. I try to step around Alistaire, but the air around us crackles, and time seems to stand still. "We're leaving," he says as his body once again touches down on the ground. "Go grab your things or come without them." I stand there, frozen in place by what I see now that he's moved.

Statues of the women stand around the room, their faces frozen in various shocked expressions. *Tía* Helga's anger is palpable, as if it's able to penetrate whatever spell they're under. The head priestess's eyes are deranged as if she's come completely unhinged. Her hand is stretched out toward where Alistaire had stood before me moments earlier, and three smoke daggers are mere inches from her fingertips. My throat starts to constrict as I realize her attack was real. She wants to kill me and is willing to go through him to get to me. A whimper leaves my lips.

Alistaire puts his hands on my shoulders. "I should not leave them frozen for too long, Josefina."

I look up into his eyes, but they are devoid of emotion. "I...What...Shit," I say, shaking my head. "What's happening?"

Go with him, Gaby's voice interjects. *Go now!*

The urgency in her voice gets my feet moving. Instead of

heading toward the stairs, though, I walk out the front door. Alistaire follows quickly behind.

"Fuck," he says as soon as we step foot in the yard. "We don't have a car." He paces back and forth a few steps before announcing to the open air, "I hate fucking teleporting!" Then he looks between me and the house behind me. With a roll of his eyes, he grabs my hand and pulls me against his chest. "You're gonna hate this as much as I do."

Three thumps sound from inside the house, and the door slams open. The next thing I know, I'm cradled in Alistaire's arms while he carries me into some cabin in the woods.

CHAPTER 21
SIREN'S SONG
ALISTAIRE

I stop my pacing. Fuck, I haven't paced this much in a century. My eyes cast upon the bed and the subtle rise and fall of Josefina's chest. The use of her untrained magic has always exhausted her, but teleporting had her collapsing in my arms. I just wish she'd wake up. It's been nearly twelve hours, and the need to see the light in her eyes gnaws at me. Thus, I pace the length of the room along the foot of the bed at the same time my demon paces inside of me, both of us watchful of the woman in our care.

We should have...

"Don't start this shit again, demon," I say under my breath. We've been having the same argument for hours. He tells me what I should have done before we arrived at the house, and I argue that there wasn't time. He rages about what could have happened, and I explain that we had been there to stop it. Then, he proceeds to tell me what he would have done had he been in charge. "We can't go back in time, and I would not have done things differently," except maybe redoing that moment I had her in my arms, my lips pressed against her skin. I don't say that last part aloud, but the demon purrs in agreement. All these years, he's never responded to me unless I spoke aloud. Lately, however, he seems to know my thoughts without me having to speak them. Do I dare hope that after almost half a century, perhaps, we are becoming more than parasite and host?

Josefina stirs, and I freeze my steps. She sighs, and goosebumps break out along my flesh. The sound is like a siren's song calling me, though I've already chosen to follow her against any sense of self-preservation I might have. Without conscious thought, I make my way to the side of the bed to the armchair that still sits where I held her hand for most of the first ten hours. She murmurs quietly. Nothing decipherable, just the subtle sounds of her dreams, dreams I wish I were in. And then, she starts thrashing, hands waving, legs kicking. She doesn't scream, but her face contorts in surprise and agony. I touch her shoulder, hoping that the surprise of my touch might bring her out of whatever fearsome event is playing in her mind. Rather than calming, she goes completely still except for the quickened breaths signaling her growing panic. Soft tendrils of shadows creep along the headboard.

Help her, my demon roars. *Protect her.*

"From her dreams?" I have many skills, many goddess-given powers, but dream walking isn't one of them. I brush her hair back from where it's fallen across her forehead. Leaning close, I whisper against her ear. "Come back to me, *muñeca*. You don't have to stay in that dream." She trembles, but I can't tell if it's from my voice or whatever is happening in the dream. The smoke edges closer to me. I'm not afraid of it, not afraid of her, but I worry at whatever is prompting her power to seep through. "Josefina," I coo, "*abre los ojos.*"

Her head swings back and forth again, and she opens her mouth. Rather than the scream I expect, she calls my name. By the time I register that she's calling for me, she grabs at my hands that are still on her and pulls me closer. My knees hit the bed, and my chest is hovering above hers.

"Please, Alistaire. *Ayúdame*," she says on a hushed whisper. "Make it stop."

The hands that had been pulling on mine, reach up, brushing their way up my chest before wrapping around my neck. Her nails graze my scalp, and I barely hold back a groan. *She's not awake,* I tell myself, but the admonishment doesn't stop my cock from hardening, especially not when her breath warms my neck where I'd opened my collar hours ago. It also doesn't stop my demon from preening.

"I need you," she says and pulls on my hair, dragging me further onto her and the bed.

My demon and I both growl at the sensation. A shuddering breath leaves her lips against my ear, and I lose my fight with propriety. Wrapping my arms around her, I climb onto the bed and settle myself against her side. She tries with all her strength to hold me over her, like I had been, but there's no way I can lay my body flush against hers face-to-face and trust I'll remember that she's asleep. The demon rumbles, grumbling as much as Josefina.

"I need you to wake up," I whisper, stroking my hand down her side. I tell myself it's to comfort her, to coax her from the dream that still has its claws in her, but it's only a half truth. I touch her because I can't help myself. I need her to wake up, so I can know how much of her need matches my own.

She wants us, the demon teases, and Josefina rolls into me. I pull her closer and allow my hands to trace from her shoulders to the crease right above her ass. Each caress is a knife, torturing me with aching need. She snuggles in, and I feel her relax for the first time since the dream took over. If this is what it takes to calm her mind, I'll gladly cut myself open. Her arm wraps around my back, and her hand follows my up and down motion, the cadence matching her breaths, slow and steady. I press a kiss to the top of her head once I know for sure she has fallen back into a dreamless sleep. It doesn't take long before I follow her.

CHAPTER 22
THE SWEETEST TORTURE
JOSEFINA

Sun warms my face, though the rest of me an inferno. My body presses against something hard, and my brows furrow. The scent of sandalwood and amber fills my nostrils, and I stifle a moan. My eyes fly open at the realization that I'm not only pressed against a hard body, I'm practically laying atop a hard male body. Not just any male body but the one I've dreamt about for months. My leg straddles one of his, and my thigh is laying across his length, his very hard length. Heat pools deep in my belly, and I try to close my legs to ward off the pulsing need, but all I end up doing is humping his leg. Heat fills my cheeks, and though I think he's asleep, I keep my face averted from his. *Fuck.* I need to extricate myself from his arms.

Slowly, I pull my top arm free from under his and lay my hand on his chest. Energy sizzles in my palm where it touches his skin. His button-down shirt is wide open, leaving him bare from the waist up. The way my body responds, though, we might as well both be completely naked. I try to lift my leg over his, but the hand pressed against my lower back holds me in place. All I manage to do is rub myself against his muscular thigh. Another moan breaks free, and I quickly bite my lip. His body trembles, and I'm acutely aware of how his stomach muscles quiver beneath me. Holy hell, this man is going to be the death of me.

The hand on my back moves, fingers splaying along the top curve of my ass, and my back arches. My body's betrayal does little to calm the heat between my thighs, and I squirm again, unable to hold still. This time, the shuddering in his body is coupled with a sudden intake of breath. I close my eyes as realization settles over me. Alistaire is awake, and I'm here using him as my own private sex toy. My cheeks that were already pink are probably scarlet at this point, but I still tilt my face up to verify what I already know. Another grave mistake as I take in his dark eyes and flared nostrils.

"I'm sor..."

I can't get the words out when his delicious tenor sets me aflame. "Muñeca, I told you that if you want something, all you have to do is ask."

Images of Alistaire intricately tied in my shadows has my pulse racing. There's so much I want, but I can't formulate words as his hand presses into the flesh of my ass, pushing my core down onto his leg. All I can do is whimper.

"*Dime qué quieres.* Tell me what you need," he says, his scorching gaze burning into me.

My mind fights against his pull, against this desire that seems to always crash through me when he's near, but my body is tired of fighting it. His hand trails up from where it was caressing my ass until his fingers slide into my hair, grasping tightly, a silent command. I try to shake my head no, but his grip tightens. His other hand reaches down and grabs the thigh laying across his groin and pulls me completely on top of him. My mouth flies open. Whether in surprise or need, I don't know because he pulls my mouth down to his.

If I thought our previous kiss was intense, this one shakes me to my essence until the entire world fades away. We're no longer two people laying on a bed inside a cabin surrounded by trees. We are fire and light, smoke and shadows. With each stroke of his tongue against mine, I lose track of where I end and he begins.

I suck in a deep breath when he releases my lips, but the reprieve is fleeting as he trails hot kisses down my neck. His hands are everywhere and nowhere at the same time. He cups my face, runs his hands through my hair, caresses my arms, and squeezes my ass, but it's not enough. I want more, need more. My legs spread until I'm straddling his hips, and he groans against my skin, my name floating from his lips like a prayer. All I can think is there are too many layers of clothing between us.

"I need you naked," I pant out, barely able to breathe.

A feral sound, more animal than human, rumbles from his chest, and suddenly his bare skin slides against mine unencumbered. I gasp at the sensation of his hard length against my pussy, and then I rock my hips, feeling the friction I've been needing. Pleasure ripples through me, and I moan in response.

His eyes are closed, but the look on his face is both ecstasy and agony, which halts my movements. Insecurity blooms in my chest as I stare at him. When his eyes open, however, they're glowing in a way I've never seen before. His hands grip my hips, and he pushes up, sending a shiver through my core at the power emanating from him.

"Take what you need," he growls out. "Use me for your pleasure and let me watch you come undone."

Holy fuck, that is the hottest thing I've ever heard. I sit up fully, allowing him to see every inch of me. All my rolls and dimples are on display, and he licks his lips like he'd give anything to have a taste. Emboldened by his response, I grab his hands from where they rest on the curve of my hips and pull them up to my breasts. At first, he cups them softly, rubbing his palms against my sensitive nipples. My body comes alive at his touch, and when he rolls the hardened nubs between his thumb and forefinger, squeezing until just a hint of pain peeks through, my eyes roll back. Once again, I rock against him, rubbing his entire length against my wet slit, teasing the part of me most in need of attention.

"You're so fucking beautiful, Josefina."

I slide my hand between us and start making slow circles on my clit as our hips rock together. He bites his lip, and something inside me wants to bite it myself, but I like the way he's watching me too much. The fact that his gaze keeps going back and forth between my face and where my hand is bringing me to the brink is adding to the experience. It's like he can't take it all in. I look down to watch his hands kneading my breasts. He lifts one of them until it's close enough for his fingertips to tap my chin, and I quickly pull the nipple into my mouth. The moan that leaves him pushes me right over the edge, and my entire body vibrates.

It's several minutes before the tension releases. I pull my fingers from my clit and instinctively go to bring them to my mouth, watching as his eyes follow my movement, but he grabs my wrist.

CHAPTER 23

SHOW ME WHAT'S REAL
ALISTAIRE

Mine, the demon roars, lashing against the force that keeps him bound to me.

I agree emphatically. The sweetest torture has been watching, and feeling, Josefina get herself off without taking over. My cock aches as if it's been beaten and strung up, yet it strains for more. Her wetness has me soaked, and I would bathe in her again and again. I would willingly give myself over to her slow and deliberate grinding if it meant being able to watch her shatter, to hear her moans. I'd do it all with my hands tied behind my back. But when she dares to taste what is likely akin to the ambrosia of ancient myths, I can't let her.

"Let me," I say with more vehemence than intended. Her head tilts, and her chin lifts in defiance, but her heart rate spikes. I feel it between my fingers where I hold her wrist. *"Por favor, muñeca.* Let me taste you."

She says nothing, but the tip of her tongue slips along the seam of her lips. When I pull on her hand, she lets it go slack until it's mere inches from my face. We stare at each other in a battle of wills, but I will win this prize. Lifting my shoulders from the bed, I come within a hair's breadth of her palm and let my nose blaze a trail up to the tip, taking in the exquisite scent. My eyes drift closed as my mouth opens, taking her fingers in as far as they'll go. My tongue slides between the two digits, and her breath hitches. I tighten my lips and suck gently, savoring the taste of her.

"Alistaire." Her voice is enough to have me ready to embarrass myself.

I pull her fingers from my mouth, never losing eye contact with her. "*Dime.* Can I have you?"

Something in her eyes says she wants to say no, and I brace myself for the answer. Rather than say no, though, she leans down and presses her lips to mine, running her tongue along the seam of my lips.

"I need your words, Josefina."

She smiles and then bites her lip. "I've dreamt about you for so long, professor. Show me what's real."

My demon howls in delight, and I want to follow suit. Instead, I simply flip her over and kiss my way down her body. Her breasts are deliciously full, and yet naturally soft. I nip and suck at her nipples until they're peaked and puckered. I love the feel of her soft abdomen and take time to explore it with my tongue, laving around her belly button until she laughs.

"Stop. That tickles!"

I chuckle but give her a light reprieve and continue making my way down to her pussy. She's trimmed but not completely bare. I love the feel of her soft hair against my face, but it's her smell that drives me wild. I press my nose at the top of her slit, right below the softest part of her and inhale.

"Alistaire."

That's it, I think. *Keep calling my name.* I push her thighs out to the sides and feast my eyes on her. "*Por* Umbra, you're absolute perfection," I say with reverence. I lock eyes with her and watch as her cheeks tinge pink before dipping my head down and running my tongue up her slit, pressing between her lips until the tip flicks along her bud. Some sound comes from my mouth, but I'm not sure if it's a growl, a moan, or something more feral. All I know is that tasting her is better than anything I've ever experienced, and I don't want to stop. Using my hands, I spread her open to me, and I feast.

I don't come up for air until Josefina's hands yank on my hair. Looking up toward her face, my eyes are blurry unable to see her clearly. It's like I'm drunk on her. "Fuck me, Alistaire. I want to feel you inside of me." Is this a dream? I can hardly believe my ears, but then she pulls me up her body, and the prickles of my scalp let me know this is very much real. Then, my cock lands along her wet slit, at the same time that her mouth meets mine, and I can't think of anything else. I adjust my hips slightly and position the head of my cock at her entrance before pushing in slowly.

"Fuuuuuck," we both say in unison.

Then, I'm kissing her again, our bodies moving together in a dance of give and take. She meets me at every stroke, and it's like an out of body experience, like when I release my demon but without the searing pain. This is the most exquisite pleasure. She is slick and hot and tight, and the way we're going, I'm not going to last long. I reach between us and press my thumb against her clit before making light circles in rhythm to our strokes. Her breathing becomes more ragged, and I lean back on my heels, so I can control the cadence as her movements become more unsteady.

"That's it, *Muñeca*. Come for me."

And she does as soon as the words leave my lips. Her hips buck, and her walls squeeze me tight, pulsating along my length. I try to continue pushing through her orgasm, but she clamps down on me tighter, and I'm lost. My entire essence dissolves into atoms, and when I come back together, she is peppering my face with kisses. The feeling is so intimate that I almost rear back. It's not like everything we'd just done wasn't the most intimate I'd ever been with anyone, but this feeling inside me, this contentedness of being skin to skin with her as we both come down from the high is almost too much to wish for. Even my demon is quiet and relaxed.

I pull from her arms and stand up from the bed. A frown comes over her face, but I can't respond to it as panic sets in. *What am I doing? What have I just done? I'm supposed to be her protector. My job is to keep her safe.* I slip into my pants and head out into the night air running from her call. Unfortunately, I can't escape the demon as easily as I can escape from her.

You're an idiot!

"¡Cállate!"

Go back.

I don't respond, but I don't have to. He knows what I'm thinking. I do, however, slow to a walk and call forth my sneakers. Who cares that my feet are filthy and likely still bleeding from running through these woods. I deserve far worse for what just happened.

She wanted it. She asked for it.

I shake my head. If she knew what I've done and what I must do. If she knew about this demon inside me. If she had been thinking clearly when she awoke, she wouldn't have.

Go back now. You left her alone in a strange place unprotected. Go back now or set me free.

"I won't let you anywhere near her," I bark out at the disembodied voice.

Then do your fucking job and protect what's ours.

CHAPTER 24
SURPRISE TEA
JOSEFINA

I sit and stare at the door for the longest time willing Alistaire to come back inside and talk to me. How could the perfect alignment of stars explode into a gaping black hole of despair? I could come up with a million reasons why I shouldn't have let him touch me, why I should have kept my distance and cultivated the distrust that had erupted in my heart the moment he walked into Helga's house with the head priestess. Not one of those reasons felt sufficient when his hands were on me and our bodies were entwined, but now, with the familiar sting behind my eyes, I question the strength of my own self-preservation. When I can't wait any longer without breaking down, I head into the attached bathroom and let the shower wash away the tears that escape.

Alistaire still hasn't returned when I exit the bathroom, but my overnight bag is laying on the bed. *How the hell did he do that?* No sooner have I thought the words than my eyes search the quiet cabin bedroom and notice the smell of herbal tea wafting in from another room. My body tenses. Though I'm hopeful it will be Alistaire on the other side of the wall, something in my chest warns that it's not. As quietly as possible, I pull a pair of leggings out of my bag and slide them on. I definitely don't want to walk into an ambush naked. My thoughts travel back to the moments before Alistaire whisked me away from Helga's house. Shadowy daggers had been aimed directly at Alistaire, at me, and though they'd seemed incorporeal, there was a sickening thud when they hit the wall where we had both been standing moments before. Shit, I hadn't gotten to ask Alistaire how he managed to get us out of there.

The air is a little chilly, but I don't want anything impeding my movements should I need to defend myself, so I put on a tight-fitting crop top. Tying a sweatshirt around my waist, and slipping some soft sneakers on my feet, I pad to the half-open door. From what I can see through the crack, the room is empty, but there's a faint rustle of paper and tinkle of metal hitting glass. Whoever is here has made themselves at home with a cup of tea. The irony that we had all just sat down to scones and tea or coffee flicker in my brain, and I cringe. I have no desire for a repeat this morning. Pulling the door quietly, I open it a bit more to peek around the corner toward the sound and gasp.

"Close your mouth, *sobrina. Te va a entrar una mosca.*"

I purse my lips tightly together. "What are you doing, Tía?"

"Having a cup of tea. Here, have one with me."

My head tilts at her nonchalant manner as if I wasn't attacked in her house just yesterday. "I meant how did you find me?"

"We are witches, you know?"

My eyes roll, but a smile tugs at the corners of my lips. I take the cup of tea she offers me and sit at the rustic table with one leg twisted up underneath my ass like I'm trying to make myself more compact. Her eyes take me in, however, and it's obvious she reads the gesture for what it is—fear.

"Was anyone hurt yesterday?"

"Yesterday?" she asks. "What happened yesterday?"

I eye her suspiciously. Though this morning felt like a dream, there's no way I imagined the battle in her living room. I know she's older than Poppa, but I don't think she's old enough for senility to have set in. "The war in your house? The head priestess?"

"*Qué* war *y* war. No one has seen that old bitchy bitch in days."

Days? Have I been here for days? Was I asleep the whole time? I try to think back to our arrival, and all I can picture is Alistaire carrying me into the cabin. At least until I woke this morning splayed across him. My cheeks heat at the memory, and Helga eyes me with a smirk. I take a sip of my tea, trying to distract myself from the replay of me writhing against his hard length, but it's not helping.

"I was surprised to find you alone. Where is..."

I cut her off. "How did you find me?" I know I've already asked the question, and she's not given me a straight answer, but now I need to distract her from that line of questioning. "Do you have a GPS tracker on me?"

"*Qué es eso?* What's a GPS?"

"Never mind, *tía*. Just tell me how you got here."

"*No importa*. The important thing is that I found you, and you are safe. Could you imagine what your *papá* would think if I told him we lost you?"

If she had asked me that question two weeks ago, I'd have had no doubt that Poppa would've moved heaven and Earth to find me. He'd have screamed down the entire state. After finding out he'd known about me having magic and tried to keep it from me, I'm not so sure. Would he be glad to have me gone, to not have to worry about his witch of a daughter? After all these years of telling me that magic doesn't exist, of trying to force me to stop making candles and deny my affinity for paranormal things, how would he respond to the news of my disappearance?

"*Tía*, was my mother there?"

She turns her steady gaze on me, and her countenance turns serious. "Was she where?"

"Was she there when you stole my magic away?" I ask around the knot in my throat. "Did she know what I was?"

Helga's eyes hold so much empathy, I nearly break down from the weight of it. My mother had been everything to me as a child. She taught me so much, and she encouraged my creativity. When I wanted to start making more than the taper candles we'd burn at the dinner table, she took me shopping for vessels, and she introduced me to various herbs and essential oils to create different scents. She was the one who told me the properties of those scents and how they could affect people emotionally. I never imagined that my emotions would play a role in that imbuement process, and I'd like to think she would have told me if she had known. But her knowing would make my father's betrayal even harder to accept.

"*Ay*, I could ring your father's neck for keeping you in the dark so long. Even shadows need a little light to exist." Her lips purse, and she fiddles with the cup in her hand like she's trying to work out a puzzle. I know that practice well. Poppa has always done the same thing when trying to solve a problem, especially when I'm the problem. I have the same ritual when there's something I just can't figure out. In fact, I had been making the same tapping and rubbing pattern on the blanket while I sat on the bed earlier. Shaking my head to clear the thoughts of Alistaire, I force my eyes back to meet hers. She must take the movement as impatience and sighs.

"Josefina, you have to understand, your *papá*, he," she pauses before continuing, "he always felt out of place within the coven. And, sadly, there were some members of the family who made it so much worse."

"He told me the family disowned him or took away his birthright. I never really understood what he meant because he wouldn't talk about it other than to say we were our only family."

Hurt flashes through her eyes, and, for the first time, I see how much she cares for my father, her brother. "Daegal is my twin. I would never have allowed anyone to chase him off or deny him his rightful place in the family. He is de Umbra, even if he doesn't have the goddess's magic."

"But our last name is Exposito," I interrupt, trying to make sense of what she's saying.

"¡Qué foundling y foundling!" She waves a dismissive hand, and her lip curls in disgust. "How dumb to pick that last name. He always said he felt like the goddess had abandoned him and that the family treated him like our mother had found him in the woods." She takes a sip of her tea, swirling it so quickly in her hands that the cup begins steaming again. My eyes open wide at the trick, and she laughs before turning serious again. "I tried telling him that he was as much a part of this family as I was, but he decided that if he was going to be mundane--his words--then he would live in the mundane world." She scoffs, and her eyes take on that faraway look people get when they're remembering something.

"Tía, if he felt that way, there was a reason."

"Yes, the reason was that he was jealous," she said, slamming down her cup of tea so hard liquid sloshed over the side. "We all knew and had been told from an early age that the reason there were so few males around was because our magic is passed down as part of the priestesshood. That is why we have the Rite of Ascension to solidify our magic in honor and servitude to Umbra." I stare at her wide-eyed, but she continues on undeterred. "He knew that he would likely not have magic, but he thought that if he prayed hard enough, if he made promises to the goddess, and if he studied everything with me, he would be blessed to ascend. When he didn't, he grew angry, and every bit of teasing became a personal slight he began to blame on the goddess until he decided to abandon her altogether. He abandoned me with her."

The pendulum swing of her anger and hurt reminds me so much of my own dueling emotions that I reach out and lay a hand on her shoulder. In an effort to both distract her from my father's choices and redirect the conversation back to my question, I ask again, "And my mother?"

She blinks, clearing the glassiness in her eyes, and picks up her tea, once again repeating the process of heating the contents. I can't help but wonder how many times she has to reheat her tea on a daily basis. Once the steam begins anew, she holds the cup in her hands as if they've grown suddenly cold. When her eyes finally meet mine again, I get the feeling she's gone through the process of weighing her words and resigned herself to a tipped scale.

"Corinne was beautiful inside and out. Though I only got the chance to see her twice, we bonded over our love for Daegal." I smile, thinking how wonderful it is to have someone else with fond memories of my mother, but Helga doesn't return my smile. Instead, her expression turns weary. "I really wish to choke your father for making me tell you all this." The disgusted look returns with the sneering lip curl that must be genetic. "Yes, your mother knew you had magic, her magic, but she did not know you'd have shadows. No one knew until the day your father called me for help."

"When I was a kid?"

"No, Josefina. We didn't know you had shadow magic until last week."

I opened my mouth to say something and then closed it again. Last week? How long have I been here in this cabin? Again, my thoughts drift to Alistaire, but I have to reel myself back in.

"Wait, my mother had magic? That can't be right. Father always said magic didn't exist. He wanted me to give up my candle making and stop decorating for Halloween. He was adamant that it was all a hoax. How did he marry a witch?"

"Easy. He didn't know at first. She kept her magic hidden from everyone for years. Even at their wedding, I had no idea. Normally, I can sense someone else's magic, and there was nothing. She was as mundane as your father, and I was happy he had found his match."

Tears well in my eyes. My mother had kept her magic secret,

and then my father had turned around and hidden mine as well. Was there nothing in my childhood that was real? I slump back in my chair.

"Don't judge your parents too harshly," Helga said, startling me. I had almost forgotten she was still there in the slippery slope of my dark emotions. "They were each protecting themselves and the people they loved, or so they thought."

Her ominous tone brings me fully back to the present. "What do you mean?" It makes sense that he might've thought he was protecting me from the pain of not having magic, but my mother would have known I'd inherit hers, right? Was it possible she had hoped I wouldn't? And why would she have wished to keep it from me? So many questions run through my mind, but I doubt my estranged aunt would have the answers. So, I settle back and wait for her to answer the only question I expressed.

She takes in a deep breath and opens her mouth when the door crashes open. Alistaire, a panicked look on his face, stands in the opening, his eyes blazing red and blood dripping over the rim of his tennis shoes.

CHAPTER 25

DEMON EYES
ALISTAIRE

The demon's warning hits a nerve. As much as I hate to admit it, he's right. I can't protect her from miles away. That was the whole problem with me being called before the council and her disappearing before I could return. A snarl leaves me, and I can't tell whether it came from me or the demon. I take off running back toward the cabin.

You could get there faster.

Fuck. He's right again. I hate fucking teleporting, but something sends shivers up the back of my neck. There's someone else in the woods. Some kind of magic. I flash to the edge of the clearing outside of the cabin and listen.

Someone's inside with her.

"I know," I snarl, trying to hear beyond the walls. The only thing holding me still is the feel of her magic, calm and waiting. I try to reach out and feel the other entity in the house, but it's shadowed. Either she doesn't know she's not alone, or she's comfortable with that person. My hackles rise at the idea of her being content with someone else in my safe space. The space where she forever marked my soul.

What're we waiting for? The voice yells in my head. I can feel him pacing, and it's urging me to act.

"Shut up! I'm trying to get a read on the magic inside."

Shadow magic. Are we going to let those bitches hurt her?

It doesn't make me feel any better to learn he's come to the same conclusion I have. "She's calm," I say in response, trying to keep my own discomfort at bay. I don't like to walk in on situations I can't control, and with this woman, I seem to always find myself in uncertain situations. No sooner do I have the thought that something shifts in her magic. I can feel the stirring in her.

Fuck it! I flash to the door and use my own shadows to blast it open. My heart pumps in anticipation of a fight as I take in the room. Nothing is out of the ordinary in the sitting area, though the door to the bedroom is open. I pivot toward the kitchen at the sound of clinking dishes, and there sits Josefina, her eyes wide. Next to her is Helga, a smirk on her lips before she sips from the mug. Locking eyes with Josefina, I feel for the outpouring of her magic I've found each time it's stirred. She stares back in apprehension, and I tilt my head to the side, trying to read her mind. Never before have I wished for that particular set of skills, but with her, I want to know it all, even what she's unwilling to tell me.

"I was wondering where you'd gone, Alistaire," Helga says, her voice cheerful and welcoming, as if she's playing hostess in my fucking cabin.

Instead of responding, I ask Josefina if she's alright. She stays frozen in place and doesn't respond. I take a step forward, and she physically shrinks back. *What's happening?*

"If you could turn off the demon eyes, I'm sure my niece would feel much better." My eyes widen with surprise. "You didn't know either?" Helga assesses me for several moments. "Interesting."

I turn toward the mirror over the mantle, and, sure enough, my eyes are glowing blood red. I step in that direction, turning away from the women. "Are they always like this?" I ask aloud, though not to anyone in particular.

"If you're asking if they've always been like that, then no. They were, however, glowing when you decided to show off in the middle of my living room."

That statement brings me back to the present situation, and as soon as I realize she isn't a current threat, I watch my eyes dull and return to their evergreen shade.

"What are you doing here, Helga?" I turn to see her smirk return, but this time there's a spark of indignation in her eyes. Though Josefina remains stiff in her seat, her shoulders aren't as tight, and I breath a small sigh of relief before turning my attention back to the witch at her side.

"You forget your place, young one. I am still a high priestess of Umbra, and you are still Umbra's servant and Protector of the Priestesshood, are you not?"

I stand a little straighter, thoughts clashing through my mind. My loyalty is to the goddess and her priestesses, but I cannot allow any of them to hurt Josefina. She has also been chosen by the goddess. At least that's the argument I would make aloud if forced. There's so much more to my feelings for her, but I haven't made sense of them myself, let alone formulated a way to explain it. "Yes, High Priestess," I say reluctantly. "I still have to ask, though, why are you here in my cabin? Or, better yet, how did you find my cabin?" The priestess nods in acknowledgment of my false contrition and my question, though there's no indication she plans to answer. My eyes drift to Josefina who turns her head toward Helga. It's hard to tell if she's trying to avoid my gaze or eagerly awaiting her response as well. Something tells me there's a little of both in the gesture.

"As a high priestess, I do not owe you an explanation for anything, Alistaire, but I will give it because you protected Josefina against the head priestess's misguided wrath." She stands and grabs another mug from the cabinet before gesturing for me to take a seat. Again, I bristle at how comfortable she is in my house, rummaging through my cabinets as if she owns the place. She pours water from the kettle into the mug and then swirls it in her hands until steam wafts from the top. "It should not be surprising that I have access to a scryer. Likewise, you should not be surprised I would have looked for her. She is de Umbra, and we take care of our own."

"Take care of..." I start, and she cuts me off.

"Like I was telling Josefina, that entire situation was an unfortunate misunderstanding." She turns to look at Josefina. "Had you not turned your magic on us, I would have been able to talk the head priestess down. Why did you not pull them back when I told you to?" Josefina's lip quivers under Helga's pointed gaze, and I respond, so she doesn't have to.

"She doesn't know how yet."

Both women turn their eyes on me, Josefina with a scowl and Helga in surprise. "What do you mean?" she asks and then repeats the question to Josefina. "What does he mean you don't know how to pull your magic back?"

CHAPTER 26

PROTECTIVENESS AND PORTRAITS

If I thought the man unnerved me before, seeing him come in with eyes blazing was enough to have me questioning every life decision. "Does every person affiliated with this goddess of yours have eyes that change colors? I watched Elinora's, and yours, *Tía*, change to black when your magic engaged. And now," I say, turning my attention on Alistaire, "yours were some kind of Halloween animatronics red." To his credit, Alistaire manages to look sheepish rather than smug. My aunt, on the other hand, is curiously pensive.

"You don't," she says simply, and my mouth gapes open. "Your nails don't turn black either. It's one of the reasons the head priestess freaked out so much. You show no outward signs of your magic. It's simply there." She rests her chin on her thumb and rubs her index finger back and forth below her bottom lip. "Now, tell me about your control."

I snort a laugh. "You mean lack of control." My shoulders lift and fall, as if the shrug can convey every bit of fear and frustration I've experienced during each time my magic roars to life and refuses to retreat when it's no longer needed. "Professor Seagal," I say, gesturing toward Alistaire with my thumb, "had to stop it from attacking my ex-boyfriend. Or rather, it had already attacked him. The professor kept it from doing whatever it had planned to do. In fact, he stopped it another time as well."

"I should've let it destroy its target both times." His jaw is set, and though his voice is firm, there's something uncertain in his aura. I have no idea how I can read him, but there's an emotion emanating from him that I can't quite capture. When I turn to look in his direction, however, he diverts his face away.

Tía Helga lets out a laugh. Alistaire and I both snap our attention back to her. A smirk sits firmly on her lips, and her eyes sparkle with mirth, but I can't think of anything either of us have said that's funny. My brows draw together, and she laughs aloud again. "¡*Qué* professor *y* professor!" She points a finger between the two of us. "His protectiveness and your nakedness when I arrived says you two are much closer, unless *él es profesor de* fucking." Her brow lifts in challenge, and I gasp.

"*Tía*!"

"What? Do you deny it? Either of you?"

"That's none of your business, High Priestess."

"Isn't it though?" She swirls her tea that is once again full, though she hasn't returned to the stove to pour another cup. "As a high priestess, I answer to Umbra, and am responsible for our younger members. Josefina is my responsibility."

"No, *Tía*." I stand from the table, placing my hands along it's edge. "Who I fuck is no one's business but mine." No sooner have the words come from my mouth than I cover it with my hand. Did I really just say that to Poppa's sister? An apology is on my lips when she bursts into laughter so hard tears start streaming down her cheeks. I look toward Alistaire, and he shrugs, though the corner of his lip lifts. The two of them are pissing me off. "I don't know what's so funny, but none of this answers the question of my mother and her magic, or why you're here." I don't yell, but I keep my voice steady, wanting them to know I'm not joking.

Helga sips her now steaming tea and relaxes her face back to its neutral facade. "No one knows for sure what kind of magic your mother had, at least not with any certainty," she says with a shrug. "We assumed it was light magic due to your affinity for candle making and the ability to pour more than wax into the candles, but I was unable to find anything in our histories about light witches who couldn't heal themselves."

I close my eyes for a few moments, swallowing back the irritation at how little I know about magic and this family, about myself. A tingle runs up my spine, and I look up to find Alistaire's eyes fixed on my face. Concern and empathy swirl in his beautiful green eyes, a far cry better than the red they had been when he first got back to the cabin. I have so many questions for him too, so many things I want to say, but not with *Tía* Helga here. I realize with a start that she's continued talking all this time, but I have no idea what she's said. My brain had totally shifted from the conversation at hand to the one Alistaire and I need to have.

"*Tía*, not to be harsh, but why are you here? You don't seem to have any specific answers for me. You've told me that the head priestess trying to kill me was a misunderstanding, though I can't understand what you want me to do with that information. And you don't seem overly concerned about anything, which, honestly, is irritating." I stand up to refill my mug, but before I can push my chair back in, there's a steaming hot cup of tea sitting in front of me. "What the hell?"

Helga winks, and I purse my lips. Her theatrics aren't helping at all. Diverting my gaze from her and not wanting to look over at Alistaire for fear I'll lose myself in thoughts of us, I take in the room. The door to the bedroom is still slightly open, but it is the only room closed off from the rest of the small cabin. Considering the size, the galley kitchen is spacious, and it opens directly out to the small dining area where we're all seated and a spacious living room with a huge fireplace. Above the fireplace is a painting that has my breath catching. Before I realize what I'm doing, I've crossed the room to stand in front of the fireplace staring up into the eyes of someone who looks like me.

The hair, fanned out around her head, is much darker than mine, but her blue eyes are exactly like mine, except they're glowing with a radiance I could only dream of. Her gown flows down her body, floating around her sumptuous curves to cascade around her feet where she floats above the ground. The colors are vibrant reds, blues, yellows, and orange, similar to depictions of the mythological phoenix. Her face is round with high cheekbones, and I can almost feel her energy wafting from the painting.

"Who?" I ask softly when I feel Alistaire walk up behind me. His breath hitches, drawing my attention from the painting to his face.

"I...I don't...I never..." he stammers, and it not like he's trying not to answer. It feels as if he really doesn't know how to answer.

"Where did you get that painting?" Helga asks, coming to stand next to us.

"*Tía*, you have absolutely no shame, walking into someone else's house and..." the reprimand dies in my throat as she turns on us, eyes and fingertips black.

"Where did you get that painting?" she asks again, shadowy wisps wrapping around her hands. Though it's obvious to me that she's directing the question at Alistaire, he still steps in front of me, pushing me behind him with his hand.

"I meant it when I said I would not let anyone hurt her." His voice is menacing, and I feel the shift in energy when his magic engages. When she does nothing more than stare at him, he answers her question. "I didn't get it anywhere."

"Liar!" Helga fumes, taking a step forward.

Alistaire's body stiffens and again, he moves to step in between us from where I had shifted to see around him. His head shakes back and forth. "I painted it nearly twenty years ago."

My hand reaches out for his arm as questions form on my tongue, but I don't get the chance?

"When exactly? This is important, Alistaire."

CHAPTER 27

AM I MISSING SOMETHING?

ALISTAIRE

My eyes shift from the high priestess to the portrait that's hung on my wall for nearly two decades. I feel just as connected to her today as I had when I'd first painted her. Something in her eyes calls to me in the same way the woman standing behind me, radiating heat that threatens to consume me, does. The priestess shifts her stance and lowers her black-tipped hand, drawing my attention back to her as I mull over her question.

"I'm not sure of the exact day, but it was probably eighteen years ago." She doesn't say anything, just watches me as if waiting for me to elaborate. "I was stuck here and had a vision of a beautiful woman floating through the air as if she were coming through my dreams. I couldn't stop myself from painting the vision and she's been there above the mantle ever since."

"Did you know? I mean, did you notice?" Josefina asks, and I don't know how to answer her.

Of course, I noticed the similarities, but how could I have explained to her that nearly twenty years ago, I had a vision of a woman who looks eerily like her? How do I explain that I started dreaming of her years ago before I even knew she existed? Our ages are already a subject I'm afraid to broach, especially since it's uncertain she realizes how old anyone in the coven really is. The only one who looks her age is young Alma, and that is only because she hasn't ascended yet. Once that happens, her aging will slow tremendously until it stops altogether. Fucking Helga is nearly 160 years old, though here, she can barely claim fifty. That's the power of the Ascension Umbra blesses them with.

"Was this before or after?" Helga asks, and I'm not sure exactly what she means.

I open my mouth to respond, but the hair stands along my nape at the same time my demon stiffens along my spine. Spinning toward the door, I place myself between the two women and whatever is coming. Time seems to stand still as I search for the source of the magic that first alerted me to another unexpected visitor. Once again, it is familiar and yet uncomfortably misplaced here in my sanctuary. The thought no sooner enters my mind when recognition hits and my whole body stiffens.

Without a word or permission, Helga pushes past me and yanks the door open. Head Priestess Adaire nearly tumbles through the now open space before catching herself on the door jamb. Her eyes narrow, and I prepare myself for another showdown between the two women. A quick look over my shoulder says that Josefina is readying herself too, though the eye roll I barely catch says she's more frustrated with the older witches than she is nervous.

"Don't you know it's rude to eavesdrop at someone's door? I would have thought you'd learned that lesson at my house the last time we were all together." Helga's hand is on her hip, and her brows raise. At least the one I can see in profile does.

"If I didn't know any better, Prima, I'd think you were conspiring against the coven, against our goddess."

"¡*Qué* conspiring *y* conspiring! You've always been so damn worried that someone might want your job. Nobody wants that responsibility. We just want you to stop being a bitch."

Adaire's lips purse, but she makes no other move. It's times like these I wish I could read minds rather than energy. Unless she fully engages her magic to attack, I've never been able to predict what she might do next. Hence the demon now cowering inside me while simultaneously seething at the second uninvited guest of the day.

"Head Priestess, what brings you to my door?"

Her eyes turn on me, and I feel the moment she recognizes the portrait hanging on the wall. Her eyes darken, and my arms go wide, trying to make sure Josefina remains behind me. Rather than stay back, though, she steps forward until she's whispering at my shoulder.

"What is it about the portrait? Am I missing something?"

"I don't know," I say honestly.

"Where did you get that painting?" She takes a step forward into the cabin, but Helga steps in front of her.

"We were just having that very conversation a moment ago, Prima. He claims to have painted it himself."

"*¡Mentira!* No one in this realm has seen her."

That statement gains my full attention. Seen who? The only person I recognize in the portrait is Josefina, and I caught sight of that unmistakable likeness the first time I saw her on campus in that crowded lecture hall. Other than the light hint of magic I'd sensed from her, it was the vision, the dream that drew me to her. Even if I hadn't been sent to watch over her, though I had little idea why she needed protection, I wouldn't have been able to keep myself from her for much longer.

"Can you two please stop speaking in cryptic messages only you seem to understand? Since you both presumably came here to find me, and since you both seem to have the audacity to call someone a liar in their own home, maybe you could let us in on whatever the fuck you're talking about."

The two women look at each other, and my eyes close as I take in a deep breath. Something about her sass sends sparks through my veins at the same time I would rather not have to threaten the lives of the very women who hold my life and family legacy in their hands. I turn my head slightly and look down to find Josefina standing at my side with her hands on her hips, and it's all I can do to not teleport her somewhere far away, so I can kiss the exasperation off her lips. She paints a fierce picture, but she is in no way prepared to take on two high priestesses of Umbra, especially not without having completed the Ascension rite yet.

"*Cálmate, muñeca.* I doubt they will respond well to being challenged. If you want answers, maybe we try something different."

CHAPTER 28

DECEPTION AND DESCONTROL

JOSEFINA

What is it about a man telling us to calm down that does anything but get us to calm down? These women are so overwhelmingly wrong with their intrusions and name calling and how they act like they're the decision-makers for everyone. Again, I can't help but understand why my father chose to leave this place and move hundreds of miles away to start a new life. *Tía* Helga is at least affable, but this head priestess whose name I don't even know is an absolute bitch, and yet I'm the one who needs to calm down. Nope, not happening.

"Before you start doing all your dark finger pointing and pupil-blowing, eyeball-changing thing again, would you at least tell me what this whole priestess thing even means, and do you have a name?" I direct the question at the head priestess, "Because I'm not going to call you by a title I don't even understand in context." At my side, Alistaire sighs, and I can almost feel his eyes rolling, though I can't see them.

The head priestess's eyes travel from me to Alistaire, and then she levels a glare on my aunt. "Are you telling me *esa malcriada*... Your brother didn't teach this child anything? You haven't told her a fucking thing?" I bristle at the pejorative and open my mouth to speak when *Tía* Helga responds coldly.

"It's not like you gave me a chance, Adaire, barging in and throwing shadow daggers around my fucking living room. He," she says, pointing at Alistaire, "could absorb your daggers. My wall, on the other hand, could not."

Daggers? Was that what hit the wall after we left the house? Wait, was that what hit Alistaire when he leaned his body back into mine? I feel my eyes go wide, but he catches my attention and shakes his head, once again trying to keep me from saying anything more. I wouldn't have gotten the chance anyway because the head priestess's attention turns back to him.

"You didn't tell her anything either?" she spat at him, nearly foaming at the mouth.

"What did you want me to tell her?" he asks calmly. "You said my job was to protect her and keep an eye open for the release of her magic. I did that. When I saw the extent of her shadows and her inability to control them, I sent her home to her father thinking he would reach out to the family." Adaire, whose name I finally know, glares between him and *Tía* Helga, but he continues on, his voice unwavering. "By the time I saw her again, you had called me back here. I barely got the chance to hear what had happened in San Antonio before I left to answer your summons. When, Head Priestess, should I have taught her all she needed to know?"

I want to be angry at his words, at his open agreement to me being so naive to everything, but I can't because the only thought dancing through my mind is him pushing me against the wall and our lips colliding in a kiss that had me weak in the knees and breathless.

Thankfully, my aunt responds, pulling me back from that delicious memory I'd like to live in more than this awkward moment. With hands on her hips, *Tía* Helga confronts the head priestess, "And here you are, once again, barging in and interrupting, so why are you here, Adaire?"

I watch the indignation rise in the head priestess's face as her nostrils flare and her face tinges red. "I am looking after our family's best interests. I am doing my job the goddess bestowed upon me."

Tía Helga lifts a brow, and I feel my own lift along with her. No one gets to address the fact that I am technically family and have also been blessed by the goddess, though, because Adaire turns her attention back to the original question. "Where did that painting come from, Alistaire?"

He stiffens, and it's not the same type of stiffening I've seen when he feels offended or disregarded. This change is unnatural.

"Alistaire?" I say quietly, my hand lightly grazing his arm. When he doesn't respond to his name or my touch, my throat constricts. Something is very wrong. "Professor?" I eke out as the air seems to close in around me. The shift has the hair on my arms standing up. Something close to a snarl rolls up from his throat.

"*Déjalo*, Adaire. Give him a chance to answer on his own."

My attention switches back to the two older women. What does that even mean? To answer on his own? *Tía* Helga looks distraught, and I see her start to shift position, raising her hand, the swirl of gray smoky tendrils creeping from her fingers. My eyes take in the head priestess, and it hits me that the magic she's using isn't in the shadows. Well, maybe it is, but it isn't flowing from her fingers, and that horrific weight of power sucking the air from the room is beyond the shadow magic I've experienced since Elinora first showed up in San Antonio. No one's magic has felt like this.

"What are you doing to him?" I cry out as well as I can with my lungs constricted. She doesn't even turn in my direction, and that's when I notice it. Unlike what I've seen with everyone else, her eyes aren't the pure black cabochons of engaged magic this time. Instead, they are a glimmering green with a thick black rim. *What is happening?* I look from her to Alistaire and see his eyes transfixed by her stare. For the first time since my shadows decided to make an appearance, I feel the release. They caress my bare feet and legs as they rise up around us. Poppa had told me to give the shadows direct orders, but it's hard to know what to say directly when I have no earthly idea what it is she's doing.

"Josefina, unless you can control them, *por favor*, let me handle this," *Tía* Helga pleads, but she's taking too long to do anything.

Alistaire's body is vibrating, and I can only imagine he's trying to fight against her hold on him. I don't want to hurt her with my shadows, I just want to break the connection, to stop him from hurting. My eyes drift back to his and catch the subtle shifting in them as his head tilts slightly in my direction. Hold on, I mouth to him and push all my thoughts into commanding the shadows to create a barrier between her and us.

Adaire must sense my shadows because she takes a step forward. That's when my aunt moves in closer and lassoes her smoky tendrils around Adaire's body, pinning her arms to her sides, but it's not her arms I'm worried about. It's her eyes. My shadows continue to rise in front of Alistaire, but they're not moving fast enough.

"Answer me, Alistaire. You answer to me!"

"Adaire," *Tía* Helga yells, "he does not. He is a servant of the goddess just as we are."

"I am the High Priestess of Umbra, and he is mine to command. I will not abide his lies and endangerment of our family. We will never be weakened again, especially not because someone forgets their place."

I continue willing the shadows to rise. This woman is unhinged, and I'm not strong enough to drag Alistaire's body out of the house. Please. Please. I'm begging at this point as the tension on the other side of the shadows rise as well. Adaire wriggles, trying to break free of Helga's shadows, but my aunt is strong.

"It's you who seems to forget your place, to forget our purpose."

Adaire's head snaps around toward my aunt at those words, finally breaking the tether between herself and Alistaire. He begins to slump where he stands, and I quickly wrap my arms around him, putting myself between her and him, pulling his face down to my chest, so she can't lock her eyes on his again. I still have no idea what she was doing to him, but I know it had something to do with that stare. The intensity. Her eyes. The vacuum effect on the room. It felt like she had been sucking out his soul.

"I got you," I murmur, holding onto him to keep him upright. Behind me, on the other side of my shadows, the argument continues.

"How dare you say that to me?" she asks before a pregnant pause that has my nerve endings tingling. Her next words make my blood run cold. "This is about her. I should have done something about her a long time ago."

"What are you saying?" I hear my aunt ask since I can no longer see them behind my wall of shadows. I don't know her well enough to read the emotion in her words, but there is a darkness to her voice.

"Did you think I didn't know what you'd done? You hadn't gone to see your worthless brother in years and suddenly you're traipsing off to Texas. No, not just traipsing, portaling, and using my daughter to do it without even telling me."

Alistaire begins to stir in my arms, a groan coming from him far before he lifts his head to look at me, but I can't focus on him right now. Every fiber of my psyche is fixated on the conversation happening beyond the dark mass swirling before me. I want to wipe it away, to see their faces, to wipe away the fear growing with each exchange.

"I do not answer to you, Adaire. You are our head priestess, but you are not my mother. What the hell has happened to you?"

A vicious laugh echoes through the darkness, and a shudder runs up my spine. Alistaire's arms wrap more tightly around me as if he's wanting to comfort me before he has fully recovered. Still, the women continue their spiteful argument as if they aren't discussing me.

"What's happened to me? What happened to protecting the family, the coven, those of us who follow the goddess? Where the fuck are your priorities, *Prima*?"

The final word was spat out with so much venom I thought my skin would burn from it.

"This family has always been my priority."

"Then why hide that *malcriada* from me, from the coven?"

The stone that has been sitting in the pit of my stomach grows, weighing me down and making me want to hurl. Everything in me screams for them to stop. My body trembles with the realization that I don't want to hear any more, but I can't speak, can't move, and it's not Alistaire's still-weak body holding me in place.

"Why bind her magic?" Adaire's question is like an arrow through my heart. It pierces it's target, and a tiny whimper of anguish leaves my mouth before I can stop it.

There's a gasp before my aunt responds. "You have no idea what you're talking about," she finally says, and though her words come out solidly, there's a tremble in them.

"Unlike you, Helga, the others prioritize the family, and they don't keep secrets."

"Josefina is family." This time, her voice is strong, and I feel the whiplash of her roiling emotions because mine are also all over the place. The ache of finding out that I've had magic all along, and the hurt of knowing I've never been acknowledged, let alone accepted, is balanced against the knowledge that my aunt did something to me out of familial love. "Did you torture her for the information?" That question pulls me out of my spiral. Torture who? Is torture something they do here?

"Do you think I would torture my niece? Like I told you, *Prima*, you are the only one who keeps secrets here."

Tía Helga snorts a laugh. "You're sorely mistaken if you think that's the truth. So she just came out and told you, huh?"

Her voice has shifted again, this time it sounds more resigned, and my mind starts trying to make sense of the accusations they've thrown at each other like they've handed me a bunch of puzzle pieces to put together. All I have to do is find the patterns. I don't know the family tree to know exactly how everyone else is directly related. The tight-knit connections that come from addressing everyone as either *tía* or *prima* makes it hard to parse out the details. I know that Serafina is Helga's daughter, but Poppa is her only sibling, so she's not the one they're talking about. Raquel, who I only saw for that short period and had little interaction with is Adaire's daughter. The resemblance is stark. They could be twins if not for Raquel's dyed hair. Then it hits me.

If no one else in the family knew I existed before I showed up in Onyx Junction, why would my aunt send someone else for me, someone who didn't seem surprised to meet me. Elinora. They have to be talking about her. If she already knew who I was and that something had been done to my magic, her behavior in San Antonio and responses to my magical *descontrol*, as she called it, make more sense than they did in the moment. It would also explain the way she looked at me with a twinge of guilt after she came to get me in Houston. Fuck, this is a mess.

I barely conclude that Elinora knows far more than she told me during the entire drive here when the continuing conversation breaks through my replaying of events. "She being your niece is the only reason she's still alive. That and her magic being bound." What? My heart starts racing at the implication. "If she cannot be contained...if she cannot control herself, then I will not be so merciful again."

"Merciful? You tried to kill her in my house. You tried to kill Alistaire to get to her."

"Ha! Who do you think told him to protect her? Me. Why do you think they know each other at all? Because I sent him there. What good would a demon-possessed guardian do me if I killed him? None."

Each successive question and answer is a gut punch. Though the last one tears my empathic soul to shreds, my heart had already shattered. In my arms, Alistaire shifts, and I realize I'd loosened my grip. When I look down, his eyes lock with mine. Guilt and anguish are written across his face, and it's the final straw to my tenuous control. Tears stream down my cheeks as sobs wrack my body. The shadows blocking us from the two women begin writhing wildly, but it's hard to figure out if all the movement is really happening or just a refraction from all my tears.

"*Muñeca,* look at me," Alistaire says softly, though not quite a whisper.

I shake my head. I don't want to look at him right now. I don't want to be here. I want to go home and be alone to, fuck, I don't know. Put myself back together? How the fuck will I ever be myself again when everything I thought I knew, thought I was, is a lie? I'm a witch of some sort, but not like my mother. She was some other kind of witch, but my father didn't know, but he knew about me enough to call my aunt, and she did what? She fucking took it all away somehow? My throat constricts at the gravity. I've had a sense of loneliness my entire life because of the isolation from any extended family, but it was nothing compared to the absolute desolation of finding out it was intentional.

Alistaire pulls from my limp arms, his hands gripping my shoulders to steady me. If I wasn't reeling from everything that's happened, I'd probably find the gesture endearing. I'd swoon at the fact that he's brushing off his own pain and discomfort to comfort me, but I can't. Not now. Not knowing that him showing up every time I needed him was less kismet and more nefarious. I was a job to him. He had been sent to... To do what? Protect me? Protect me from what? I never even saw shadows or had my emotions get carried away until I met him, until that day he sang to me.

"Josefina." His voice is soft, coaxing, and yet maddening. How dare he? My eyes snap up to his with a glare. "Please. *Por favor.*

Give me a chance to explain much better than those two are doing," he says, pointing his thumb over his shoulder.

Again, I shake my head at him. I don't want to hear what he has to say. What can he say? Can he say that his being outside my tent to help me celebrate the loneliest of birthdays was fate? Can he say that showing up at the bar was coincidence or taking me home after finding me in the alley with those guys who tried to attack me was more connection than just kindness? Can he say that the way he worshipped my body this very morning wasn't part of the job?

"Everything you're feeling right now, and I'm sure you're feeling everything, is all valid. You have every right to be angry, confused, hurt, disappointed, and whatever else is roiling through that beautiful head of yours, but you're only hearing bits of the story, *muñeca*."

"Stop calling me that," I say to the floor because I can't bear to look into his eyes. "I'm not a doll. I'm not a toy to be played with. I'm not delicate or breakable."

He says nothing at first, but then he sighs. "No, you're none of those things. I've never thought any of those things, but if you want me to stop, I will."

The tears start streaming hot and heavy again, and I can't stop my lip from quivering. Behind the curtain of shadows, the argument continues, but I can't hear them. The storm swirling inside me is too loud. My head reels, and I close my eyes against the impending nausea. A shiver runs through me, and I'm suddenly hot and cold at the same time. My breaths quicken, and my heart races. I've only passed out once before that I can remember, but I know it's coming. The last thing I remember is Alistaire's booming voice yelling my name.

CHAPTER 29
FEAR AND REMORSE
ALISTAIRE

"Josefina!" I call out as her eyes roll back in her head, and she starts to drop to the floor almost before I can catch her. I grab her and pull her into me, though I'm still dizzy from the force of Adaire's compulsion. That shit is disorienting and leaves me reeling for a good twenty minutes or so, but none of that matters right now because the only person I need to be coherent for is lying in my arms. Passed out and vulnerable. Thankfully, her heart rate has slowed down, but with that forced relaxation, her shadows have begun to fade, diminishing the safety barrier she put up between us and the witches on the other side.

Helga notices us first, her eyes widening in surprise, then concern. Finally, she turns her face to Adaire and a vaguely concealed threat leaves her lips, low and sharp. "If you even try to harm her, I will ruin you." I have no idea what she means by that, or what she could possibly do, but her words help relax some of my initial concern about our protection dissipating when I can't free my hands to fight off whatever projectiles or spells might come our way. I could flash us out of here, but we both have too much stuff in this house right now to keep them from finding us.

When the swirls of her shadows are nothing more than a thin

fog, Helga sweeps them away with her hand, and steps toward us. "What happened?" she asks, the concern evident. My own concern mingles with hers, and a knot forms in my throat, making it impossible for me to answer. The truth is that I don't really know what happened. One moment, she was protecting me, cradling me in her arms, and then she was frozen in an emotional breakdown until she just collapsed. Goddess that was fucking scary.

An unfamiliar burning stings the backs of my eyes, and I blink them hard. Once. Twice. Wetness caresses my cheek, and I want to brush it away, but I can't let her go. Helga's eyes flit back to Adaire whose face has softened slightly, and the head priestess nods once. Empathy pours from Helga, and she's by my side, her hand on Josefina's head faster than I can blink. I sink down to my knees, holding her against me, until I can sit with her in my lap. I probably should've chosen to sit on the sofa or a chair, but I couldn't will my feet to move.

Helga's other hand comes to my shoulder. "She's breathing, and her heartbeat is normal. Her skin is a bit clammy, but she will be alright." She says the words to me, yet it feels like she's also trying to will herself to believe it. "*Está bien,* Alistaire. I think she just passed out." I look up into her warm caramel eyes and swallow, trying to dislodge the lump holding both my words and my breaths back.

I repeat her words finally, and the tears take over. "She's fine."

It's been ages since I've cried, decades at least, but maybe a century or longer. I can't even say I remember why it happened the last time, maybe my father's death, maybe my mother's leaving. I don't know, but the feeling is so foreign that its presence now makes me angry. The fact that I'm crying over Josefina who's cradled in my lap when she should be on her feet demanding answers is killing me. We just talked about how strong she is, and yet, at this moment, she's fragile, delicate. I turn my glare on Adaire.

"This is your fault!"

At first, she stiffens. Whether it's from my words or the look I've leveled on her, I'm not sure. Until the other day when I declared my unyielding protection of Josefina, I'd never before defied the head priestess. My entire childhood had been preparation to serve the goddess and protect the coven like my father and all the fathers before him since the coven came to this realm as exiles from Illorum where they had once served a different goddess. I never got the whole story of the exile, but that didn't matter. I had pledged my loyalty and my life to their service, and I have been faithfully serving my post, taking on the powers bestowed upon our family ever since my father died.

"Watch yourself, Alistaire."

I avert my eyes from her, but not out of deference. No. She's already used her compulsion on my once, and while her powers aren't strong enough to make me do something physical, I need my head clear. I shake my head and give a sardonic laugh.

"Head Priestess, I would have answered your question. Hell, I had answered the question less than fifteen minutes before you stormed into my house. I'd have told you the truth, but..." I pause to look up, hoping she's actually listening to me, "but you chose to compel me, to try and pry a different answer from me that doesn't exist." She scowls, but I continue on. "I pledged my life to Umbra. I pledged my service to the protection of this coven, of this family, but you do not own me, and you do not control the demon inside of me." I watch as understanding dawns on her face.

"What demon?" Helga asks, shock evident in her tone and by the look on her face. "What did you do, Adaire?"

The head priestess says nothing, just stands there. A derisive laugh comes from me before I turn my attention back to Helga. "Our leader thought it a good idea to infect me with a parasite who now runs havoc through my body and mind. He's also very protective, angry, and determined." I cut my eyes to Adaire and sneer. "And he doesn't like you." Adaire sputters, worry emanating from her as she eyes me nervously, likely drawing the same conclusion that I have. My demon protected me from responding to her compulsion, though he couldn't keep it from freezing me in place.

Once again, Helga's eyes go wide. "You did what?"

"I told you that I will always do what needs to be done for the goddess and our family." Though she says the words with vehemence, the certainty with which she says them wavers. She is unsure under Helga's scrutiny.

"How? Is it reversible?" Her mouth opens and then closes again, like she wants to ask a litany of more questions but thinks better of it. After a couple seconds, though, she levels one more at the head priestess. "Why would you do that to him?"

Adaire sits on the ottoman directly behind her, and I hold my breath. Though she looks defeated, I know better than that. She is never down for long, and she's good at hiding her intentions. It's how she managed to infect me in the first place. Taking a deep breath, she lifts her eyes to mine for a brief moment before turning to face the other high priestess.

"Do not judge me too harshly, *Prima*. It was not my intention to hurt Alistaire, but I did not lie when I said I did so for our family, for the goddess."

Helga looks in my direction, sadness visible in her eyes. Maybe I was wrong in my thinking that Gabriela is the only empathic person in the entire coven. Helga might not know what happened or why, but her support has me breathing a little easier. I nod my thanks and shift to a better sitting position with Josefina cradled in my arms. I need to hear what the high priestess has to say, but my priority is this beautiful woman who held me up for the second time when Adaire bombarded me with her magic.

For the briefest second, my mind slips to thoughts of my father, and I wonder if he had been subjected to similar treatment during his tenure as guardian. He had always been reverent in his discussions of the coven, especially of the high priestess he'd served, Adaire's mother, Tempris de Incendia, no, de Umbra. In fact, there was a time when I wondered whether he'd been secretly in love with the woman. No, I can't imagine she had treated him as harshly as Adaire has done me. Would he be heartbroken about the way things have changed, or would he somehow think me responsible? Thankfully, Adaire starts talking again before I can spiral on that thought.

"When our mothers came from Illorum, the goddess blessed them with a guardian and bestowed that guardian with the training and powers needed to protect us."

"I know this."

Adaire cuts her off with a wave of her hand. "Yes, you know they exist, but you were not there to hear *Mamá*'s lament that they were human, dying too quickly, and leaving her responsible to protect and train their sons before they were ready to take up the mantle." She rings her hands together. "Alistaire's father lasted far longer than most. He had been able to train Alistaire with the skills needed, and he was here for my transition to Head Priestess. But his human body wouldn't last forever. He had been my quiet protector, mentor, and guide through it all, and then he was dying."

Once again, the sting of tears assaults my eyes as she recounts her own fear and loss. I had no idea she revered my father so much. My heart aches anew for my own loss of the man who had been my compass for so long, and now I wonder at the depth of their relationship.

"I promised Brevard that I would take care of his son and ensure that the goddess's blessing made him strong enough to withstand whatever came his way. As I watched Brevard wither away in his illness and thought of Alistaire becoming our guardian and how very few lived to old age, I got scared. *Me dio miedo* that Raquel would not have anyone to help her transition to head priestess, that she would be left to learn and train, protect and monitor at the same time on her own."

She raised imploring eyes to Helga who remained steadfast,

letting her get it all out, and I was grateful. All these years I've been angry at her for what she'd done to me. All these years fighting this demon to maintain dominance over my own psyche. All this time having no idea why she chose to punish me. I might not understand her reasons or forgive her in the end, but I need to know why.

"I begged the goddess to bestow longevity on him, to remove the limits of his human life."

"You asked the goddess to make him immortal? Adaire, that can't be done. We're not even immortal."

Adaire swallows, and I see the remorse written on her face. This is the first time I've ever seen her demonstrate anything other than control and contempt. "I know," she says, "but I was desperate." She takes in a deep breath and lets it out slowly. She seems to age significantly in the span of that single breath as if the weight of what's coming next is too heavy a burden.

CHAPTER 30
TOGETHER YET ALONE
JOSEFINA

"Wake up, child. You're sleeping through the good part."

The voice is muffled, soft and sweet, but unclear, as if I'm hearing it through water. I try to open my eyes, but they're sealed shut like when you've slept long and hard. "I can't open my eyes," I whisper, not sure where I am or who I'm talking to.

Whoever is talking to me laughs, and the sound is both alluring and unnerving. "You can. You just don't want to. You just stood up to some of the strongest witches in your realm. What have you to fear here?"

My realm? Here? I will my eyes to open, but nothing happens. Panic begins to creep up from my stomach as I realize that not only can I not open my eyes, but I don't feel my arms or legs. I feel nothing except an emptiness in my abdomen slowly being suffocated by fear.

The sound of the woman...person...entity...I'm not sure who or what is talking to me, but the sound of them sucking their teeth at me has irritation mixing with the fear. "I find it hard to believe that a Daughter of Umbra would be so weak as to let fear determine her fate." She pauses for a moment, and I somehow sense her closeness as if she's leering over me. "Ah, but you are not just a Daughter of Umbra, are you?"

The smell of a candle just as its wick fizzles out assaults my nose when her breath touches my face, and my eyes fly open. My chest seizes as I stare into my own face, or one that is so similar I'm unsure if it's a reflection.

"There you are, daughter. I was wondering when I'd get to meet you. Time passes so strangely in your human realm, like the snap of a finger here, and yet, it feels like I've been waiting for ages." There's no emotion on that face, which tightens my chest even more. I've never been so emotionless, so desolate. "Do you recognize me?"

I start to shake my head, but her eyes harden, a flicker of fire alight in their pupils. I huff out a breath, as much to steady myself as to buy time to create an answer. "You look like......me," I finally say, and she smiles, though her face remains impassive. How is that even possible? There is a fire in her eyes, but the rest of her face appears lifeless, moving normally but portraying nothing.

"Ah, and you have seen me elsewhere, not just in your reflection, haven't you?"

It takes several moments of working through my thoughts to land on the... "The portrait on Alistaire's wall. That is a portrait of you?"

This time, when her lip quirks up I feel something besides the stony indifference, and I know that me being here is not a good idea.

Alistaire

Helga moves to Adaire's side and puts a hand on her shoulder. The tension in the room may have lessened with the head priestess's confession, but my body feels like a bow strung taut, like I could snap at any moment. My demon must feel it too because he's pacing, his energy growing exponentially, making my skin stretch too thin until I'm watching for fissures to open and the truth of what I am now to spill out onto the floor. Then Josefina shifts in my arms, her body twitching as if caught in a dream. Her eyes dance behind their lids, and her breaths pick up. I pull her tight against me and once again wish I could whisk her away, but we both seem to be captive to this moment...together yet alone.

Adaire's voice breaks through my melancholy, and I refocus on the conversation happening a mere 10 feet away. "Umbra told me that she had no control over the lifespan of humans. She said there was nothing she could do to help, but I couldn't accept that. I couldn't accept that there was nothing to be done and that Brevard's son could be here today and gone the next." She looks in my direction, but her gaze seems to go through me as if she's seeing something, or maybe someone, else.

The head priestess continues her lament, but I'm no longer listening. Instead, my mind tries to piece together the picture she's painted of her relationship with my father. My mother left not long after I was born. According to my father, she hadn't understood what it meant to be the wife of a guardian or that my father's loyalty would be to the goddess first. When my heart broke to learn that she had left us, my father told me she'd wanted to take me with her but it was forbidden. *Our bloodline belongs to Umbra* he'd said, his voice somber. I'd taken his tone to mean he regretted having to make that sacrifice, but maybe it was resignation, an understanding that he was destined to be alone. Turning my attention back to the priestesses, I can't help but wonder whether he was ever really alone.

"So, I found a scholar, someone old enough to know the old texts and to have heard the old tales. He told me that the only way to extend a human's life is for them to either lose their humanity, like vampires, or to become host to another being with a longer lifespan." She looks between Helga and I, her eyes pleading. I stare back at her, brows furrowed. Does she really expect me to agree she'd made the right choice. Either I had to die, or I had to be possessed. No, neither of those options is one I would have chosen for myself or anyone else.

"I wanted to keep you alive. Letting a vampire turn you was too risky. Too many humans completely succumb to a full death, or they become untethered. You... Well, I couldn't take that chance."

Incredulity courses through me and anger flairs. "You had no right," I say quietly.

Her shoulders droop slightly before she stiffens her spine and draws them back. "I gave you added strength, more powers, and a longer life."

"And I'm supposed to be grateful that you used me as an experiment, so I could be your servant for longer than was my duty? Am I supposed to appreciate the daily loss of myself as this demon and I meld together? Should I not have had a say in what happened to me?" The demon whimpers inside me, but I don't have the energy to tend to his needs right now. I already know he hates Adaire as much as I do, though his reasons might be different. That doesn't mean he gets to decide how I feel about this situation.

"He's right, Adaire," Helga interjects before the head priestess can respond. "We were exiled from Illorum along with our mothers for the acts of one priestess. None of us were given a chance to choose or repent. We've remained exiled for centuries now. Why would you condemn him to a legacy like that?" Though her voice is soft, the question hits its mark, and tears stream down Adaire's face.

I want to feel something for the head priestess, but I don't have it in me. Her selfishness has ruined my life, and her treatment of Josefina and her father before her is responsible for whatever is happening with this precious woman in my lap who continues to whimper lightly and tremble all over.

"You do know that had I not given you that demon, you might not be alive now to protect her." There is a barb attached to that last word, but I can't tell if it's meant for me or Josefina. Either way, my demon snarls, and I narrow my eyes at her.

"*Prima!*" Helga yells. "It's time to go home. You've done enough damage here."

She must have been reading my mind because I was seconds from telling them both to get the fuck out of my cabin. I want them both gone. I need time and space to process. I need to be able to focus on Josefina and figure out how to pull her from whatever dream state has her. Adaire lifts her chin defiantly, more like a petulant child rather than the nearly two-centuries-old head priestess of the goddess Umbra. It would be laughable if she wasn't causing so much havoc in the lives of others.

"I'll leave when he answers the question. How did you get that portrait of Incendia?"

CHAPTER 31

INCENDIA

JOSEFINA

"Walk with me, daughter." The goddess holds out her hand, helping me to stand. "You have lain here long enough, and it will be time to return to your realm soon."

"Where are we?"

She smiles, a hint of teeth showing but her eyes never change, those emotions a steady blank slate that makes my insides curl. "We're in Illorum, the home of your foremothers, all of your foremothers."

"I don't understand."

She pats my hand where it sits at her wrist. "So much has been taken from you, daughter. So much was taken from all of you when you were taken from me."

My brows furrow at her riddle-like statements. The repetitions and phraseology twisting and turning in my head, but I dare not say anything for fear she will leave me alone here. Here. Where is here? Illorum. The name frolics in the back of my mind like it's searching for a soft place to rest. It dances back and forth, flickering the way candles do in a light wind. Shadows dance around it, weaving through the trail of light left in its wake. A tune plays in the background, and I find myself humming along, coaxing words from their hiding place in my memories.

Illorum, the home my ancestors spurned
Illorum, the place I hope to return
Illorum, please wait, don't forget about me
Illorum, I'm late, but I've got the key

Momma's voice sings through my thoughts, bringing tears to my eyes. She would sing this tune that I thought was nothing more than a made-up lullaby each time we made candles. There would be the most serene look on her face as she dipped into the wax and sung along.

"My mother knew of this place?"

"Your mother was born in this place. Just as your grandmothers and their grandmothers. She was a Daughter of Incendia, as you are, but you are so much more than that now. You have both the light and dark in you, fire and shadow. Who knew that the petty grievance of a lover's quarrel would create such an amazing creature."

Though her face remains impassive, there is a sarcastic lilt to her tone that catches me off guard. "Daughter of Incendia?" I ask, not having heard that name before.

"I am Incendia, the Goddess of Fire, and your mother was one of my priestesses, as was her mother before her."

I look up into her flickering irises and recognition dawns on me. One day, Poppa caught me staring into my reflection in the mirror behind where two candles burned. He quickly blew out the candles and shuffled me off to bed. I spent the night listening to the muffled voices of my parents arguing, and that was when he started trying to steer me away from the candles that I love so much. But what I remember most is watching the lights flickering in my own eyes as I stared at myself, much like the reflection she presents standing in front of me.

"You were there," I say. "Watching me through the mirror, staring back at me beyond the flickering candlelight."

"I've always been here, child. Always waiting."

"Why?"

"Now, that is a question to be answered another day. For now, know that your purpose is greater than what any of the de Umbra coven try to tell you. They were once mine too, you know." I open my mouth to ask another question, but she holds up a hand. "Another day, perhaps. First, there are things you must do, like complete your Ascension."

"Ascension?"

"Yes, you must take your place as a Daughter of Umbra."

"But..."

"You are mine, daughter, but you must also accept my cousin's gifts. The shadows are drawn to your light, to the flickers of your flame, but they will only follow you if you accept them as well."

"Another riddle?" I ask with a scowl.

"A lesson. The first of many." She leads me back to the room where I'd first awoken. "Now, sleep here, so you may awaken at home."

A listaire

"Incendia," I breath out. Though it's barely audible, both witches look at me. I know the name. Of course, I learned the name from my father, but I had no idea who the woman in my dreams was when I'd painted her. Now, it makes perfect sense. Well, it makes sense who she is but not why she came to me. My demon lets out a sigh that is almost a purr of contentment. I'd always heard that demons were cursed souls, but sometimes I swear this one is actually a cat of some sort—fickle and assholish but vigilant and possessive. He gives a low chuckle that vibrates up my spine, and my lip quirks up on one side.

"What's so funny?" Adaire asks.

I look up at her with a smirk. "When you decided to curse me with eternal life, or whatever the fuck this possession is, did you ever once think 'Hey, where's that demon from?'" Her brows droop as she mulls over my question, and from the corner of my eye, I notice Helga's head snapping to her.

"You gave him a demon's curse?" Helga asks, almost appalled at the idea. *You and me both*, I think to myself.

"No," I say with a mirthless chuckle. "She cursed me with a demon." Within me, the demon balks, but I ignore him. He and I have begun to work through our forced proximity within the confines of my body and mind, but that does not mean that I don't still resent the intrusion.

"Are you fucking kidding me, Adaire? He's lying, right? Please tell me he's lying." Her tone isn't angry. It also isn't quite the surprise I'd have expected.

I let my eyes fall on hers and flick the demon's shackles just a bit, enough to have my eyes turn red. Helga and Adaire both gasp, and Adaire jumps up, her hands splaying cautiously. Her fear has me laughing out loud.

"You created this. Why so worried? Wasn't this what you wanted?"

She scowls, but I laugh again. It's so ridiculous that she cringes at one little glimpse of my demon, but she's the one who gave him to me like a pet I can never outlive.

"Alistaire," Helga admonishes. "I understand your frustration, but Adaire is still our head priestess, and you will be respectful." I scoff but say nothing more when she turns back to her cousin. "I'm going to assume he's telling the truth since you haven't refuted it. Does the goddess know you considered her gifts to Alistaire insufficient?"

Adaire gasps and then snaps her mouth shut. Holy shit! I hadn't even thought of it that way. I've been so angry and felt so disrespected that I hadn't considered Umbra's response. If I'm being truthful, I believed it sanctioned by the goddess and resented her too.

"She told me she couldn't help," Adaire says, "but she didn't tell me I couldn't find another means."

"Do you really think that her telling you she can't do it means she condones the act?," Helga asks. "No, of course you don't, which is why you haven't told her. Assuming, she doesn't already know and isn't looking for a way to punish you. By the goddess, *Prima*. Wait, are you the only one who knows what happened?"

The head priestess stares at her cousin for long enough to make me uncomfortable. The unspoken words thickening the air throughout the cabin until I wonder if she's not going to answer at all. As I watch and wait, my breath held in anticipation, Josefina's body jumps, and I barely hold her still, afraid she'll fall off my lap or hit her head on the furniture next to us. Once I have her steadied again, I look down, and her beautiful blue eyes stare back at me. She blinks a few times as if trying to reorient herself. I give her a tentative smile, but gesture for her to remain silent when Adaire opens her mouth to speak again.

With a sigh, she breaths out a simple "No." Helga stands, hands going to her hips before she begins pacing back and forth from the sitting area to the kitchen. It would be comical if her super speed hadn't kicked in until I began to wonder if she might literally wear through the floor. "Stop and listen, please. I needed some help. Artificial possession requires a spell stronger than I can produce." She holds up her hands. "You know I'm just not good at that." Helga's feet stop moving so quickly her body tilts as if she's about to topple forward from the brake, and she stares at Adaire, watching and waiting. Then Adaire says the eight words that might just cause the roof to explode off the cabin, "I took a page from your book, *Prima*."

Josefina

I take in slow, even breaths. My stomach lurches, and my head spins as I come back into my body. At least, that's what I assume is happening to me. When I finally open my eyes, I'm surprised to find Alistaire holding me cradled against himself. He hasn't noticed me yet, his eyes transfixed on something happening over my shoulder. I don't know how long I've been laying here in his arms, but my body aches. Still, I don't move. Nausea threatens, and I don't want to break his concentration. Though sound hasn't returned to my consciousness, whatever is happening is intense from the look on his face.

When the sounds from the room finally blast through, my body jerks involuntarily, drawing his attention. His eyes go wide, and then he smiles. I breathe a sigh of relief, feeling whole in more ways than one. But he doesn't pull me tighter or kiss me or even say anything. Instead, he gestures for me to remain silent before turning his attention back to the room. That's when I hear Adaire's contemptuous tone, "I took a page from your book, *Prima*." My brows furrow, and my nose scrunches. Are the cousins still arguing? No, they couldn't possibly still be arguing after all these hours.

"*¿De qué hablas?* I have never gotten involved with demons or any of that shit."

"Language, *Prima*," the head priestess says sarcastically, and my eyes roll.

"I am not one of the girls, Adaire."

"*Qué* girls?" Her brow raises in challenge, and I think to tell them both to stop acting like children when the conversation shifts until my name pulls me from my still groggy state.

"Get to the point," *Tía* Helga retorts.

"The point is that I'm not the only one using magic beyond my control. You found a way to bind Josefina's magic. That took a pretty powerful spell, right?" Adaire snorts a laugh. "Neither of us have been great at spell work, so it didn't take a genius to figure out who you had assist in your secret."

I quickly close my eyes again in case either of them decides to look toward where Alistaire still holds me. The house could cave in, and I'd still be homed in to hear this explanation.

"That was to protect her, not to enslave her. You don't curse someone with a demon for protection."

"*¡Qué protección!* She nearly killed multiple people with her shadows, and from what I hear, it wasn't even the shadows you bound." There's a slight pause in the conversation, and it takes all of my willpower not to open my eyes. Thankfully, the silence only lasts a few moments. "What exactly were you called for that first time, Helga? What was Daegal afraid of?"

My breaths freeze, and I squeeze my eyes shut. Alistaire's thumb sweeps back and forth against the skin of my upper arm where he's holding me. The gentle movement ticks the minutes like a clock's pendulum as I wait.

CHAPTER 32

AN ACT OF LOVE

ALISTAIRE

This conversation is absolute torture, and if the tightness in Josefina's features are any indication, she's in turmoil too. Still, the two women volley accusations back and forth without saying anything directly. Between my anxiety over how these answers might affect Josefina and the erratic pacing of my demon, I want to scream at them to spit the shit out already, but I hold my tongue. I've spent my entire life knowing that every single one of these women is stubborn as hell. It's in their DNA. With that thought in mind, I look down at Josefina's beautiful face, and I have to smile. There's a level of stubbornness in her too, but those glimpses of defiance turn me on more than piss me off. The same cannot be said for the elders.

"It wasn't Daegal who called me," Helga says, breaking the silence, and time stands still. I can tell Adaire is just as shocked as I am, and Josefina has gone deathly still. "Corinne was the one who called me."

The next twenty minutes make me angry and break my heart all at the same time. It's like the women have forgotten Josefina and I are here in the room as they discussed hidden identities, magical gifts, and temperamental goddesses. Josefina silently sobs in my arms. Even my demon is subdued throughout the entire ordeal, and I finally feel something more than overwhelming resentment at his presence. He's keeping me settled while I hold my *muñeca* and try to be her anchor within the waves of emotion washing over us all.

"You see, blocking her magic was an act of love, a request from her mother. We have always been so sure that magic wouldn't be passed down through the males in our lineage that I had no way to account for her possibly having shadows. The bonding was supposed to allow her to live out her life safely as a mundane without Daegal ever finding out that Corinne was a cursed Daughter of Incendia as we all had been at one time." Helga stands and starts pacing. "She knew she didn't have much longer and didn't want him to resent her after she was gone. She didn't want Josefina to fully awaken alone. In Corinne's own words, 'it was better to have no magic than to be alone when the flames consumed her.'"

"By the goddess, that is..." She pauses, her breath hitching with emotion. "I'm not sure I could have denied her either. The secrets, though, Prima. We have all pledged to keep no secrets from each other within the coven."

I look up in time to see Helga glare at the head priestess, and I nearly laugh. Emotions are definitely high when I can't maintain an even keel. I was trained to tamp down my emotional responses. A guardian must be level-headed. All decisions must consider how they benefit or potentially harm the coven or somehow dishonor the goddess. That day I sang to Josefina in her tent was the first time I'd felt any spontaneous emotion since my father died...well...other than anger and fear. Those emotions have been my regular companions since the possession. My mind wanders through the years and all my training. Then I flash to the day I was blessed by the goddess to take my father's position. That proud moment didn't last long as it was shortly followed by the possession spell I endured that gave me this demon. Finally, I land on the day Adaire sent me to Houston for the first time.

There was an air about the head priestess that I couldn't quite understand. She had been unreasonable with everyone who'd come to see her. I had already determined that the day was a rare one anyway because she'd kept me by her side the entire day. Normally, I was only called when there was something for me to do. I'm not a glorified bodyguard, at least not in the strict definition of one. A guardian protects the best interest of the goddess and her priestesses, not individuals, so I was completely caught off guard when Adaire sent me to Texas to watch for one young woman who might have untrained magic.

It took an entire year before I found her, or should I say felt her. I walked into the lecture hall the same way I had many lecture halls on the campus. As an adjunct professor, I used my early career status to gain entry into various classrooms and content areas looking for this one woman. No description. No details. No name. I was simply told that she would show up on that campus as a student and my job was to watch for any signs of magic. I didn't need any signs. Her magic called to me like a siren, and it was all I could do to not turn around and stare at her throughout the entire lecture. Instead, my entire body sizzled at the feel of her eyes on my back for the full hour. Then, when I caught a glimpse of her, a manifestation of the woman from my dreams, I was a goner.

Still, her dual nature explains why the essence of her unreleased magic was so strong, like a potent perfume. It's truly surprising other paranormal entities hadn't seeped from the woodwork to claim her. Or maybe that was the power of the bonding, and it was only because of my demon that I could sense her. My jaw ticks as I mull over that thought. If she hadn't attracted others, there must be a reason why I couldn't seem to stay away, why I'm still drawn to her.

Silence descends on the room again, and I realize I haven't been listening to the women anymore. Looking up, my eyes meet theirs, and it's like they're seeing me for the first time. My demon lifts his head and stiffens as he recognizes the change that's taken over. Even Josefina stirs under the heavy weight of the moment.

"Leave my house," I growl out, tired of them and their back and forth. Tired of their bullshit. Tired of being unable to comfort the woman in my arms. Josefina's palm lifts to my cheek, once again trying to comfort me when her whole world has been shuffled around because of the actions of her parents and this coven. I should be comforting her, not the other way around.

"Josefina!" Helga cries. "Thank the goddess, you're awake. How are you feeling?" She steps closer to us, leaning down as if to touch her, and a snarl leaves my throat, causing her to jump back.

Mine, the demon inside me growls, and I'm in complete agreement with him. Adaire's eyes flash black, and Helga looks stricken, but I couldn't give two fucks. *Estas viejas* have done enough damage for one day. Shit, for multiple lifetimes. They both look toward Josefina who wriggles herself out of my grasp, leaving me as empty on the inside as my arms.

"*Tía*, what did you mean about the flames consuming me? You've told me so little and kept so many secrets, but I need to know."

Sadness shows in Helga's expression, but instead of answering, she shakes her head, and I have to bite my tongue. After all this, all the bullshit, she still won't directly tell Josefina the truth. "It doesn't matter," she finally says. "It can't happen now."

"With all due respect," I say, standing to help Josefina get to her feet after having been passed our for so long, "how do you know that for sure?"

"Watch yourself, Alistaire," Adaire admonishes, likely hearing my frustration.

Though she seems deflated after all the revelations and reprimands, I don't back down. "*Mira*, it sounds to me like neither one of you did your due diligence before playing with magic you can't control, so *perdona el desconfío*," I say with a shrug. Josefina sways on her feet, and I pull her into my side. "We could probably trust you more if you'd have actually included us in the conversation, or even willingly accepted that maybe, just maybe, you made a mistake."

At my side, Josefina lifts her eyes, looking from one priestess to the other. Neither elder says anything until finally she groans at their reticence and storms off into the bedroom, slamming the door behind her.

Adaire opens her mouth to say something, and I hold up my hand. "You had your chance. Now leave." Indignation surges in her cheeks, so I let my eyes turn red to match, a challenge to the power she thinks she has over me. No doubt, I'll have to answer for my behavior before Umbra, but I will not beg forgiveness from Adaire.

Helga puts her hand on Adaire's arm. "*Tiene razón, Prima.* Today has been a lot for everyone, and it's been too much for some of us." She then turns her attention to me. "*Cuídamela.*" I say nothing, but when she looks like she's wanting to say more, I nod in confirmation simply to get her to leave faster. The fact she has the audacity to think I wouldn't watch over Josefina pisses me off. "Oh, and Alistaire," she says as she pulls the head priestess toward the door, "she has to complete the Ascension rite. There's no protecting her from that. No spell. No wishing. No amount of anger or resentment. Umbra will require it. Please talk her into returning, so we can prepare her."

Though I've never been privy to the specifics of the ritual, I had heard of one witch refusing to ascend. According to the story I overheard, her shadows had literally torn her apart. I shudder at the thought of Josefina being destroyed by her own magic and swallow the lump in my throat. "How long?"

Adaire's answer comes on the wind as they're both swept out of the house, "Three days."

What the fuck? My eyes go wide, and my heart races. Is that three days to get back or three days before the ritual? I look toward the bedroom and will my breaths to slow. Closing my eyes, I send a prayer to the goddess. *Umbra, give me strength to face down this woman and talk her into pledging herself to you.* As the words float off, my eyes catch on the portrait above the mantle. Incendia stares down at me, a warning in her fiery eyes. Neither goddess will forgive me if I get this wrong.

CHAPTER 33

GIVE ME THAT LEG

JOSEFINA

I have no idea how long I've been here in the tub when the front door slams shut. Ten minutes? Two hours? Time is irrelevant as the day's events play through my mind at a merciless speed. Everything is a blur, and yet I can't seem to stop the constant loop. I slide further down in the water when the air cools my skin enough to cause goosebumps, but then I'm suddenly too hot and need to sit up to keep from melting.

The shift in energy tells me the two witches have left the cabin and the immediate area around the cabin. I don't know that I've ever noticed how magic feels or considered that a shift in energy might be something more than just my imagination, but this change is unmistakable. It's like the knot that had been tied around my chest relaxes slightly, and I'm able to take a deep calming breath for the first time. Holding in the air, I slide under the water, inundating myself completely and shutting out all the world's noise.

When I come back to the surface, warmth cocoons me, and I let out an audible sigh as Alistaire's hands begin massaging my shoulders. He slides his feet down into the tub on either side of my hips while his hands work magic on my taut muscles. A moan escapes my lips followed quickly by a slight giggle. He kisses the top of my head before removing his hands from my shoulders. I start to protest when he squirts shampoo into my hair and begins working his fingers through the tresses. Holy fuck. If 'I've died and gone to heaven' was achievable while still breathing, Alistaire washing my hair would be my heaven. I moan again, and this time he laughs. The sound is musical and life-giving.

"Fuck, I would let you do this every day," I say before my brain registers the words, but I won't take them back.

"Done." His answer comes just as easily. "Now lay back."

I relax back into the water, and his hands work through the strands, rinsing the shampoo out before he motions for me to sit up again. Just as meticulously, he works the conditioner through my hair, running his fingers between each strand. The man is a dream. After the second rinse, the sound of another bottle opening and closing rings through the silence of the bathroom. Then his hands and a cloth are roving over my body, starting at my neck and working ever so slowly down over one shoulder and then the other. He pulls up each of my arms and runs the sudsy cloth over every inch before repeating the movements. I wait with bated breath to see where he's going to go next.

The water must be boiling because I am on fire. I can't think straight, and my breaths are ragged. His hand grabs the rag and slowly drags it across my chest, just above my breasts, and my breath hitches. The exfoliation only adding to the sensations. He slips the rag between my breasts, stroking from just above my belly button up to the tip of my neck, and I have to wet my lips. Just when I think he's going to run his hands across my already peaking nipples, he pulls his hands away, and I whimper at the loss. Again, he laughs, and I have the urge to elbow him in his... I don't even finish the thought when two cloth-covered hands assault my breasts.

Fuck me, the sensation is exquisite. The cloths have just the right amount of roughness to them to match the pressure of his strong hands as he kneads and squeezes. I squirm in response, and then he pinches both of my nipples through the rag, nearly sending me over the edge.

"Alistaire," I say, his name a plea and praise at the same time.

"*Muñeca,* my name on your lips is the thing dreams are made of."

A twinge of guilt filters through the arousal-filled haze. I'd been angry earlier, but I definitely did not want him to stop calling me *muñeca*. I'd willingly be his toy and let him play with me all day long. His hands washing my hair and caressing my body are an act of claiming because there's no way I'll be good for anyone else after him. I can't lean into the negative feelings, though because his hands trail down over my stomach, lavishing attention on every roll and dip between my breasts and where I need him to touch most.

Leaning back against him, I'm keenly aware of the fact that he's still fully dressed, and his clothes are soaked. He doesn't seem to mind, though, as his hands continue exploring. Then he gives me a direction that has me soaked in a way that has nothing to do with the water I'm lying in.

"Give me that leg."

listaire

The need to push her over the ledge is driving me mad. I want her undone. I want to feel her release and then hold her until she falls asleep in my arms like she's meant to, not like she'd been most of the day. The fear of having her with me and yet so far removed is unbearable. Add to that, all the lies, secrets, and ways the two priestesses have fucked with our lives. I'm surprised I'm still able to think coherently. But right now, the only thing I want to think about is making Josefina cry out my name.

She tentatively pulls her knee up and out of the water. I'd not been able to have her in many positions like I'd wanted to this morning before I'd panicked, but I'd seen enough to guess at her flexibility. I grab the outside of her thigh and pull it high, trying to ignore the ache in my cock at the need to slide inside her in this position. She lets out a small squeak of surprise but doesn't try to pull away.

"Good girl."

Her gasp at my praise has all kinds of thoughts playing through my mind, and my demon purrs in anticipation. It's unnerving to feel him as part of me, responding alongside me, and yet recognizing him as his own entity. I push all thoughts of him to the side and refocus on the beautiful woman at my fingertips.

"Does my *muñeca* have a naughty side to her?" I ask, dropping my lips to the rim of her ear. Josefina shakes her head slightly, but I see her lashes flutter from my vantage point. Every move she makes, no matter how subtle, is mine to observe, and I will willingly explore every inch, every desire, every need she has. "*No me mientes*, Josefina. Your body gives you away," I say with a tweak of her nipple before returning to my job of washing her from head to toe.

Running my hands up and down her leg, I revel in the feel of her twitches when my fingertips graze the skin behind her knee and the instep of her foot. She's too enthralled in the experience to complain about the slight tickling, and I have a feeling her heightened arousal makes the tingles less pain than pleasure. The light moan she releases has my body responding, and I have to remind myself that this is for her as I give the same attention to her other leg.

This time, when I swipe the rag down from her red toenails to her thigh, I let the cloth drag across her slit, tickling along her exposed clit. Her breath hitches, and I smile. "Hold your leg up for me." She tilts her head back slightly, and I hold her gaze for a several seconds before sliding my hand around the outside of her thigh to push my fingers further between her legs and squeeze her inner thighs. My knuckles graze against her pussy, and her eyes flutter. "Eyes on me, *muñeca*." The gorgeous blue irises lock on my face, and her pupils widen. My fingers slide along her slit, as I cup her plump lips. My mouth waters with the desire to drown myself in her pussy. "You're so beautiful, Josefina. So fucking beautiful." Her lip quirks up on one side, but I don't give her time to focus on my words. Instead, I slide two fingers into her, eliciting a gasp.

"Alistaire," she breaths out, but it's not enough.

I need to hear her scream my name not just whisper it like a secret. My fingers work in and out of her tight pussy while my thumb finds her clit, making small circles. Water splashes over the sides of the tub as she writhes, and her leg starts to drop. I stop my movements, holding myself perfectly still within her. Her hips start to move, trying to find the friction I'm withholding. I grab her chin with my other hand, turning her face fully in my direction, and I shake my head at her.

"What did I say, *muñeca*?" Her brows furrow, and mine lift in response. Then I let my gaze glide down her body to where her leg is bent, knee nearly back in the water. When my eyes find hers again, her nostrils flare. Whether with need or defiance, I don't care. She purses her lips, and I smirk. This challenge is already won, and we both know it. At least that's what I think until she opens her mouth.

She bites her lip and flutters her lashes. "You said I was naughty, professor."

I can't tell if it's me or my demon whose tether snaps, but a growl leaves my lips moments before my mouth crashes onto hers. My hand that had been holding her face dips down to knead her breast, rolling the taut nipple between my thumb and forefinger at the same time the fingers of my other hand work in and out of her at a pace that has her moaning within seconds.

"Yes, Professor. Please."

"Please what?"

"Make me come." No shyness. No uncertainty. Nothing but unwavering need, and I want nothing more than to fulfill her desire.

I curl my fingers, so they rub along the spot that has her panting and use my thumb to rub her clit. At the same time, my other hand leaves her breast and comes up to wrap around the base of her neck. "Fuuuuck," she breaths out, and time stands still. Nothing else exists except the feel of her. The tightening of her muscles. The bob of her throat as she swallows beneath my palm. The sting of her nails digging into my forearms as she comes undone.

CHAPTER 34

STOP BEING NICE

JOSEFINA

Adrenaline courses through my veins, shocking me awake. The room is dark. Silent except for the sound of Alistaire's breathing. *What in the world was it that woke me, that has my heart beating wildly?* I take in the shadowy room, half expecting something to manifest from the darkness, but there's nothing. Even my own shadows lie dormant. Then I feel it.

The bed starts to quake. My first thought is to grab for Alistaire, but the moment my hand touches his chest, fear fills the room. His body jumps, and his arms thrash wildly. I manage to put up my hands to protect my face, but the worst isn't over. Suddenly, he lets out a guttural scream of terror and agony that freezes my soul. His head swings back and forth against the pillow. Tears stream down his face, and my own eyes burn. When he starts thrashing again, I reach out and try to hold his arms in place, putting my weight against him, but it doesn't stop the mayhem happening.

"Alistaire," I whisper, afraid to scare him more than he already seems to be. When nothing changes, I say a little more forcefully, "Professor, please." Still, he continues to pull away from me, flailing at whatever demons are plaguing his mind. "Please," I cry out, my fear awash with his.

There's a shift as power surges through the room, my power. Shadows pull from the corners and crawl along the furniture. Tendrils wrap around him, coiling like a snake and pinning his arms to his half-naked body. I fold myself over the shadows, covering him like a weighted blanket and holding on until he settles. I have no idea how long it takes, but eventually he lets out a sigh, and his body goes slack. Several minutes, maybe an hour, pass before his eyes blink open and find mine. He wets his lips with his tongue and says my name. It comes out as a question, though he's not asking who I am. He's taking in the scene before him...well...on top of him.

"Shhhh Professor," I say before he can ask any other questions I might not be able to answer, and he might not be ready to discuss.

Smiling down from where my body still pins his tied-up form to the bed, I lower my lips to his. My kiss might not be able to take away the nightmares, but it might relieve some of the residual emotions still haunting his eyes. Whatever happened to him, whatever he was reliving, was terrible. His lips open at my prodding, and I nip, lick, and suck my way to another sigh from him. It's a gift I want to receive over and over again. I want to be his safe harbor, the light in his darkness. He's not the only one able to care for and protect another.

"Muñ..." I cut him off with another kiss.

When I let us both up for air again, I give him an ultimatum I doubt he'll oppose. "Unless you're going to tell me what you want me to do to you, Professor, *no digas nada.*"

He clamps his lips shut, but the glint in his eyes says he's weighing the options. I watch him with one brow arched. Finally, he nods in acquiescence, and I kiss him deeply, a reward for being a good boy. The thought sends heat to my core at the same time I want to laugh. I have never been dominant. Hell, I don't want to dominate anyone. But there's something about this man giving himself over to me, being tied in my shadows, even if it's for our mutual protection, that is a heady experience.

"You've been so good to me," I purr, kissing my way over his jaw and down his neck. "Finding me when I need you most." My shadows recede from his chest as my lips find the hollow at the base of his neck. I lick along his clavicle, slowly working my way down. "Making sure I'm safe from myself."

Crawling backwards, I, and the shadows, make my way down to his stomach, which quivers at each flick of my tongue. His breaths come out in pants, but they're much different than they had been earlier. This time, there's no fear, only anticipation. His beautiful eyes are almost completely black, glowing with a hint of red, which I've come to learn is him trying to hold himself back. I'm not arrogant enough to believe he couldn't easily overpower me and my shadows, especially since my control of them is tenuous at best, but I somehow know he won't unless I ask him to. So, I continue my exploration of his body.

"You let me use your body for release when I'm wound too tightly to function, and then you become everything I need." Though his hands are free now, he doesn't move. When I kiss right above the waistband of his boxer briefs, even his breaths still. I slide them down slightly until just the tip of his fully erect cock peeks out the top. "Let me be that for you now. Use my body to come back to yourself, so we can make sense of it all together." He groans in response, and I pull the tip into my mouth, swirling my tongue around it.

The musky scent of him mixed with the taste of his skin has me clenching my thighs and wanting to climb on top of him. *This isn't about me*, I remind myself and pull him completely out. The man is so damn beautiful from head to toe, inside and out. No matter the nightmares plaguing him, his actions show who he is, and I can't get enough. Wrapping my hand around his shaft, I pull it forward, and he sucks in a breath. I smirk, locking my eyes with his, before trailing my tongue from base to tip.

"Goddess," he murmurs, and a jolt of power zings through me.

I slide my hand up and down his shaft, squeezing when I get to the base. Then I take each of his neatly shaven balls into my mouth. I've never before felt comfortable, felt safe enough to explore my own sexual fantasies with a man, but Alistaire has me needy. I want to make him feel as good as he did for me last night. I want to find what he likes and be that for him. Fuck, I want to lose myself in exploring him.

"Josefina, fuuuck..."

That exultation is like gasoline on the fire burning inside me. I glide my tongue up the length of his shaft and take him into my mouth, positioning us both, so he slides all the way to my throat. Breathing through my nose, I hold him there for several seconds, relishing in the range of emotions that travel across his features. He never takes his eyes from my lips, but he loses himself for several moments until I pull back, streams of my saliva tethering his cock to my lips.

"*Demonios*, that is the sexiest fucking thing I've ever..."

I swallow him back down before he can finish the sentence. I don't want to think of anything else he's seen or done. I don't want him thinking about any other experiences. I want to be it for him because he is it for me. Pausing for a second, I let the truth of that thought wash over me. Maybe it's the way he protected me with his body against Adaire's magic, or the way he held me while I walked with Incendia. Or maybe it's the way he cared for me afterward, never asking anything for himself. Whatever the reason, something has changed, and this thing between us is less of a simple crush and more of a need. I need him. Tears burn the backs of my eyes, but rather than letting them fall, I channel that energy, those emotions, into showing him how I feel.

"Muñeca, your mouth." I purr at the praise falling from his lips, and he growls, grabbing my head but then letting go to clench the linens bunched beneath him. "So fucking beautiful stretched around me."

The fire inside me burns with the knowledge that he's holding back. His words aren't quite as naughty as they might be, and he's gripping the blanket for dear life when he should be pulling my hair. I want him to let go, to use me, to make us both forget. I pull off of him. "I told you I'm not a doll, Professor. I won't break." He stares down at me, a war happening behind his eyes before they flash red.

A listaire
    Esta mujer. This woman is going to be the death of me. She's playing with fire, calling for me to let go. The tether on my demon is threadbare, and he's champing at the bit to be freed, to have her. Yet, she keeps pushing me. The grip she has on my cock is coaxing, and the work her lips and tongue are doing on the tip have me barely holding on. Now, she wants me to... to what? Fuck, I don't even know, but I want to do it, whatever it is.

Do it, the demon rumbles.

Shut up, I tell him, barely keeping myself from saying it aloud. He chuckles, and anger flares.

Stop being nice. She doesn't want nice.

She deserves nice. She deserves love.

Hmmmm he mocks. *We can love her without the niceties.*

'Fuck me,' I hiss, and Josefina's eyes widen before drooping with her growing arousal. That look is the final straw that pushes me to wrap my fingers in her hair, holding tight without pulling. Her moan elicits an anger-inducing *I told you so* from within my head. *Por Umbra,* I'm going to extricate this fucking demon from me if it's the last thing I do. He chuckles again at the same moment

Josefina rakes her teeth lightly along my shaft, and I damn near convulse from the pleasure.

"Do that again, and I'm going to finish before you're ready to stop," I rasp out, pulling her hair hard enough for her to release my cock.

Josefina smiles up at me. The little witch has the audacity to smile at me. The growl that leaves my throat is unearthly, but her response drives me. She moans, and I climb to my knees, ready to fuck her until she screams. When she trails her eyes down my body to land on the cock she'd just had in her mouth, though, I pause. Licking her lips, she gets up on her hands and knees, and lifts her eyes to mine, a spark shining in those now blue-black irises.

"Fuck my mouth, Professor."

Breaths. I have no breaths. Fuck, I've forgotten how to breathe. Four little fucking words have reduced me to a gasping fish, my mouth opening and closing. Then the minx giggles before circling her tongue around the head of my cock again. Yeah, there's no way I'm surviving this woman.

Give her what she wants, asshole.

Her mouth slides down my shaft, and her ass wiggles in the air, taunting me. I reach down and give it a swat, eliciting a moan from her around my cock.

"You like that, little witch?" I ask, watching her face for the truth. "You want me to play rough with you?"

In the most unusual paradox, her cheeks turn pink with embarrassment at the same time her eyes darken with desire, and her lips clamp tighter around my shaft. There's absolutely no turning back, no walking away, no letting her go. She's a fucking dream in the nightmare that is my life. I grab her hair in my hands, weaving the tresses between my fingers, and I give her what she wants until I can't hold back any longer.

As soon as my balls tighten in warning, I try to release her, but she doesn't stop. "*Muñeca*, I'm about to come," I say, my voice husky with the need to release. Rather than pulling back and letting go, she wraps her arms around my hips, digging her fingertips into my ass to hold me closer. "Josefina," I say, trying to free us both, but she's not having it. Pushing me into her throat, she purrs, and the vibrations send me over the edge. I roar with my release like a wild animal going in for the kill, and she takes every drop of me. I'm lost to this woman. She might not realize it, but she owns me completely in this moment, and I don't know if anything will ever be the same.

CHAPTER 35

NOW WE'RE TALKING
ALISTAIRE

"Tell me about what happened when you passed out."

We're sitting on the sofa, listening to the crackle of the fire I started about an hour ago. We've been sitting in relative silence since leaving the bed this morning. Breakfast, tea, and cuddling, all happening in silence as the hours tick by. My mind, however, has been anything but silent. It's screamed at me to tell her how I feel. It's warned me of Adaire's 3-day countdown that's now fewer than 48 hours. It's whined about the reality of having to leave this oasis. And it's reminded me that's there's more at stake than these feelings between us.

That's been the hardest part. Yesterday, I'd run out on her in a panic because of my feelings. Today, I want to bask in them, but our reality won't afford us that opportunity. So, I've held her quietly against me, taking in her scent, and the feel of her in anticipation of losing it all. The what-ifs have me choking on the knot in my throat. What if she doesn't feel the same? What if she's scared away by my nightmares and the demon inside of me? What if she doesn't accept her Ascension and Umbra's gifts? What if Incendia sends someone else to watch over her?

No. I won't even accept that last one. I will kill anyone who tries to get close to her. The demon's head perks up at that, agreement emanating from him. He, of course, would be glad to kill anyone for nearly any reason. I think to tell him so, but it'll start an argument I don't want to have right now. So, I turn my attention back to Josefina and the question that's been on my mind for hours.

She looks up at me with her big blue eyes, and uncertainty flits across her face. I flinch. It hurts to think she might not trust me enough to answer the question.

Would you tell her about your nightmare? The demon taunts. *Will you tell her about me?*

That's the important question, right? Will I eventually tell her about the demon? Yes, I have to. It would be unfair to not let her know what she's dealing with, though I'd rather not. The nightmare, however, is another story. She doesn't need to relive the possession with me. It's bad enough to know he's always here. The details of how he got here are terrifying. I'd rather spare her that.

"I'm not even sure myself, honestly. It felt like a dream and yet not. I woke up in an empty room and then was taken for a walk."

My brows droop. "Taken for a walk."

"There was someone there. She called herself Incendia, like the portrait," she says, gesturing to the painting above the fireplace. "Supposedly, the witches in our family once followed? Worshipped? Served? Fuck, I don't know. Anyway, whatever relationship they have with that goddess they deal with now, they did the same for Incendia."

I chuckle at her choice of words. "You seem skeptical."

She huffs out a laugh of her own. "Well, after being told magic doesn't exist and religion is bullshit my entire life, it's hard to turn around and accept that there are these goddesses who give us gifts in exchange for...what?" She waves her hands around with the question. It's hard to remain serious when she's so animated in her disbelief, but there are things she needs to know.

"Our, well, their relationship with Umbra is different from

most human religions. The gifts given by the goddess are primarily for protection. They are her priestesses, but they are not her apostles nor out to tell the world about her. In fact, part of my job as guardian is to keep others from finding out about them, about her, and trying to steal those gifts for themselves."

She sits up, taking her warmth away. Confusion mars her beautiful features, and I try to find another way to explain it. It's not like I get lots of opportunity to talk about the goddess and the relationships we have with her.

"Umbra took pity on the coven when they were exiled from Illorum, giving them shadow magic, and choosing my ancestors to be their protector." Her brows furrow, and I can't help but smile. There's so much she doesn't know, so much that was kept from her, and yet she's unbothered. "You are a beautiful enigma, *Muñeca*. Just taking it all in without actually taking it in. Your skepticism is both refreshing and worrisome. Like your aunt, I'd like to have words with your father."

That statement gets a rise out of her. She stands and places both hands on her hips, and I smirk. There's nothing intimidating about this woman. Her soft skin and supple curves make me hard. Even those damn ropes she makes with her shadows are a fucking turn on. Otherwise, I'm more scared for her than of her at any given moment. Still, I hold up my hands in surrender.

"I'm simply saying that by keeping all this from you, he's put you in a precarious position." Her head tilts to the side, and I grab her hand, pulling her back down against my side. "You will ascend, with or without the help of the coven, and with or without the goddess's blessing, but it will be far messier, and much more painful." She tries to pull away from me again, but I hold her still. "Shhh *deja explico* before you bite my head off." I wait for her to settle back in, and then I explain.

In order for any of my story to make sense, I have to start with my family's involvement with the goddess and our relationship with the coven. "My father had been a fourth-generation guardian, and he passed down much of what he'd learned to me. Sometimes, I'd have questions that he couldn't answer. There were always questions to ask, which is probably why I make a good professor. He, however, would get exasperated with me and send me to Hylee, Gabriela's mother. She'd gladly answer all my questions. It was her mother, after all, that caused the coven to be exiled here in the human realm after all."

"What's with that whole exile thing? Who does that?"

I chuckle. "Deities may be more powerful than us, *muñequita*," I say, kissing the tip of her nose where she stares up at me, "but they can also be ruled by emotions. So, as the story goes, Yovizna, the Goddess of Water, on behalf of a spurned priestess, asked that the entire coven be exiled and stripped of their light magic because that priestess's husband had an affair."

"With Gabriela's grandmother?" Her hand goes to her chest, obviously scandalized on Gabriela's behalf. "Wow, old people sure know how to cause trouble."

A full belly laugh bubbles out of me. "About that old thing. There's probably something else you should know." She sobers, and I almost hate to tear away at her innocence like this. "The Daughters of Umbra don't age like humans," I take a deep breath, ready to add that I don't age like a human either, at least not anymore, but she doesn't give me a chance.

"What the hell does that even mean?" There's that skepticism again. I don't want to take that from her. It's protective to question things. If I had asked more questions before simply accepting Adaire's promise that the potion she gave me would make me a better guardian...

What? The demon scoffs. *Do you think you'd still be here, still alive, still strong enough to be what she needs? Ha! She'd look at you like an old man with one foot in the grave. She'd be vulnerable to the humans, the supernaturals, and the coven.*

I close my eyes against the truths I don't want to face. If I were alone, I'd rail at him, but Josefina wouldn't understand my frustration. She would think I'm yelling at her when it's the fucking voice in my head that's making me crazy.

When will you accept that this fucked up situation might be far worse? He asks, and I groan. *Together, we can protect her, keep her, worship her.*

Never before has this demon considered us a team. He's been just as antagonistic toward me as I am about him. At least, he had been until Josefina. In fact, the only time he's asked to be released has been to look for her. The only time he's shown any interest in anything has been her. But he's not fought me for her. He's fought me when I've run from her, when I've turned away, when I've been uncertain about her.

We belong to her, he says, *and together, we will protect her from everything that might want to cause her harm.*

I can't argue with him. I'd already accepted that I would take on the entire coven, even Umbra herself, to protect Josefina. To hear him say it, though, strengthens my resolve. Nothing and no one will touch her and survive.

'Now we're talking.'

"We've been talking," Josefina says, and I blink at her multiple times trying to make sense of her statement before I realize I must have said that shit aloud. Dammit!

CHAPTER 36
MR. RED EYES
JOSEFINA

The last forty-eight hours have been a blur, a painful blur, and though I'd like to stay hidden in Alistaire's cozy cabin, there's no way to put off the inevitable. "The Ascension will happen whether you accept it or not." Those words keep playing in my mind as Alistaire drives us back to my aunt's house in the car I didn't even know he had here since he simply flashed us to the cabin that day. He can't tell me what exactly the Ascension rite will entail, but the story about the only witch his grandfather had known to reject the rite was scary enough to make me rethink not returning. So, here we are, driving back through town, crossing the river I only vaguely remember from the day I drove in with Elinora, and pulling up in front of *Tía* Helga's house.

A flash of light from the attic window catches my attention as I step out of the car. I can't tell who it is looking down, but I can feel their stare. Alistaire steps up next to me and puts his hand against my lower back. When I don't move, he leans down and says something about everything being alright, but I don't catch his words. The shadows moving behind the figure in the window are unusual.

"Who is that?" I ask. I don't expect him to necessarily have an answer, but he knows the family better than I do.

"Who, *muñeca*?" Tilting my head up, I wait for him to follow my gaze. "*Qué demonios?*"

"Demons? In my aunt's house?"

No sooner do the words leave my lips than a scream echoes out from the backyard. I take off running, unsure whether the yard is accessible from the side of the house or not. Alistaire could easily make the trip in half the time I do, but he's grabbed my hand and matches his pace to mine. Concern mars his face, and I wonder whether I shouldn't have just sent him in to help. It's not like I'll be any good to anyone. My heart stammers inside my chest, and I feel my shadows prickling for release, like they do every time fear gets its claws into me. Then we round the corner, and run into a family reunion, full of laughter.

Serafina stands next to a man at the grill, her hand on his shoulder, and *las primas* sit around a blazing fire pit in the middle of the yard. Alma perches on the arm of an empty Adirondack chair, her face pointed toward the deck that leads into the house. A shrill voice echoes from that same direction and is quickly followed by cackling laughter from everyone.

"*Por Umbra*, Moisés, you scared the fuck out of me!" Isabella slaps at the chest of a man whose hands hold her shoulders. The smile on his face drops when his eyes, his very red eyes, turn toward us.

Alistaire stiffens, and he steps in front of me, but I won't let him take the attack again like he did with Adaire the last time we were here. Peeking around his body, I catch sight of Serafina with her hand on the other man's chest when he tries to step past her. His eyes also glow red, and it doesn't take much to imagine Alistaire has turned his on as well. And that's when it hits me, *demonios*. If witches are real, demons must be real too. And holy fuck, I've been fucking a demon. No, no, no. This is not good. I step in front of him, turning my back on the others to look up into Alistaire's face.

"Look at me, Professor," I coo, trying to break the tension of the trio staring daggers at each other. Please, for all the goddesses in this world and the next. "*Por favor.*" Those words get his attention, and he shifts his gaze to me.

"They're demons, Josefina. You're not safe."

His voice is deep and authoritative. If we were anywhere else, I'd probably be a puddle, but not here, not in front of these women. "Have you seen yourself, Mr. Red Eyes?"

"That's enough posturing, boys," a voice filters through the tension. "Don't make me tie all of you up. I might enjoy that more than you think." I turn around to see Elinora staring down the three men, one at a time. She barely spares me a glance, and frustration at her slams into me.

Ignoring everyone else, I walk up to her. "I need to talk to you."

"Careful, *Prima*. You might not want this smoke." Though her voice is teasing, I feel the tension coiled within her, and guilt tints her caramel eyes.

"I don't expect an apology, I say quietly, but I do expect answers." She nods before addressing the rest of the group.

"Can we please eat, drink, and be merry?"

Alistaire

The witches may have broken the immediate tension, but they've done nothing to reduce the unease I feel with these two creatures around. Since when do the Daughters of Umbra fraternize with demons? The two demons get together, chatting with each other and cutting their eyes toward me. As I watch them, Josefina accosts Elinora, and suddenly, I'm wondering if we made the right decision by coming back here today.

"Josie," the young one yells, genuine affection in her voice, as she runs to hug Josefina. The disarming of her defenses that happens in the wake of that hug would be comical if it wasn't so sweet. I can't hear the words they exchange, but it's obvious they've shared some kind of bonding moment in the short time Josefina was here before everything blew up.

Serafina walks up behind Alma and puts her hands on the child's shoulders. "Go help your *abuela* bring everything out to the deck." I can't hear her words, but I read lips pretty well, another positive outcome of teaching younger adults who think they can get away with so much shit. When she moves to talk to Josefina, however, I can no longer see her face. I take two steps forward, planning to stand at Josefina's side when the air shifts, and one of the demons appears next to me.

"I wouldn't if I was you," he says.

I raise a brow but don't turn my head toward him. I won't let Josefina out of my sight, especially not with these demons around. "And you think you're gonna stop me."

"If I have to. You see, that woman she's talking to is mine, and I won't let anything hurt her."

"Interesting since I've been protecting this family for decades, and I've never heard anything about you."

His eyes flare, cutting through the first moments of dusk. "Who the fuck are you?"

"You first," I say, turning to face him while keeping Josefina in my periphery.

Neither of us get to say another word before a cool hand touches my arm, and I notice another on his. "*Fíjense*, if you don't put your proverbial dicks away, I'll have Elinora put them on the grill." The demon's eyes fade a bit, and I shake my head.

"Now, Gaby, you know that shit doesn't work on me."

"What?" she says, batting her lashes. "I didn't do anything."

At those words, the demon pulls from her grasp, a scowl plastered on his face, and I howl out a laugh. Everyone's attention turns to us, and Gaby lifts up her hands in surrender. "If he beats your ass, you asked for it," which only makes me laugh harder.

"Word to the wise, don't underestimate any of the women here. They all have some secret act they're willing to pull on the unsuspecting. Most often, they're harmless, like Gaby's attempt to send calming vibes, but *algunas*," I say, cutting my eyes toward Elinora and Raquel who stand side-by-side watching us. "Some of them really will cut your dick off and make you say thank you for the privilege."

Gaby giggles, and I give her a wink, but the demon in front of me looks completely perplexed. I shrug and turn to find Josefina and Serafina both staring at us, matching smirks on their faces.

"Well, demon, it looks like our women have decided that we're more entertaining than attacking each other."

His head turns in their direction as he responds. "Yeah, I can't tell if they're waiting for us to declare war or what?"

I give him another shrug. "I wouldn't be surprised if they aren't hoping we'll fight it out, so they can watch."

The other demon steps up on his other side with a rumbly, "I overheard someone taking bets on whether or not shirts would come off."

My eyes roll. "Fucking Hijas de Umbra."

They both chuckle, and I have to hold myself back from laughing along with them. Finally, the one who claimed Serafina holds out his hand. "Joaquín Santos, demon-cursed, middle-school teacher. This here," he says, gesturing toward the pirate-looking demon beside him, "is Moisés."

"Death demon extraordinaire," he chimes in cheerfully, though there's a hint of malice in the way he says his title. I'm not sure title is the right word, but I don't care enough to ask. "Now, why don't you tell us what kind of demon you are, so we can all get back to enjoying ourselves since it appears the witches don't want us to kill you."

"I'm not a demon," I declare, though I know they can already sense something in me the same way I sensed them as soon as we walked around the house.

"Bullshit," Moisés says, his tone never shifting.

I smirk. "I'm not," I say, crossing my arms. Both men look at me skeptically.

"If you're not a demon," Joaquín says, playing mediator, "then what are you?"

"I am the goddess-blessed, human guardian of the de Umbra coven." Both men open their mouths to argue, but I hold up a hand. Looking around, it's obvious the women have gotten bored watching us, and I let out a sigh. "And I've been cursed with a demon."

"¿Cómo?" Joaquín asks, completely taken aback, which is funny considering he's demon-cursed, essentially a demon himself.

"Say that again," Moisés demands.

"I was forcibly possessed by a demon, neither of us willing participants."

Both men let out a whistle, and for the first time since Adaire cursed me, I feel like someone understands me.

CHAPTER 37

TEENAGERS AND MIRRORS
JOSEFINA

Serafina stares me down as soon as Alma's out of earshot, and I raise a brow. At first, she doesn't say anything, just watches me like she's trying to put a puzzle together, and I'm the piece that doesn't quite fit. When the words come, I almost choke in surprise.

"*Mira*, I'm sorry for being a bitch that day you came." My smirk makes her laugh before she clarifies. "Okay, I'm not sorry for that. I know I can be a bitch, but I am sorry for the way I treated you."

Spending that night in Alma's attic room gave me some perspective into Serafina's behavior, so I don't hold any of it against her, but it's nice to get the apology. "No worries. There seems to be a lot of shit to deal with around here, and my surprise arrival was just one more cherry on that shit pie."

"That's one way to put it," she says with a light chuckle, the tension finally leaving her features. "Anyway, it looks like we're going to need to run interference between our men, so we don't need any animosity amongst family."

"And you accept me as family now?"

"*Cuidado, Prima*. I apologized. I won't be doing that too many times." I laugh, and she joins me. "*Familia es todo. Mamá* was wrong in keeping you and *Tío* a secret. Now that you're here, though, you're one of us *y punto.*"

"So, what's with the demons," I ask, changing the subject.

"I could ask you the same thing, though I had no idea Alistaire had any demon in him."

I look over her shoulder to where Alistaire and one of the demons stands chatting, their relaxed stances a facade. Alistaire is coiled like a snake ready to strike while he watches me and the man at his side simultaneously. I'd laugh if I wasn't also worried about what might happen if either of them makes a sudden move. Then the third one saunters over, and the hair on my arm stands.

Serafina has turned to watch the interaction from my side. "Fucking Moisés is going to stir the pot, watch."

"Should we step in and stop it?"

"Nah, if they're going to be stupid enough to fight outside *Mamá*'s house with all of us standing here, they better at least strip down, so we can enjoy the show."

"I'm guessing the clean-cut hottie is yours?" Her eyes cut to me, and I can't help but giggle at the flash of jealousy in her dark brown eyes. "You can't expect anyone not to notice, especially not when the three of them stand there looking like gods. Scary as fuck demon gods, but gods nonetheless."

She smiles and bites her lip when the three men look up in our direction. "Dark and delicious," she agrees.

Alistaire's eyes on me sends a shiver up my spine and heat down to my core until I'm ready to close the distance.

Then a scream rings out with my name attached.

"Alma," Serafina gasps out before running full tilt into the house with me right behind her.

Alistaire

The cousins all take off running into the house at the same time, leaving us frozen in place for half a second. Then, the demons at my side disappear. *Fuck, I hate teleporting,* I manage to think before following their trail up into the attic where Alma sits in front of a large mirror.

"*Pequeña*," Joaquín says, his voice much calmer than he feels. His chest heaves, and his fists clench, at the same time that his jaw ticks a steady rhythm, all signs of fear. What he's afraid of, though, I can't tell. It's just a teenager and a mirror. Then I see something move within the glass, and I step forward.

"Where's Josefina?" Alma asks, her tone whimsical, like she's excited for Josefina to come up here.

"Alma," Serafina pants from the door.

Alma turns around as if finally noticing that her small room is suddenly full of people, and her head tilts in confusion. "Why is everyone up here? I just called for Josefina."

"No, *pequeña*, you screamed for her like something was attacking you," Joaquín says.

Josefina steps forward. "Are you okay?"

Alma's eyes light up. "There you are! I wanted to show you something, well, someone."

Serafina and Joaquín exchange looks, and the hairs on my neck stand up. They know something, and I'm not sure I like the implication.

"Stand down," a voice says from my shoulder. "You and your demon. Your girl's gonna want to see this." When I turn to look at him, Moisés grins, and I roll my eyes. I don't trust this demon as far as I can throw him, though I'd like to test that part of the equation.

Another voice pierces the relative silence that has taken over the attic. "Everyone back downstairs. Joaquín, the steaks will be briquettes if you don't go check on them."

He starts to protest, but Helga shoos him and Moisés down

the stairs with the rest of the coven, leaving the five of us up here. She looks at me with a question in her eyes. I set my jaw and plant my feet. I'm not going anywhere. If Josefina needs me during any part of what's happening, I will be right here. Helga sighs and turns her attention to Serafina.

"Sera, let's give them a moment." Her voice is much softer than I'd expected, as if she knows it will be a fight to get the witch to leave her daughter. "We already know she's not in danger here. You can even sit on the stairs outside if you need to be close, but this isn't about us."

Alma turns toward her mother and smiles. "I'm fine, mom," and the earnestness of those simple words has me relaxing.

Finally, the two witches leave the room, Helga laying her hand on my shoulder before walking out the door. I don't hear whether they stop on the stairs or make their way completely down to the others because my eyes are transfixed on the form moving through the mirror. It's out of focus, like an old tv that needs to be smacked a couple of times to jostle the tube, but something has my demon sitting up with an awareness that holds my attention.

CHAPTER 38

I KNOW YOU

JOSEFINA

"Josie, come sit by me," Alma says, her eyes shining with excitement.

I watch the play of light and shadows swirl in the mirror, surprised that I'm not as afraid as I probably should be. It's not normal for items in a mirror to move like that, and every other time smoke has moved along a mirror, it was a warning of something else about to happen, often related to the man standing near the door. Maybe it's his presence that has me relaxed since he's often been the impetus for the shadows, but I can't help thinking it's something else.

When I don't move, Alma gets up and grabs my hand, pulling me to where she was sitting and then down to the floor with her. She turns back toward the mirror. "She's here. You can show yourself."

"Alma, who are you..." my words trail off, and a sob lodges in my throat, as the figure stops swirling and comes into view. The image immediately goes squiggly again, but this time from the tears spilling down my cheeks. I open my mouth, trying to push out words, but the air is stuck in my lungs. This is impossible. How? How is this possible? The woman staring back at me, the one with a face as familiar as my own, smiles, and all the air I'd been holding whooshes out on a single word, "Momma."

Alma claps with glee, "Oh good, you recognize her. She wasn't sure you would since it's been so long, but I told her that you look a lot alike." The girl is rambling now, but I can hardly pay her any attention. Every fiber of my being is focused on the image of my mother swaying in the mirror.

"Can I talk to her?" I ask, my voice barely above a whisper.

My mother's smile is wide when she nods, and Alma is nearly vibrating when she says, "Oh yes, she can hear you." I don't have the heart to tell her I was hoping to be able to hear Momma's voice, not whether she can hear me. I miss the lilt of her tone whenever she would suggest something new. Like every time we'd make a new candle, or I'd suggest a new scent, she'd always turn her encouragement into a question as a way of making me take responsibility for all my choices. Would I own it or change my mind? It was empowering for a ten-year-old, though I probably would've hated it in high school. Still, I'd have given anything to hear her say, 'Do I have this right?' or 'So, what you're wanting to do is...'

"I can hear you, Fina." The sound of her nickname for me coming from her lips shatters me. My shoulders heave and tears fall like rivers across my cheeks.

"Oh no," Alma says, sitting up on her knees to wrap her arms around my shoulders. "I didn't think this would make you sad"

I shake my head at the sweet girl, unable to trust my voice or that any words I say will come out in the way I mean them. Thankfully, I don't have to say anything because Alistaire responds without leaving his post. "I don't think she's sad, Alma. It's just a lot. Imagine if you hadn't seen or heard from your mom in twenty years, and she suddenly spoke to you."

"I've never not seen my mom for more than a day."

"And you were still glad when she returned, right?"

She nods in my periphery, but I can't take my eyes off my mother, afraid she's going to disappear.

"I've always been here, Josefina. Always watching over you. Always looking for ways to ensure you were okay without me."

My head swivels back and forth of its own accord. Nothing has been okay since she died. Poppa changed, became more somber and less whimsical. I've been lost without her guidance to help push me forward. Stuck. I've been stuck. At least, that's how it felt until a certain someone walked into my tent that day and sang to me. I look back over my shoulder quickly, my tear-filled eyes taking in Alistaire's watchful stance, sympathy oozing from him. It helps to know he recognizes the gravity of this moment for me and is here to make sure I'm alright. He winks, and my lip quirks up before I look back at my mother whose gaze has followed mine. Her smile is soft as she takes in the man who has earned my heart.

She nods a couple times in his direction as if giving some silent sign of approval, and I smile. I don't need her approval, at least not for choosing Alistaire, but it feels good to have it. "Alma, can you leave me alone with my mother for a few minutes, please." Alma looks between me and the mirror before agreeing. I don't watch her leave. I trust that she'll respect my wishes and not linger around outside.

"I miss you," I say. "I miss you so much, Momma." Her lip quivers, but she blurs through the tears once again until I'm able to get myself under control. The hand placed lightly on my shoulder helps with that endeavor, allowing me to take in the moment. Finally, I say the words that have been haunting my mind since she first came into view. "I have so many questions."

She smiles, though it is not a happy smile. "I know, and I'm sorry I left you behind with so many unanswered questions, so much unsaid. In trying to protect you, I took so much from you, and it didn't even work."

"Why? Why didn't you tell me?"

Tears fill her eyes. "Your poppa didn't know what I was. He

had done everything he could to escape the supernatural world, to live a mundane life. I didn't even realize all he'd walked away from until our wedding when I met your *Tía* Helga." I nod, understanding that it was a big secret to keep from him. "Then, when you imbued your dislike for that teacher into the candle, he flew off the handle. He screamed and cried and yelled about how it was never supposed to happen. How you couldn't possibly have done it and that something must have been faulty in the wax or the wick or the jar. He wouldn't have listened, and I was afraid he would have rejected both of us."

"Poppa would never..." I say, wanting to defend him, but I'm not entirely sure she's wrong. I remember how angry he was when he got that call from my teacher. He'd thought I'd intentionally added something to the wax to make the smoke, and he wouldn't accept that I had no idea how it happened.

"So, I called your *Tía* and asked for her help to bind the magic you'd inherited from me." She turns pleading eyes up to me. "We had no idea you would inherit gifts from your grandmother as well. Helga was sure that their bloodline only passed through female descendants."

Everything she's said thus far makes sense and matches what I overheard during the argument in Alistaire's cabin and what Incendia told me on our walk through Illorum, but still, I struggle to understand how, if my magic was bound, the goddess found me. "Incendia told me that I had already received her gifts."

My mother stiffens, and a gasp leaves her lips at the same time Alistaire plops down onto Alma's bed behind me. "When did you see the goddess, Josefina?"

I tell her about the argument between Adaire and *Tía* Helga, recounting how I passed out and found myself in the goddess's presence. I share how the goddess had called me 'not just a Daughter of Umbra.' "She'd said I had a greater purpose than either title would allow, though the cryptic tone did more to frustrate me than anything. Why make a statement like that without actually answering the question?"

"If the goddess came to you and told you to complete the Rite of Ascension, then that, *mi'ja*, is exactly what you should do."

The urgent desire to dig my heels in and refuse is so strong, but I know that's just my spitefulness at being kept in the dark for so long. I hate not knowing what I'm walking into. I mean, I went into teaching because I knew what to expect, and I could plan for the unexpected because nothing was ever too far out of the ordinary. I continued making candles in the way Momma had taught me because it was like a warm hug from her every time one of the scents hits my nostrils and the flickers catch my eye. My near-on obsession with the sexy professor behind me was one of the first impromptu things I've ever done. Still, I've already decided to accept Umbra's gifts. It's the whole reason we came back here and didn't immediately return to Houston. While I have no intention of staying here in Onyx Junction, this is something I must do before I return to my life.

We sit there for another thirty minutes or so revisiting the highlights of my life that she's missed. I introduce her to Alistaire, though without details of our relationship, simply because we've not discussed it ourselves yet. Her response to his greeting, however, catches both of us off guard.

Alistaire

"I know who you are Alistaire Seagal, Son of Brevard, Servant of Umbra, and Protector of the de Umbra Coven. I know you and your demon."

What the fuck? I snap my mouth shut when Josefina turns toward me, her eyes wide. Confusion and pain mar her beautiful face. *Your demon?* she mouths, and I swallow, trying to express the apology I can't bring my mouth to form.

"How?" is the only word that escapes my lips as I wade through the devastation on Josefina's face.

She snorts a half laugh. "I said that I would always protect my daughter." Her voice that had been soft and loving until now turns stern and powerful, the voice of a high priestess. "Not only have I watched over Josefina and Daegal, but I've also watched the de Umbra coven, not trusting them to leave my family be. Not after finding that the head priestess had been monitoring her all these years." Her face takes on a hard edge. "Had I still been alive, I'd have challenged her directly, but I couldn't. So, I watched and waited. I recognized the demon in you, guardian, so I begged my goddess to intervene."

Intervene? Not only do I not understand how she'd found out about my possession but how she intended to intervene. "Why, then, do I still have this demon inside of me if you had planned to intervene?" The question is a challenge, likely disrespectful, but I wonder. I'd like to know why someone who could have possibly relieved some of the pain of possession and frustration of carrying this demon with me daily for over fifty years didn't.

Again, her blue eyes fall on me, a tiny flicker glowing within them, though there's no warmth in her expression. "You're a much stronger protector of my daughter, Daughter of Umbra and Incendia, with that demon who was hand-picked by Incendia."

The demon whimpers, like it physically hurts him to hear the story. He hadn't chosen this life any more than I had. We are bonded together because two witches decided to play goddess. Not for the first time, I wonder who the demon had been before the ritual that bonded him to me. We've spent so much time at each other's throat, vying for dominance, that I don't even know if he had a name before he invaded my skin and burrowed inside my psyche.

"Momma!" Josefina's cry cuts the tether on my sanity. "You allowed him to be cursed? You played a role in it?"

"No. He was already possessed when I found out, but I investigated the specifics of that possession to ensure your safety," she says without remorse. "To ensure the flame of Incendia within you remains lit." Her eyes blaze when they land back on me. "I did not expect you to seduce my daughter, but..."

"Momma, stop!" Josefina is on her feet, staring down at the mirror with her mother's image. "What is wrong with you? Binding my magic? Lying to Poppa? Participating in Alistaire's torture? I don't even know you anymore."

Corinne Exposito de Incendia deflates at Josefina's admonishment, and I recognize the choices for what they were—a mother's love for the child she couldn't be there to protect. I send soothing thoughts to the demon who remains curled around my spine. He doesn't deserve my scorn, nor does Josefina's mother deserve my hate for her involvement. I won't lie and say I'm not still pissed at Adaire and her arrogance, but even she had her own reasons for initiating the ritual. Goddess knows, I don't agree with them, but it helps to know it wasn't a frivolous decision. Besides, this demon and I have something in common, we're both head over heels for the woman staring down her own mother in defense of us.

"And what of the demon, Momma? Was no choice given there either?"

"No," I answer for her.

A sob is Josefina's only response, and I barely make it to my feet before she falls into my arms. I wrap my arms around her, holding on tightly to the woman falling apart from the same news that has started to put me back together. I let my gaze shift to the ghost watching us from the mirror, and a silent acknowledgment passes between us. An apology I'll never hear, and a promise she doesn't need to. When her image fades from the mirror, I kiss the top of Josefina's head and lead her downstairs to the cacophony that will hopefully distract her from the pain, at least until we're alone again.

CHAPTER 39

ALL OF THE ABOVE

JOSEFINA

There's something to be said for time that both flies by and passes at a snail's pace. That's how today has gone. When Head Priestess Adaire told Alistaire I had three days to return, I didn't realize she literally meant there were three days before we began preparing for the Ascension rite. So, today's job is to find a dress for the event because, apparently, I have to dress up as if having my *Quinces* all over again, not that I had anything formal back then either.

"Come on, *Prima*," Gabriela calls from fifty feet ahead of me. She's far too excited for this mall excursion. I'd literally rather do anything else.

"Ugh, I hate the mall. I hate shopping. I hate trying on clothes. Can't I just wear one of my boho skirts and a black top? We are witches after all, right?" I ask the last question more softly since we're in public, but she still laughs aloud as if we're at a comedy club instead of my worst nightmare.

"*No te hagas.* It'll be fine. There's this great plus-size shop here that sells formalwear. Nothing like the bullshit stores that existed for my ascension, and my *Quinces*. Every fucking dress I tried on felt like a burlap sack. Now, I come here to try on the gowns and feel like a princess. So, no, you cannot wear all black and ride in on a broom. *Una moto*, on the other hand? That you can definitely ride."

I shake my head at her antics, but I also can't hold back the laughter. Of all the cousins, Gaby is my favorite next to Alma. First of all, she's nice, which I cannot say about everyone, and she's funny, like legitimately has me rolling funny. That's why I agreed to take on this task with her as my partner. That and us wearing about the same size. If anyone would know where to find something appropriate in our size, she'd be the one.

"Now, I'm not gonna lie. Normally, I buy my clothes online. There are usually so many more options and different colors and sizes, but we don't have time to wait. We have to find something for you today, and it has to fit off the rack."

I groan at that last part. It's hard enough finding casual clothes that fit off the rack, let alone anything formal. In fact, every single pair of slacks I wear to work have had to be hemmed and taken in a bit in the waist. Not much, but it's hard when your ass rides low and your stomach high. Clothes, even at plus-size stores, don't size for various body types.

"Fine," I grind out when she ignores my latest complaints. "Are there any parameters I need to know? Anything that will help this trip get over faster?"

She smiles, grabs my arm, and pulls me down a side hallway off the main corridor to a store in the far corner. I huff. "So, they hide the fat chicks in the corner, huh?"

"No, silly. This entire wing of the mall belongs to this store." My eyes must pop out of my head because she lets out a full belly laugh and continues dragging me through the entrance.

When we step inside, it's otherworldly. They have everything from lingerie, leather, jeans and cocktail dresses to wedding gowns. The mannequins all have fuller figures with different shapes, some top heavy, some bottom heavy, and some just round the middle like that furniture commercial's tagline. My mouth is wide open when someone approaches to ask if we need any help. "It is a lot to take in at first," she says with a smile. "Don't worry, you'll get over the shock of the entry as soon as you try something on and see how perfectly it fits. Our owner is a sorceress with ensuring we have something for everyone."

I cock a brow at Gaby, but she shrugs saying nothing, and I'm left wondering whether the woman has just told me the owner has magic or if it is simply a figure of speech. I take back all those good thoughts I had about Gaby. She's a total bitch like the rest of them. My quiet chuckle gets a side-eye, and I shrug before following the saleswoman to the back of the store where the formal gowns are displayed.

"Do you have a preference of color or style? Anything you definitely don't want?"

"She doesn't want to look like some dowdy old spinster," Gaby says before I can even think of an answer. I roll my eyes and groan, eliciting another round of laughter before Gaby adds a more serious answer. "Our family color is purple, so maybe we can start there?"

My head tilts to the side, a question on my tongue, but then my phone dings, drawing my attention.

NAUGHTY PROFESSOR: Found anything yet?

ME: The store of every fat girl's dream.

NAUGHTY PROFESSOR: The kind I'm in or...

ME: All of the above.

NAUGHTY PROFESSOR: I want to see.

ME: With me in them or...

"Let me guess that a certain guardian can't stand being left home alone while you're out shopping." Her tone is accusatory, but the smile on her face is affectionate.

The smile that had formed during our exchange slowly fades at her prodding. After learning what some of our family members have done to him, I've become extra protective. No one will ever hurt him again if I have anything to say about it, and they damn sure won't do it in my name. So, when my phone dings with his response to my question, I ignore it in favor of making sure Gaby understands that he is not to be fucked with.

Gaby holds up her hands. "*No te preocupes, Prima*. I like Alistaire, and I hope you make each other very happy." She starts to walk off toward a couple of racks while the saleswoman ushers me toward the dressing rooms, but she turns around to add, "Oh, and if you ever need blackmail info on embarrassing shit he did in childhood, I got you." And then the door is between us, and I'm trying on gown after gown, as if there's no end in sight.

I'm exhausted by the time we leave the mall and return to *Tía* Helga's house. Everything is quiet for the first time since I arrived in Onyx Junction, and I climb my way up to the attic. Thankfully, Serafina and Alma have gone home, and *Tía* Helga is either asleep or chooses to leave me alone. As soon as I enter the upstairs room, my eye catches on the big mirror that still sits against the wall at the end of the room. It's been covered with a blanket since the day I spoke with my mom, but the shiver that runs through me says she's still there waiting for me to approach her again. Tonight, will not be that night.

Falling onto the bed, I pull my phone from the pocket of my jeans I haven't bothered to remove yet. A twinge of guilt runs through me when I see Alistaire's final response sitting on the screen.

NAUGHTY PROFESSOR: All of the above.

I unlock my phone and type the most honest thing that comes to my mind.

CHAPTER 40

MISSED TEXTS AND MATH JOKES

ALISTAIRE

I should be asleep. Tomorrow is the Ascension rite, and I'm to be there as security to ensure no one interrupts. I've heard enough stories to know that nothing ever happens to disrupt the rite, but still, my father had to stand outside each one, and I'm expected to do the same. This time, however, my heart will be inside those doors, between those four walls, and amongst the women who have no real loyalty to her. Not standing by her side will be much harder than anything I've been called to do in Umbra's service.

Then, there's the fact that she never answered my text from earlier. I know that she was busy finding her gown for the rite, but I didn't think she'd just be inaccessible. I'd spent most of the afternoon sitting on my hands to keep from party crashing the dress-shopping excursion. Though she wasn't alone, she wasn't with me, and for some reason, that just doesn't sit well.

Ours, the demon grumbles, and I growl right along with him, though that single word makes me smile at him. Something has shifted between us since that conversation with Corinne. It no longer feels like a battle for dominance anymore but an understanding that we may not have wished for this, but we both want the same thing—Josefina, safe, secure, happy, and with us. I can only hope that she feels the same way because he may become absolutely unbearable if she doesn't.

Pouring myself a glass of whiskey, I stretch out on the couch and let the burn of the liquor settle into my stomach, anything to reduce the feeling of emptiness without Josefina here by my side. After all these years of being alone, even since this demon became my constant companion, it's crazy how quickly I've grown accustomed to her presence. I don't even want to sleep in my own bed because her scent lingers. Truth be told, I want to whine like a petulant child, but I won't do that. I'm Alistaire fucking Seagal, Son of Brevard, Guardian of the de Umbra coven, and losing my fucking mind for this woman I shouldn't have ever touched.

If my father could see me now, he'd beat my ass. He made it very clear when I became friends with Gaby that we were not to even think of the de Umbra women as anything more than priestesses of our goddess. 'They are off limits,' he'd say repeatedly. It wouldn't matter that Josefina didn't grow up in this world, didn't know her family or her place as a member of the coven. The only thing that would matter is that I knew, and I overstepped that line. Hell, I didn't just overstep it; I demolished it. Staying away has been a struggle since the moment I saw her in that class, and then I felt her shadow's caress in that tent. I've not been the same since. She is everything to me, and I'm willing to lose the goddess's favor to have her.

Several moments, maybe hours, pass until I'm staring into the bottom of the empty glass. Is it my first glass? I can't remember. My mind tries to piece together the past several hours, but everything is a blur. I consider trying to go to bed but reject that idea quickly. I'll get no sleep at all in there surrounded by memories of her. Instead, I grab the tv remote, but before I can press the button, my phone dings, and I'm teleporting before the dots on the screen can manifest into a second message.

MUÑECA: I need you.

MUÑECA: ...

Josefina

Seeing the read receipt come through on my message is only a good thing when it's followed swiftly by a response. He doesn't respond, however. I send a second message, and that one sits on 'read' as well. What in the hell could he be doing? Stop it, Josefina. Not everything is about you. Maybe he's busy. Maybe he has other things to attend to besides you. Maybe he hasn't just been sitting around all day waiting for you to finally answer him.

"Maybe I'm fucked," I say aloud to the empty room.

"Si tú quieres," says the voice that melts my heart.

If that's what I want, indeed, I think to myself as Alistaire walks out of the shadow looking like the most delicious dream I never want to wake from. He smiles at me, and I smile back, stretching out my arms to him from where I lay on the bed. Without waiting, he climbs onto the tiny bed, his body weighing me down and warming me up. I wrap my arms around him in the best way possible, or rather, the only way I can with how we're situated, and just take in the feel of him.

"Rough day?"

"Excruciating. You?"

"It doesn't matter. Everything's better now."

If someone were to ask me who said what tonight, I couldn't even tell them. It's enough to know that we both suffered in the other's absence, and lying here together on this single bed neither one of us fit well on makes it all go away. When my breath hitches with emotion, he shifts, trying to find a new position, but I don't release him. There's no way I can let him go tonight now that he's here.

"*Muñeca*, don't let me crush you." I nearly laugh, but he wrestles us around until, somehow, I'm splayed out on top of him.

"But it's okay for me to crush you?"

"You couldn't," he says with a smirk, "but I'd gladly let you try."

I slap at his chest playfully. "Not here in my *tía*'s house!"

"I thought you'd never ask."

Within the next breath, possibly the next heartbeat, we've gone from that tiny bed in *Tía* Helga's attic to his king-size bed in the cabin, both of us naked. No awkward fumbling. No storming emotions. Just calm understanding. The moment his fingers graze against my bare flesh, I breathe a sigh of contentment. Here is exactly where I need to be, and he is who I need to be with. I don't even have to question it. My heart and body are of one accord, and when his mouth follows the trail of his hands, I open for him, offering everything I am.

I'd always imagined that being claimed by a man would be hot and heavy, a clashing of sweat-drenched bodies like they describe in romance novels or show in movies. Alistaire and I have had moments close to those, but none of them have felt as profound as this slow and deliberate joining. He slides inside, stretching me until we are one in the same way my magic is a part of me and his demon is a part of him.

"I felt like a piece of me went missing when you stopped responding to my texts." His breath grazes my ear, and his lips slide along my neck. "The number of times I had to stop myself from tearing down that mall brick by brick to get to you is irrational."

A giggle bubbles up from my chest, though there's nothing funny about the way he slides in and out of me or the way he hits that spot deep inside that leaves me breathless. "Did you just make a math joke while making love to me, Professor?"

"Is that what I'm doing, *Muñeca*?" His voice is low and gravely, sending bolts of pleasure to my core. For a moment, I forget what I'm saying, but he's hovering over me, watching and waiting for a response.

I stare into his eyes that are both dark with lust and glowing with something more. "Making me love you?" He stops breathing, stops moving. I grab his face with both of my hands and run my fingers through his hair, pulling him closer and saying one little word, "Yes."

CHAPTER 41

TELL ME ABOUT YOUR DEMON

JOSEFINA

Maybe it was wishful thinking on my part, but multiple orgasms and laying in Alistaire's arms after hearing his professions of love haven't helped lull me to sleep. My chest tightens with each tick of the clock as if I were walking to the gallows in a few hours and not into my power. I guess it doesn't help that morbid thoughts continue to run through my mind because I have no idea what I'm walking into. Will the rite require some type of bloodletting like the ones we learn about from ancient civilizations? Or maybe we'll have to sacrifice an animal. I don't think I can bring myself to slaughter anything fuzzy. Maybe it's like a gang, and we have to get beat into the coven, and by beat, they attack us with their own shadow magic to test the strength of ours. No, there's no way Serafina would let Alma go through with it if that were the case. Fuck, I need to go to sleep.

I roll onto my side if for nothing else than to have a different view than the ceiling. Shadows dance along the wall, painting a terrible scene. Bats flutter around an old church, terrorizing the people entering through the doors. Two of them dive down, growing larger until they stand as men to enter the building right before a single motorcycle parks along the street. I blink my eyes a few times thinking that maybe I did doze off and imagined the whole thing. Why the hell would I be dreaming about vampires? I've always found the lore surrounding them alluring, but this is something else entirely. When I reopen my eyes, the wall is blank, the only shadows resting in the corners. Yep, my imagination is on one tonight.

An arm wraps around my waist, pulling me back against his warmth, my ass folded against his semi-erect cock. Heat pools in my core at the contact. How I'm not satiated, I don't know, but there's something about the possessive way he's wrapped around me that has me wiggling back. He chuckles. "You need sleep, *Muñeca*. You have a big day ahead of you."

"Tell my brain that," I whine.

Alistaire kisses the top of my head and lets his hand slide down to my hip. "I'm not sure your beautiful brain is going to listen to either of us."

"Me either. So, maybe fucking me into a coma will work instead." I try to sound hopeful, but he just laughs again.

"I think you did a better job of that than I did. Have you slept at all?"

He slides his arm under my head, and I snuggle into him before shaking my head in response. "I just wish I knew what to expect."

"I know." He kisses my head again. "I wish I could tell you what will happen, but guardians aren't allowed inside during the rite. Our job is to ensure no one enters besides the family."

"Wait, you can't be there with me?"

"I'll be right outside the door."

"But..."

"I hate it as much as you do. It's going to kill me to stay out there, but I will also have the added stress of keeping Joaquín from storming in as well."

"What if those witches try to kill me? I'm still not entirely sure they accept me as family, let alone as one of them."

"They won't do that at the altar of Umbra." He says the words, but I hear the uncertainty in his tone. Even he's not sure everything will go well. I find myself wanting to reassure him, though I'm the one who will be at the mercy of Umbra and the coven once those doors close. I hate the fear oozing from him and that he's having to pretend for my sake.

"Even the shadows are conspiring against me tonight," I say softly.

"What do you mean?

"As if it wasn't bad enough to have morbid thoughts about all the horrific things that could happen during the rite, shadows danced across the wall in a scene of bats and vampires terrorizing a church."

"Huh? Vampires? at a church?"

"Doesn't make any sense, right? *Me vuelvo loca.* That's the only explanation I can come up with."

He snorts. "You're not going crazy, *amor.* You're just nervous, and rightfully so. I am too, and I'm not the one preparing to stand before Umbra."

"But you did it already, right? Isn't that how you got your magic?"

"Are you sure you want to hear about that right now? I'm not sure it will make you feel any better or help you get some sleep."

I roll over to face him, wrapping an arm and leg over his body. "I don't see me getting sleep any time soon anyway. Tell me about your experience." I snuggle my head up under his chin and whisper, "please."

Alistaire

I'm never going to be able to tell this woman no for anything. I already see it now, and if we ever have kids, it's all over for me. The demon's head lifts at the thought of kids. That response is going on a shelf for discussion later.

Demons can't have children, he says, sadness in his tone.

It's a good thing I'm not a demon, I answer back to my silent companion before planting a kiss along Josefina's hairline. I'd do anything to not have this conversation with her, to not share the truths that might change how she looks at me.

She loves you, the demon reminds me.

Yes, but will she still love me when she knows about you? What about when she finds out exactly what my role in the coven is and who I answer to? Will she trust me to protect her when she finds out that the head priestess who literally tried to kill her less than two weeks ago holds my leash? He whimpers but remains silent.

"My rite was pretty straight forward," I say aloud to the space above Josefina's head while wrapping my arms more tightly around her shoulders. I'm not sure I can get through any of this if she looks at me. *"Se había muerto mi papá."* I sniff back the sob threatening to explode from me at the memories her question evoked and the emotions battling for purchase at the thought of her Ascension. "He was dead, his body still in repose, and I was pulled to the altar to swear my loyalty to Umbra and my life to serving the head priestess as protector of the coven."

Josefina tries pulling back from me, her head pushing against my chin, but I hold her still. She must feel the weight of what I can't say because she eventually settles back down without a word. I swallow back the lump in my throat and blink against the burning in my eyes.

"You have to understand, I'd been trained my whole life for this role. My mother left because of my father's insistence that I would carry on the family legacy. She didn't want this for me. *La verdad es que* she didn't want it for him either, but he wouldn't have ever considered leaving, breaking his vow, turning his back on the goddess who'd blessed our family for generations. I knew nothing else but how to be a guardian. So, when Head Priestess Tempris called me in to make my vow, I did so proudly."

That is the truth of my experience. I did it all willingly not knowing what my fate would be afterwards. I simply imagined that my life would be like my father's, serving the coven, the occasional late night or out-of-town trip, and a lonely existence because no human woman would want to be shackled to someone who couldn't put her first, someone who would insist their son become a guardian when his time came. I didn't even bother to dream of happiness, telling myself that being a guardian and keeping the de Umbra women safe was enough. Then Adaire became Head Priestess, and I began questioning those choices.

"The goddess gave me limited powers, just the ones I would need to ensure the safety of the coven. For example, I could hide in the shadows and clear them enough to see my way through even the most obscure space, but I couldn't create my own or control someone else's against their will."

"My tent," are the first words she's spoken since I started my story, and she's right. That is how I knew something was wrong in the space and was able to get to her without the shadows attacking me as well.

"Yes, although my powers were augmented by then."

This time, when she tries to lift her eyes to mine, I let her and answer in the easiest way I can, letting my eyes glow red. She wriggles her arm free and reaches up. Her palm on my cheek is a balm, a physical promise that she hasn't been scared away yet.

"Tell me about your demon."

I snort out a mirthless laugh. "Do you want to know about that pain in my ass or how I got him?"

Her one shoulder lifts, because it's hard to move with the way I'm wrapped around her, but I see the shrug for what it is. She's willing to listen to whatever I'm willing to tell her, and suddenly, I want to tell her everything.

Tell her how handsome and strong I am, the demon taunts.

I ignore him and decide to start at the beginning with the drink Adaire offered me one evening after chaperoning Raquel's prom and ensuring she made it home safely from the after party. "I thought it was simply a thank you. My father had spent many evenings reviewing special events with the head priestess before he got sick, so I figured that's what was happening. At least, that's what I thought until my entire insides turned to molten lava, and I was writhing on the floor of Adaire's living room. She stood over me with a vessel of some sort that she uncorked and proceeded to pour over my face as soon as I started screaming from the pain. Not long after, I passed out."

Josefina wraps her arms around me, pulling me close. I tighten my grip on her as well, though telling the story isn't as hard as I thought it would be. The memories aren't as painful as the nightmares that return regularly. Somehow, she takes the pain away. I tell her about waking up to excruciating pain that can only be described as a rearrangement of internal features. My stomach had shifted lower, and my ribs felt stretched to their limits. Even my skin seemed to be pulled taut against the bones that were now double their original size.

"Somehow, my body was making room for the demon in the only way it knew how, to stretch wider."

"Wait, so it's really like having another person inside of you."

I'm not sure whether to laugh or groan at her simplistic assessment. It's much more complicated than that. I feel the demon as if he's some kind of separate entity. Like, I know when he's curled around my spine like a snake or when he's laying across my collarbone like a cat in a tree. But the voice I hear is more internalized, as if he's a part of my psyche and yet separate enough for his own consciousness. It's like arguing with an asshole 24/7 because you can't get away from them. The number of times I've considered trying to physically cut him out of me could have me committed. At the same time, he's protected me, watching my back, and sharing in the emotions I feel for Josefina.

"It's taken 50 years, but he's grown on me. Now I only want to choke him every few days rather than every hour."

Both Josefina and the demon chuckle, and I can't help but to laugh along with them. So much has changed since I met Josefina, and even more since I've had her, since we claimed her as ours. She is the one thing we always seem to agree on.

"Does he have a name?"

That's a great question. I've never thought to ask, never wanted to think about him as anything more than a parasite I could somehow eradicate with the right remedy. I wait and listen, thinking that he'll pipe in with some smart-ass comment or a name I'd never repeat to Josefina, but he says nothing. He really is like a fucking cat sometimes.

"If he doesn't have a name," she continues when I offer no response, "then maybe I can give him one."

That piques his interest.

CHAPTER 42
DON'T WORRY
JOSEFINA

The peace I felt laying in Alistaire's arms into the early morning swiftly fades away when he teleports me back into *Tía* Helga's attic. I lay both my hands on his cheeks and stare into his eyes, willing him not to leave, though I know that's an impossible ask. His smile is tight as apprehension colors his expression. I swallow around the nerves that have returned in full force, but his kiss brings me back to the present.

"You'll be fine, *Muñeca*. Serafina would never let anything happen to Alma, so there is nothing...well...nothing terrible to be worried about...too much."

A giggle bubbles out of me at his attempts to help assuage my fears while wading through his own. He really is the best man I've ever met, and I love how much he tries to protect me in all ways.

"So, what exactly are you worried about, Professor?

He lets out a heavy sigh. "Um, not being able to be there for you? Not being able to see what's happening with you. Not being able to know that you're alright. Do I need to say it another way?"

Another giggle. "Nope, I think I understand. You're a control freak."

Laughter bellows out of him, quickly followed by an

admonishment from the first floor. "Go home, Alistaire. You have work to do today, and Josefina needs to get ready."

We both close our lips tightly, trying to hold in the chuckles and failing miserably.

"Go," I finally say, pulling out of his arms. "I'll be fine."

"I'll be there when you walk in and when it's all over. I'm not leaving until I see you safely on both sides."

He leans in for one more kiss, and then he's gone. With a sigh, I head downstairs to accept whatever scolding *Tía* Helga decides to dish out.

Alistaire

We should have just stolen her away. The demon's snarl echoes through my mind. *She shouldn't have to go through with this. We shouldn't let her go through with this. These women. That fucking witch. They don't deserve her.*

"She's pledging herself to the goddess, not them. They're already family by blood," I say aloud as I pace back and forth through the small lobby outside the sanctuary. He matches my movements by walking up and down my spine.

He scoffs in a way that's more like a growly warning than a sign of disbelief. *Family. What family? I don't trust them.*

"You know you're not making this any easier, right?"

"Who are you talking to?" asks a voice from the doorway. I turn to see Joaquín peeking his head inside and looking around as if he expects someone else to be standing in one of the dark corners and to yell about him being here.

"This fucking demon on my back," I say, letting the annoyance at today's situation paint my words. It's not the demon I'm frustrated with, but Joaquín doesn't need to know that.

"Oh yeah," Joaquín says, stepping into the lobby and letting the door shut, throwing the space back into shadows that dance in the flickering candlelight. "I forgot you have your own curse." He looks at me with a tilt to his head before asking, "How does that vibe with your goddess? I mean, demons don't usually play well with other supernaturals, so the fact that you presumably had magic before the possession is super curious."

"Do you plan to distract yourself from the anxiety running through you by asking me ridiculous questions? If so, get the fuck out now. I have enough of my own shit to contend with, on top of this fucking demon's nerves getting on mine to not have the patience to deal with yours too."

We stare at each other for several moments before he lets out an audible sigh. "It's that obvious, huh?"

I don't get a chance to respond when chatter comes from the other side of the front doors. The priestesses have arrived. As soon as the door starts to open, Joaquín fades from sight, and I shake my head, knowing his little parlor trick will not hide him from the high priestesses, especially not Adaire. Helga is the one who says something first.

"Go ahead and show yourself, Joaquín. I'm sure Alistaire has told you the sanctuary will be sealed, and anyone not allowed will be destroyed, so there's no need to pretend you're not here."

He comes back into view and glares at me. I shrug and fight to keep the smile from my face. "Perdona, Doña. I was going crazy at home and thought that seeing the place would make the wait easier."

She raises a brow but keeps her voice soft. "And now that you've seen it?"

"Me muero de ansiedad," he answers, and I snort from trying to hold in my laughter.

"Looks like you two have more in common than you thought," she says with a soft smile and a wink in my direction. "I can tell you they'll both be fine until I'm blue in the face, but you won't believe me until you see it for yourselves, so I'll simply say, smile and lend them the strength of your love when they walk through. Do not add your anxiety to their own. *¿Me oyen?*"

We both nod before she turns to enter the sanctuary, leaving us alone once again.

"Are we that transparent?" Joaquín asks, but before I can answer him, more voices penetrate the quiet of the lobby.

"You look great, regal even," one of the women say, but I can't quite recognize the voice muffled by the wooden door. "*No te preocupes.* He already thinks you're hot."

I can't hear the second voice, but I know it's Josefina. I can feel her magic pulling at mine, and I have to hold myself back from flinging open the doors and running away with her like my demon suggested earlier. Then I see her, and my breath catches. She is absolutely stunning, and Gaby, who walks in right behind her is correct. She does look regal in that dress. The bright yellow top wraps around her neck, exposing her shoulders and a tiny sliver of collarbone on each side. Then it fades to white as it hugs her breasts and drops to the floor in shimmer cascades that go from the white to the darkest of purples, the color almost turning black where it trails the floor.

"Wow," is the only word I can manage.

She stops in her tracks at my voice and gives me a shy smile.

"Doesn't she look absolutely perfect?" Gaby asks, beaming, as if she is responsible for the entire look. Who knows, maybe she is, but it's not the dress or the way her hair is swept up off her shoulders. It's the radiance of the woman I love and the boldness of her wearing the colors of Umbra and the colors of the Incendia as captured in the painting above my mantle.

"I'm not sure perfect is a strong enough word," I say, unable to keep my eyes off of Josefina. She steps closer until she's looking up at me, her lips begging to be kissed, but I don't get the chance because Gaby puts her arm between us.

"Don't mess up the makeup. Save it for afterward." Then she

pulls Josefina toward the sanctuary. In the entry, she turns to me with a smile. "She'll be fine, Alistaire. *Te lo prometo.*"

It's not that I don't want to believe her. It's that my brain and this demon have trust issues. When I turn back to see Joaquín wringing his hands, I say the closest thing to the truth that I can muster. "If there is one member of this family that I trust to tell me the truth, it's Gabriela. Our girls will be fine."

"Do you really believe that?"

Fuck, I wish he hadn't asked me that. I hate to lie. Inside, the demon laughs at me and my plight. *Fuck off*, I think, knowing he can read my thoughts, and he just laughs harder. "No," I say with a heavy sigh. "I don't, but I want to." He nods in understanding and then rushes to the door when he hears the rest of the women arrive.

"What're you doing here, Joaquín?" Serafina asks with an exasperated sigh. The look on her face, however, is more gratitude than frustration. She's glad he's here, but it's young Alma's response to his presence that makes me smile and once again think about the possibility of children.

Does Josefina want children? Would she want children with me? Would she be willing to take the chance with my curse, not knowing if our child would be cursed as well. Fuck, do I want to take that chance.

That's not how it works, the demon chimes in. *I'm a disembodied soul. Nothing to fill her up with, though I'd sure love to try if you'd let me.*

"Shut the fuck up!"

A stifling silence falls over the lobby as everyone turns to look at me. Shit, I said that aloud, didn't I? I don't even have to ask the question because the laughter roaring through my head is all the confirmation I need.

"Sorry. Arguing with a demon."

"Good to know I'm not the only one doing that regularly," Serafina says with a wink in Joaquín's direction, and everyone laughs, breaking the tension. With a quick kiss to Joaquín's cheek, she pulls Alma from his arms, and the cousins all make their way inside the sanctuary.

No sooner does the door close than the goddess's magic fills the space as she seals the sanctuary shut. From the corner of my eye, I catch Joaquín shudder from the shifting energy. I can't focus on him, though, as I try to calm my own breathing and slow my racing heart. It's that very heart telling me to smash through the door and spirit Josefina away to someplace no one can find her. Thankfully, my head knows that's not an option, so I walk over to the corner of the lobby and take a seat amongst the shadows. Joaquín follows my lead. For the next hour, there's nothing to do but wait.

CHAPTER 43
TOO SOON?
ALISTAIRE

It feels weird to be back in Houston, to sleep in the loft I've lived in for most of the past five years. It's even stranger to not spend nearly every hour of the day at Josefina's side, but she was so adamant about getting back some semblance of normal that I couldn't stop her from returning to work. I couldn't even stop her from going back to her apartment alongside the beltway. I'd tried to get her to move in with me, but she said it was too soon. Too soon?

"We've been sleeping in each other's arms every fucking night for nearly a month," I had argued, but she wasn't hearing it.

"As wonderful as that was, it wasn't under normal circumstances. It isn't how things were when we left here. I need to feel like me again, and the me who was here last had her own apartment, her own job, her own life, and a crush on a professor who showed up exactly when she needed him." We'd stood in the middle of her living room, and she'd put her hands on both sides of my face. "Can you be that for me, for now...until I get my head on straight?"

That fucking question still haunts me, still makes me irrationally angry. Even the demon railed against it that day, begging to be set free, so he could stay with her if she insisted my body left her alone. I nearly gave in, but that wouldn't have made things better between us.

So, here I am, walking through campus, my mind trying to figure out how to give Josefina the space she needs to process everything that happened while trying not to lose my mind for missing her. When a voice calls my name, I hardly notice until Taylor runs up next to me.

"Professor Seagal?"

I stop walking. "Taylor. Good afternoon."

"Sorry to bother you like this, but I can't think of anyone else to ask." She pauses, and my brows furrow. "It's just that..." Another pause, and my anxiety raises. Then she lets out a deep breath, vomiting the words she's been holding in. "I haven't heard from Josefina since the day you asked for her address." Something in the way she shifts her eyes away from me says that timeline isn't exactly accurate, but I recognize the sincerity of her worry. "I was going to ask the cops to do a health check, but I didn't want you to be implicated if she really had disappeared."

My head tilts to the side. "Implicated in what?"

"Whatever happened to her. We've been friends for a couple years now, and she never disappears. She's the most consistently accessible person I've ever known, so when she asked me for your number and then stopped answering calls and texts, I got worried. I've gone by her place, and she never answers the door. I even called her job, but they said she'd taken a leave of absence, just like..."

"Just like me." I finish for her, and she nods once. "And you don't believe that could be a coincidence?" I already know her answer would be negative, and I'm not going to lie to her when she's worried about her friend. I love that Josefina has someone who's worried about her. "Her story is not mine to tell, but let's say we found out our families are loosely related, and there was a family situation that had to be handled. We both went to take care of it, and we're both back."

"Wait, she's back?"

"Since Sunday. I'm not sure whether she's ready to be social or talk about everything that happened the past few weeks, but don't give up on her yet. Okay?"

She beams a bright smile. "Thank you, professor. I was so worried that I had missed something important, and I guess that I did, but..."

"She'll be glad to know she's loved and was missed." At least, I hope that will make her happy.

"Thanks again, professor," Taylor says as she turns to run off. Her bright energy lingering behind.

Something off about that one, the demon says, his tone uncertain.

Is that just because your cranky ass can't imagine being that cheerful? I shoot back at him as I finish the walk to my office.

No. It's because there's something off...odd...different about her. She smells weird.

You don't even have a fucking nose.

I don't have to see him to know he's rolled his eyes, and I laugh at the irony of him claiming to sense something he can't possibly experience.

I don't need a body to recognize when someone is hiding something about themself.

I can't even argue with him. He found Josefina before I sensed her magic, and he knew where she was at the Renaissance Fair before her magic called out to me. That thought sends a shiver of anxiety down my spine, and it's enough to make me pull out my phone to text Josefina as I rush to my office. Before I can get to my desk, a text message comes in from her, and I breathe a sigh of relief.

> MUÑECA: Would you like to come with me to
> San Antonio tomorrow?

I would follow you to the ends of the earth if you'd let me, I think before settling in my seat to respond.

> ME: Of course. Do you want me to come tonight or pick you up in the morning?

My breaths stall as those three dots appear and fade, appear and fade, mocking me with the hope that she won't make me wait.

> MUÑECA: You could come now?

I don't even bother responding before throwing shit into my bag and damn near running to my car. If leaving it in the parking lot on campus over the weekend wouldn't raise suspicion, I'd have teleported myself home and then to her apartment. Anything to get to her faster, but I still have to be careful and keep a low profile here at the university. So, I make the short drive to my house, throw some clothes in a bag, and make my way to her in record time.

J osefina

It takes far longer for Alistaire to arrive than I thought it would. When he finally knocks on the door, I nearly jump out of my skin. Though I can feel his presence on the other side of the door, and the shadows created by the flickering candles in front of the mirrors all signal his arrival, I check the peep hole just to make sure. The scowl on his face at how long it's taking me to answer sends heat to my core. I'm also impatient. I've missed him more than I probably should. With a quick look in the long mirror at the end of the hall, I loosen the tie on my robe and let the belt fall before opening the door.

He's through it and has me in his arms before I can breathe out a greeting. His lips capture mine in a searing kiss, and I match his need with my own. I know it's my fault that we've been separated these past few days, but I needed to clear my head. I had to work through everything that has happened this past month, including everything I've learned about him. We couldn't get out of the sanctuary and away from the family fast enough after the Ascension because of Alma's Quinces, but there was the weight of his role in everything that pressed down on me as well until I felt like I was drowning. I couldn't separate it all. The fear. The secrets. The lies. The betrayal. They were all one, and everyone involved morphed into the thing of nightmares, especially after I'd announce my claiming of both goddesses during the rite. I wasn't too sure the coven would let me live after that.

His hands sliding down over my backside to slip beneath the robe bring me back to the present, back to him. Fuck, I've missed his touch, his mouth, his calming nature. I press myself harder into him, wanting to feel every inch of his body against mine and wishing he was naked. Without thinking, my shadows glide up and around him caressing everywhere my hands can't be. They pop loose the buttons on his dress shirt, exposing his chest and taut abs, finally letting our skin touch.

"Josefina," he growls out before pushing me backwards, so he can close the door. I hadn't even realized the door was still wide open as my magic swirls around us. He either doesn't notice or doesn't care because his hands are pushing the robe off my shoulders, exposing me to him completely. Not to be outdone, I reach down and unbuckle his belt, releasing the button and the zipper to slide his pants and boxer briefs down around his ankles. The smoky tendrils of my magic slowly wrap around each of his legs, and it's like I can feel them touching his skin as clearly as my fingers grasp onto his hair and pull his mouth back to mine.

Without warning, Alistaire leans down and picks me up as if I weigh nothing. I can't hold back a tiny scream at the surprise. I've never had a man pick me up before, well, not since Poppa when I was a little girl. Alistaire is definitely not looking at me like a little girl, and dammit, I'm here for whatever he has in mind. Wrapping my legs around his hips as best I can, I cling to him like a koala, wishing we were closer still, wanting him inside me. His nostrils flare when my wet pussy slides against his length.

"Fuck, *Muñeca*, I've missed you."

I hum in agreement and let my shadows continue their trail up his legs until they're swirling between his legs, softly caressing his balls. He hisses, and a fresh wave of desire runs through me, making me impossibly wet. A tendril wraps around his balls, gently squeezing while another clamps onto the base of his cock. His moan is like the unlocking of a door, setting me free and calling me home at the same time. This man is my calm, my freedom, my home. I might have needed a couple days to separate the truth of my feelings for him from all the other bullshit disturbing my soul, but now, in this moment, everything is clear.

"Is the offer still open?" I ask, hating the trepidation in my voice.

He stills, though his breathing continues at an uneven pace with my shadows still working him between us. The look he gives me is one of confusion mixed with lust. I could make him suffer through trying to work out my cryptic question, but I don't want to wait much longer to have him inside me.

"I'd like to move in with you. I've hated sleeping alone, hated not feeling you and your magic nearby. I don't think I've ever felt more alone than these past few days after having had you with me, protecting me and loving me, this past month."

His eyes go wide with surprise, but it's surprise mixed with joy. "I could snap my finger right now and have everything at my house if that's what you want. Just say the word."

A smirk teases the corner of my lips. "Am I to assume that's a yes?" He growls out my name in warning, and I giggle, wiggling myself against him. His hands cup my ass, spreading me open, and

I moan at the friction while still surprised at how effortlessly he holds me up in his arms. "Fine, Professor Seagal, I'll move in with you, but if you don't fuck me right now, I'm going to hurt both of us because these shadows have a mind of their own."

He chuckles, the sound low and husky, as he starts walking toward my bedroom. "I thought you'd never ask."

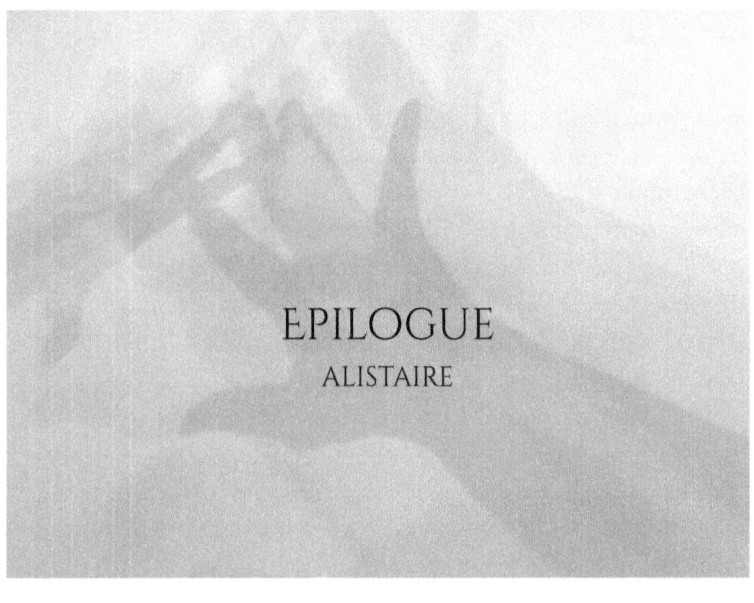

EPILOGUE
ALISTAIRE

I can't say that the nightmares have subsided. The process of gaining my demon still haunts me, the pain still a tangible memory that chokes me in my sleep like something from a horror movie. The demon himself, though... yeah, he's still a pain in my ass, but I don't necessarily hate him anymore. Josefina's presence has somehow bonded us beyond the physical and mental sharing of my body. I now feel his emotion as my own, and he has stopped fighting me for release and dominance. Instead, we both focus on her.

She sits on the couch watching out the floor-to-ceiling windows at the Houston skyline. The city is far more spread out than built up like many large cities, but it's no less beautiful. Sadly, I can tell by her blank stare that it's not the view she's fixated on. Her mind has drifted away, as it has most of the days since we came back from Onyx Junction and she moved in with me. Though she's managed to help my fragmented soul piece itself together, hers is still reeling from everything that happened before and after the Ascension.

As I pull the last plate from the dishwasher, the air within the loft shifts, nearly causing me to drop it on the floor. I immediately look around expecting to find some supernatural entity has entered our home, until I realize the demon remains unbothered. Every candle throughout the open living space flickers to life, and my eyes snap to where Josefina lounges on the couch, one leg bent up. I can't see her face, but her head is lolled back against the cushions. Closing my eyes, I take in a deep breath and stifle a groan at the scents combining through the room—jasmine and sandalwood, and the distinct smell of Josefina's arousal.

As quietly as possible, I approach the back of the couch and lean down near her ear. "What are you thinking about, *Muñeca*?" Anything I might have thought to say afterwards dies in my throat as my mouth goes dry and my cock presses uncomfortably against my zipper.

She looks up at me over her shoulder with a seductive smirk on her lips, all the while letting her fingers play beneath the waistband of the sleep shorts she put on upon arriving home from work. "I was thinking how delicious you looked tied up in my shadows that day in my *tía's* house. So much was happening that I didn't get to admire the view as much as I'd wanted."

A smile plays across my lips. "I told you all you had to do was ask."

Her head slowly swings back and forth, and I tilt mine in question. "I'm not asking, Professor. I'm telling you that I want you naked, the knots of my shadows trailing up your beautiful body."

I let out a long, slow breath, trying to control the racing of my heart. *Fuck, that's hot,* my demon says with a low whistle. He's absolutely right. My *muñeca* has never been submissive in the general sense sexually, but she's also not shown any dominance either. Our sex life has been reciprocal, each of us focused on pleasing the other, of showing our love and care through physical intimacy. Often, sex has been a way for us to ground one another, a distraction from an otherwise painful reality. The thought of giving myself over to her for nothing more than her pleasure is like a blessing from Umbra. I trail my tongue over my lips to wet them before releasing a single word. "Where?" When she points to the space in front of the windows directly in front of her, I let out a small moan. The idea that someone could see her control over me is both terrifying and arousing, but I don't hesitate to make my way around the couch to stand in front of her.

"Strip," she says, her fingers still playing along her pussy.

Torn between wanting to tease her and not wanting to wait for her next move, I begin by unbuttoning my shirt slowly, my eyes fastened on the movement between her legs, wishing she didn't have those damn shorts on. When I pull my t-shirt over my head, her eyes take me in, lingering on the dips right above my waistband before traveling up to meet my gaze. The heat in that look has precum leaking from the head of my cock. I'm surprised there's not already a wet spot growing on the front of my pants to give away how much her words and actions are affecting me.

The demon sucks his teeth and rolls his eyes in frustration. *What the fuck are you waiting for?*

Shut the fuck up. I'm getting there.

Without warning, He reaches into that shared part of our psyche and pushes his magic forward, causing me to blink. When my eyes open, I'm standing there completely naked.

You fucker, I sneer internally.

Let the games begin, he calls triumphantly, and with a gesture that almost has me thinking she hears him too, Josefina waves her hand. Clouds of smoky tendrils creep toward me from all directions. If I didn't know this woman, and if I wasn't more aroused than I've ever been, I'd probably be teleporting my ass out of there, but I remain still.

Josefina bites her lip as her chest rises and falls in time with the writhing tendrils. "You really are the most beautiful man I've ever seen, Professor," she says between panting breaths.

The moment the tendrils reach my feet, they start crawling up my legs, knotting themselves in elaborate patterns where each knot sits between a loops that goes completely around my leg. Not knowing what to do with my hands, I force myself to leave them loose down at my sides. When the knotting reaches my thighs, part of the smoke breaks off, creating two new, thicker rope-like tendrils that wrap around my wrists. These are slightly tighter than the ones around my legs, but the noticeable sensations are nothing compared to the shock when my hands are pulled up above my head, wrists binding together, and linking up until it wraps around the curtain rod.

I look back at Josefina, but she's lost in the moment. Her free hand has pushed up the hem of her sleep top, and her fingers are pinching and twisting first one nipple and then the other. *Fuck yes*, the demon exclaims in absolute ecstasy as if he can feel the tightening of my muscles, cock included. A moan leaves my lips as my own arousal melds with his, and fuck if I'm not ready to come.

"Josefina," I say, my voice a raspy whisper. *"Muñeca, no voy a aguantar."*

"You can take it, Professor Seagal. Hold on for me." Though her voice is soft and coaxing, the gleam in her eye and hitch in her breath says that she's just as close as I am. Then, her shadows wrap around my balls and twist up the length of my fully erect length.

"Fuuuck. Fuck." I swallow, my breaths heavy. She pulls her fingers from her pussy and pushes her shorts down until I can see her glistening slit. If I wasn't stuck here with my arms above my head, I'd be diving face first between her legs. "I want to taste you."

The smile she gives is diabolical, and a growl vibrates in my throat. "No, Professor. I like you right where you are. Exposed. Vulnerable. Undone." She licks her fingers, and I whine, garnering a giggle from her before she drops to her knees on the floor and begins a slow crawl toward me. My cock throbs with every move forward until I'm holding my breath as her hair tickles my naked thighs.

"You're dripping, Professor," she says with a smirk and sits back on her heels. Her face even with my cock. "Here, let me clean you up." With those words, her tongue plays along the tip of my cock, lapping up the tiny beads of precum. She moans in response, and I damn near forget how to breathe.

When she takes me fully into her mouth, retracting the smoky ropes, I don't last long at all. And when she releases my arms, I drag us both to floor, pushing her knees wide and licking up every drop of her arousal. It doesn't take any time before she's writhing beneath me, her hands fisted in my hair, and my name on her lips. Sliding two fingers inside her opening, I curl them just enough to rub that spot that will push her over the edge. This time, her release gushes all over my hands as she screams until her voice is hoarse. I kiss her, letting her taste herself on my tongue and then teleport us into the shower, too spent to carry her down the hall like I've grown accustomed to do.

Later, when we fall asleep in each other's arms, I listen to her slow and steady breathing, and revel in the fact that I get to call her mine.

Josefina

The past six months have been a whirlwind of changes and emotions. Poppa and I have come to an understanding about his and Momma's secrets, my magic, and my place as part of the coven. Of course, there were many shared tears and loud voices in the process, but we've each made concessions. I've promised to let Alice believe we're all mundane since she seems to have forgotten or blacked out the events in the house and at the River Walk. I'll gladly do that if it means maintaining the relationship with my father. On his part, he's agreed to let *Tía* Helga, Serafina, Isabella, and Alma come for a visit. I can't blame him for not wanting to see the others, especially Adaire. Those wounds still haven't healed, and I won't force him to relieve that pain.

Honestly, the head priestess and the shit she put me through is why I haven't gone back to Onyx Junction, even when she's called Alistaire to come back for some job or another. I can't bring myself to trust her no matter how much everyone swears she wouldn't go against the goddess's blessing. I still recall the way Alistaire's body had fallen against me when she'd hit him with her smoke daggers, and each time I relive that moment, my shadows ache for release. I want to hurt her, but I know that would hurt the rest of the family and upset Umbra. I'm not willing to do that, so I've kept my distance, getting to know my *primas* via text messages and video chats.

We have so much in common, it's crazy. Even Serafina and I have come to an understanding. Her love for family has made the process easier, that and the relationship Alma and I have developed. She is truly a breath of fresh air and a great mediator. She's almost as good as Gaby, though she's still limited in her understanding of why all the adults haven't fully welcomed me into the fold. It's been hard to explain, so most of our conversations revolve around high school and her budding relationship with that boy who took her to the Fall Ball. Maybe budding isn't the right word since she told me they've been friends for years, but I can't help but wonder how he'll handle her slowed aging since the Ascension. Or better yet, how will she handle watching him grow old while she remains young for decades.

I've had a similar concern about my relationship with Alistaire. I'd always known he was older than me, but I never realized how much older. The man is over a century old, a fucking human century, and he barely looks like he's seen 45. Part of that blessing came from the goddess, but he said his aging completely stopped when he got his demon. It's still so hard to wrap my mind around the fact that he has a disembodied soul floating around inside his body and playing in his mind. I won't complain, though, because that demon loves my playful side and helps talk Alistaire into all kinds of fun kinky stuff. He especially loves when I tie them up. Alistaire thinks it's because of the shackles the demon's subjected to in order to remain tethered to Alistaire's body, but I think the demon just has a little freak in him. Maybe one day I'll be able to talk Alistaire into letting me see him unleashed.

"Why are you awake?" Alistaire's groggy voice asks from beside me.

"You wouldn't know I was awake if you were sleeping," I retort.

"I feel you thinking."

I chuckle at that statement because I know it's true. I feel the same thing when he's struggling, and I always know when he's having a nightmare, though they've been coming far less frequently. "Do you remember the night before the Ascension when I couldn't sleep?"

He snuggles in close, wrapping his arm around my middle and laying a leg over mine. "Yeah. That was a very anxious time."

"Understatement. But do you remember I told you about the images my shadows created on the wall?"

"You mean the vampires at the church?"

"Yep, that's the one."

He lifts his head to look at me in the dark, his eyes glowing red. I smile, but it's empty. I can't even muster the pretense to play like everything is fine.

"What's wrong, *amor*?"

"I had a dream. It was the same as the scene from my shadows, except this time I saw who got off the motorcycle." I pause for a second, afraid to say the words and make it true.

"Who was it?"

Swallowing the lump in my throat, I finally force the name out. "Elinora."

"Are you sure?"

I nod, though he's no longer looking directly at me. His eyes are trained on the ceiling, like he's trying to reach across the distance with his senses. "I've been here fighting back the urge to call her and make sure she's okay. I mean, it's far too much of a coincidence to not be real, right?"

"Did your mother ever say anything about the gifts you received from Incendia?"

"No, why? I mean, I know about the emotions I can put into my candles, but I don't know about anything else." I still haven't told him, or anyone else, about Incendia telling me that I would be back to see her one day. Somehow, I'm able to travel between realms, but since I don't understand how, I haven't said anything. He turns to look at me again, and I try to keep my breaths normal. I'm not a big secret-keeper, but is it really a secret when you don't know anything. Still, it feels like I'm lying by omission, and I hate that.

"And have you gotten anything new from Umbra that you haven't told me?"

I shake my head vehemently, glad I'm able to answer this question honestly. "Nothing that I know of."

"You're probably not ready to hear this, but I think it's time to go back."

I wince as if struck. I'd already come to the same conclusion, but hearing him say it makes me want to argue against it. "For good?" I ask, my voice uncomfortably small.

"That's up to you, *Muñeca*. I will go where you are. If you want to keep this as our permanent home, then that's what we'll do, but if you want to fully assimilate into the coven, then I'll get the cabin ready for year-round living." He kisses my forehead. "And if, at any time, you change your mind, or you want to go somewhere else, I'll be by your side."

"What do you want, Alistaire?"

"The privilege of calling you mine for the rest of our lives, and any lives thereafter."

"But?"

"No buts... And. And I still think you need to go back and see

Xiomara. I also think you should visit the sanctuary and speak with the goddess."

"All because I saw Elinora in my dreams?"

"Because visions aren't a common blessing, and yes, because you saw Elinora with vampires."

Well, fuck!

Acknowledgments

I always say that inspiration can come from anywhere. The Daughters of Umbra series is no exception. Last year, Gracie sent us images of women consumed in shadows with a caption that said "New Series Inspo," and my immediate response was, "If you don't write it, I will!" So, here we are with a close-knit, shit-talking familia that's full of drama and sass.

Now that I've tackled the inspiration, let me address the release schedule. Gracie and I did not come out with the date for Josefina's and Serafina's release on our own. If you know us, you know this was a group decision that happened over a year ago when one member of Roberts Row suggested we plan a spooky mass release with some of our closest author friends. That one suggestion became a plan to release books together every October 13 for the next however many years of our friendship. So, be prepared! Also, I don't know where I'd be as an author, or if I'd still be an author, if not for Britton, Ashley, and Gracie. That #RowLife is real!

I also want to give a huge thank you to those who have helped get the word out about this new series. The love and support have been wonderful.

LEYA LAYNE

Leya Layne's love of a Happily Ever After started with Disney.
Then she found romance novels in her early teens thanks to a bag
of Harlequin novels hidden under her grandmother's dresser. She
got her HEA fix for the rest of her teen years thanks to a well-worn
library card. Though she is currently publishing contemporary
romances that have been described as Hot Hallmark, don't be
surprised to see her delve into historical or paranormal in the
future. The possibilities are endless, but the one thing she'll
promise is that they'll all be spicy!

Follow Leya all over social media:
https://linktr.ee/LeyaLayneAuthor

See her website for forthcoming releases and trigger/content
warnings:
https://bisabelwrites.com/leyas-content-is-for-18-only/

Coming Soon

December 2025: Magnolia Cove: A Cozy Romance Anthology

February 2025: Whiskey Falls Anthology

April 2025: Elinora

ALSO BY LEYA LAYNE

You've Got Bookmail

Shar's Story

Love with a Vengeance

Carol's Christmas Awakening

Clarissa and the Wallflower

Breadcrumbs

Cole County Anthology Series (Being Unpublished Dec 31, 2025)